unnerving

twelve stories for a monthly dose of shivers

BLUE FORGE PRESS
Port Orchard, Washington

Unnerving Eclipse
Twelve Stories for a Monthly Dose of Shivers
Copyright September 2021
by Blue Forge Press

Cover art by Brianne DiMarco
Interior design by Brianne DiMarco

First Print Edition, October 2021
Second Print Edition, February 2023

ISBN 978-1-59092-911-7

For information about film, reprint or other subsidiary rights, contact blueforgegroup@gmail.com

Blue Forge Press is the print division of the volunteer-run, federal 501(c)3 nonprofit company, Blue Legacy, founded in 1989 and dedicated to bringing light to the shadows and voice to the silence. We strive to empower storytellers across all walks of life with our four divisions: Blue Forge Press, Blue Forge Films, Blue Forge Gaming, and Blue Forge Records. Find out more at www.MyBlueLegacy.org

Blue Forge Press
7419 Ebbert Drive Southeast
Port Orchard, Washington 98367
blueforgepress@gmail.com
360-550-2071 ph.txt

*For Kelly, who taught me
to love all things weird and spooky
and for Faith
who shares my love
of the bizarre and unexplained.*

CONTENT WARNING

This book is intended for mature audiences as these stories are purposefully meant to unsettle the reader. If one month's story is too intense, skip that month. While the editor and Blue Forge Press have selected and edited each of these stories, ultimately you are responsible for curating what you read.

For a full list of triggers by story, please write to:
blueforgepress@gmail.com

table of contents

unnerving

twelve stories for a monthly dose of shivers

JANUARY

Raising Cain

Jennifer DiMarco

don't like her," I leaned in and whispered to Gwen, the round-faced blonde with the thick emerald green glasses. "I've never liked doctors."

Gwen crinkled up her button nose and gave me a playful push. "She's nice. It's just a job."

I shrugged off the friendly admonishment and smiled over at Doctor Janus (so on the nose) who'd insisted we call her Barbara the moment we'd arrived.

"I guess," I'd muttered under my breath, making Mikael snort and add, "As long as we get our two grand? I'll call her Daddy if she wants me to."

Mikael was omnisexual and I liked the way he wore baggy jeans over neon bodysuits; it made him look like an animatronic trying to pass as human.

We'd finished our intake eforms and supplied our W9s including direct deposit information and currency preference (I went with DogeCoin because I was planning a trip to Elon City on the lunar dark side and didn't want to deal with exchange rate fluctuations). After Doctor—*Barbara*—had collected our tablets and ushered us into a massive open-concept living room that resembled an upscale ski lodge, she'd excused herself to 'go fetch refreshments.' That left the five of us to snoop.

"Do you think she actually lives here?" Jessica mused, running her manicured hand along the polished cedar mantel.

"It's probably some kind of time-share for psychologists." Damien gave Jessica an unwarranted peck on the cheek—possessive as fuck, that guy—and sank down at her feet to poke at the fire crackling in the huge river stone hearth.

"Careful," Gwen cautioned her brother as he freed the poker from the rest of the tools and the iron and brass sent up a cacophony.

Damien gave her a dismissive, 'don't worry about it' wave and went back to playing with fire.

Gwen sat next to me and I liked the close warmth of her body and the way she smelled like lilacs. She seemed unsettled.

"Bet this couch cost more than our rent for the year." I winked at her and she smiled half-heartedly and nodded. We all had shared rooms in NYC Hostel #914; that's how I'd met Gwen and she'd introduced me to everyone else.

"It is nice," Gwen admitted and snuggled into the posh cream-colored softness. 'Nice' was her go-to when she was nervous. This brought her closer to me and I put my arm around her shoulders. Gwen and I weren't lovers but I thought she was beautiful and wouldn't have turned her down.

"Barbarella can keep her two grand if I can just live here!" We all laughed a little as Mikael flopped down along the matching love seat, kicking his socked feet up on one arm and letting his rainbow dreads hang over the other. "Damn. That's like a thirty foot ceiling, dude."

Mikael was studying Set Design and CAD Architecture and

was always throwing out obscure film references married with design and engineering factoids. I liked this about him because it made him unexpected and unexpected people held my interest. As soon as I knew how someone would react or what they would say, I was bored. I hated being bored more than literally anything else.

"Boredom is existential torture," I'd told Jessica once and she'd tossed her long, copper hair over her shoulder and *tsked* at me, "You've clearly never been tortured."

I think she liked being casually demeaning like that; she was a dominatrix by trade, putting herself through a double major in Persuasion and Interrogation with military and medical concentrations. You wouldn't guess it from looking at her: Lanky and thin with small breasts and eyes too big and dark for her flour-white face... or maybe you would. Maybe unusual-looking girls make perfect SM/BD queens. Not a conventional Rubenesque beauty? Try tying people up for a living!

I leaned back and rested my head on the overflowing cloud of the couch. Mikael was right. The ceiling was easily two-storeys or more with cedar hand-hewn beams carved from whole trees. I let the welcome sensation of vertigo wash over me like cold water down my spine and lifted my head slowly, letting my gaze slide down the shining red-gold of the matching cedar walls and over the twelve foot windows that kept the Catskill winter evening at bay.

"It's snowing again," Gwen told me, stating the obvious but also telling me she was watching me. She was so outside my league it wasn't funny but it still gave me a hot thrill whenever her attention was on me.

"I'll throw another log on," Barbara announced as she re-entered the hall (that's a good word for it) with a wooden tray of demitasse cups and plates of crystallized ginger cookies I could smell already. Her voice echoed a little—as did the heels of her expensive leather boots—as she crossed the expanse to join us by the fire. Mikael quickly took his feet off the furniture and sat up. Jessica sat down next to him.

"I'll do it!" Ever-eager Damien popped up like a jack(ass)-in-the-box and flashed his pearly whites at the doctor. As a professional gamer, Damien made more than most of us (last year, he'd even rented a solo room at the hostel for *seven* months) and could have been a poster child for wage inequality. Jessica would have to fuck a dozen guys up the ass to make what Damien made shooting the same guys in the head in a single battle royale round of *Universal Predator*. I think easy money makes people shallow but I'm not a gamer so maybe mashing buttons is harder than it looks.

"Thank you, Damien," Barbara smiled at him but the smile didn't reach her eyes. She set the tray down on the ornate coffee table and went about handing each of us a tiny cup of chantico and a matching china plate with three bowtie ginger cookies.

"No thank you." I took the unsweetened chocolate drink but held up a hand to pass on the cookies. "I'm diabetic."

"Oh." Barbara hovered in indecision for a moment, holding the cookies aloft on their delicate little plate. Maybe she wondered if she should apologize. Clearly she didn't understand managed healthcare; I could afford twenty units of insulin a day and dosed one unit for every five carbohydrates I consumed. Good thing I lived with islet-suppressing diabetes as opposed to weight-induced; no amount of insulin was approved for the latter. I was earning my masters in Philosophy and Anthropology but to burn off tension I ran the old New York subway tunnels six miles a day and had a body fat percentage of nine-point-two percent.

"So when do we start?" Mikael, brazen and to the point, asked around a mouth full of cookies.

Barbara settled into a wingback just across the coffee table from me, finally setting down my rejected plate of empty carbs. "You already have." Barbara pointed to her left, not looking herself.

We all looked for her.

A small, black sphere the size of a Satsuma holiday orange was nestled among the smooth stones of the fireplace. It looked like a large Sulphide marble but instead of a white clay or kaolin figurine, inside it was a reflection of the five of us—the six of us if I counted the doctor. My gaze caressed the room again; now that I saw the first one, I easily found half a dozen others. Maybe more if those knots in the beams high above us weren't old knobs of branches after all.

Jessica was making a wary face and Barbara caught it; savvy old broad that she was.

"You agreed to be monitored for the entire length of the session," Barbara explained in her perfectly modulated, firm but soothing tone. "And the session began as soon as your forms were signed."

"Which it said in the contract," Gwen pointed out diplomatically. Jessica looked at her. Gwen was third-year law and Jessica trusted her; the dom nodded and managed a smile at the doctor, obliterating her nervousness with cookies. Jessica was definitely someone who skipped reading the Terms of Service.

Silence stretched and Barbara seemed in no rush to instruct us; or maybe this extended quiet was part of the process.

Mikael broke first: "You know it snows double the national average here?"

"I do," Barbara answered, her smile painted on. I

wondered if anyone else could tell how practiced she was. Her glasses were as expensive as her boots and the furniture; unlike Gwen's sporty specs, Barbara's frames didn't feature a visible recording indicator. (Gwen's was turned off as required by Paragraph 19 of today's contract.) Unless… I looked at the shiny black eyeballs throughout the room. So many angles. Maybe Barbara left pedestrian tasks like recording to the inanimate objects. Maybe her glasses were just glasses; how archaic and quaint in the age of CRISPR2 and VAR machine learning.

"Shall we play a game?" Barbara moved us forward.

Mikael chuckled, probably at some filmography illusion only he knew. "Let's do this."

Barbara took a deck of glossy black cards from the tray that I hadn't even noticed were there. The firelight caught her just right and her coral-colored blouse was translucent for a moment. The body beneath her coiffed and pleated exterior was small, fragile even. She was probably sixty-five, maybe seventy. She handed the deck to Jessica who was closest to her, counter clockwise, on the far end of the love seat.

"*Twenty Questions*," she told us but I had a feeling this wasn't the childhood guessing game.

Jessica took the deck and held it tentatively. We were all university students; we awaited instructions.

Barbara just returned Jessica gaze, saying nothing. Again, the tension in the open hall was a pressure, like a tangible thing.

This time, Jessica broke: "So I… just take a card?"

Barbara bobbed her head demurely as if humoring a young child. She said nothing.

Jessica cocked an eyebrow and looked away from her and at each of us briefly. She turned over the card on the top of the deck.

"Wait." Damien—the consummate player in so many ways—lifted up on his haunches, balancing on the balls of his feet in a ready-to-spring type of crouch. He'd never taken a seat on the couch with me and Gwen but had stayed near the fire. Even the poker was still balanced across his knees. "What are the rules? What's the objective?"

Barbara took him in for a moment—the cookie crumbs on his polo shirt, the anticipation in his popping jaw, the twitch in his hands as if he itched for a controller or at least the deck of cards. She bobbed her head again, acknowledging his existence and his questions. "Take turns. Select a card. Answer the question honestly. There are twenty cards."

"*Truth or Dare* without the dare," Gwen defined and Barbara lifted an open hand to her.

"Yes. No dares."

"And the objective is...?" Mikael that time, curiously serious. Maybe he was thinking: *We get two thousand dollars to lie convincingly four times each?*

Barbara seemed to hear something in his voice, some penchant for deception or dramatic flare. "Honesty." She let that sink in—mundane and mediocre as it sounded—and then added, "I have never had a group of subjects finish the deck."

Subjects. I heard the word like: *Objects. Inanimate. Statistics.*

"Do we get paid whether or not we finish?" Jessica asked.

"No," Gwen and Barbara answered as one. Barbara smiled a little at Gwen and motioned for her to continue. Gwen blushed and said quietly to her friend, "That was in the contract, too."

"And if we lie?" Damien was on his feet now, pacing in tight, clipped steps in front of the fire. He wasn't even playing yet and he was thriving, in his element and ready to dominate.

"You won't be paid." The doctor left no room for argument. After all, it had all been in the forms we'd signed on the tablets... if we'd cared to read them.

"Okay." Jessica took a sharp breath and read the first card aloud: "'What was your first pet?'"

Mikael laughed hard once, like the bark of a seal. Damien's face flooded with incredulous shock. Even Gwen grinned a little and shifted beside me.

Barbara remained the same: Stoic. Still. Watching.

Jessica looked from each of us to the doctor and back to the card. "Okay. Wow." She ate the last of her ginger cookies, pretending to take the card very seriously and really think about her answer. "That would be... uh... Poppy, a silver tabby, when I was ten."

She leaned purposefully forward and set her empty plate and demitasse on the tray. When she straightened back up, she looked down at the card again, blinked, and added, "Actually, it was a hermit crab." She looked up at Barbara. A moment passed and then, "He had golden hairs on his legs and I named him Fabio. He had these really big claws and could snap a Popsicle stick in half."

Jessica looked down at the card. She ran a fingertip over the question. Maybe the print was raised? I wondered what color it was.

"I..." Jessica exhaled. "...I tucked him between my thighs one night so he'd cut off my Dad's dick." She looked back up at Barbara but Jessica's face wasn't confrontational or bold like I expected it to be. Jessica looked... surprised. "He didn't like that. My Dad. So he boiled Fabio and made me eat him."

"Oh my god...." Gwen looked green.

I was glad I hadn't eaten or even sipped my chantico.

Jessica blinked. She didn't seem to care we were all in the room.

Damien dashed in and I thought he'd comfort her, commend her bravery; they'd been dating for more than a year. Instead, "My turn!" He snatched the deck and vaulted around the wingback to return to his perch by the fire.

I watched Jessica from the corner of my eye, trying not to stare. She was still holding the card she'd selected, still focused on it.

"You didn't say we had to draw from the top," Damien announced like he'd found a winning loophole.

Barbara turned her head slowly to consider him. Her faint smile neither denied nor confirmed his statement and, emboldened, Damien slid a card from the center of the deck.

"'How many stuffed animals do you own?'" It was Damien's turn to laugh. "Damn." The question was so easy! "Sorry, Jess." But she looked at him blankly. Damien answered, "One." His smile widened, became toothy. "It's a mouse. A fucking little city mouse that chewed through my console power cable last year. I killed him, gutted him, and stuffed him with half a sock. Then I nailed him to the wall above my desk."

Damien tossed the answered card onto the coffee table. It skipped along the glass top and slide over the sharp edge onto the cream-colored Saxony carpet.

"Damien."

He looked at his sister. "What?"

Gwen looked from me back to her brother at a loss for words. How could he not know how foul and disturbing that was? Gwen shook her head. "Just give me the deck."

Damien shrugged and handed the stack of black cards to her, crouching back down to bounce and await his next turn.

Gwen looked from Damien to Jessica then shifted the deck between her hands and pulled a card off the bottom. "'Which of your friends would survive a zombie apocalypse and which would die first?'"

"No way," Damien was irritated. "That's a good one."

Gwen just seemed confused. "Assuming zombies are real..." she began.

"Duh," Damien was up and pacing again, this time holding the poker on his shoulder like a rifle.

"Right." Gwen frowned at him. "I guess Cain..." She turned to me and smiled gently, a little guilty, I think, because Jessica was still clearly so upset and Gwen's question was so removed from reality. "Because you run every day, you know?"

I did know but it was Damien who answered, "Hey!" He slammed the poker down into the floor like beating out a cadence with a cane. "I took first place in *ZombiU*, remember?"

Gwen scowled at him. "You're denting the floor, Damien."

He stopped instantly, swore, then muttered an apology, sinking back down to his crouch.

Barbara said nothing.

"How come your question is two questions?" He bitched, as if having to do more for the same money gave her an unfair advantage.

"I don't mind," Gwen offered and placed her card on the table carefully as she answered the second half. "I think I'd be eaten first because the chubby girls never live long in zombie shows."

I wanted to say something like, *Because you're sweet and delicious, Gwen!* but that sounded incredibly forward and rude and also really twisted. And I couldn't say anything because Gwen started speaking again.

"Actually, no." Gwen handed me the deck but pointed at Mikael. "It would be Mikael because he's Black."

Ouch. But true. Hollywood had its troupes.

"True dat," Mikael joked, nodding in agreement. "Zombies like themselves some dark meat!"

I cringed and drew my card from the top. The text was silver. I ran my fingers over it. It didn't feel raised. There was no discernible change in the texture between the card and the small, san serif letters.

"What's your question, Cain?" Barbara asked.

I looked at her.

"Keep it moving, bro!" Damien was impatient.

"I pass," I said and handed the deck to Mikael, not breaking eye contact with the doctor. I caught the surprise that flashed across her face but it was there for tenths of a second.

"Whoa, Cain. Man." Damien whistled. Even the (understandably) shaken Jessica was looking at me in surprise. "You are one private fuck."

"You understand if you don't answer four questions—" Barbara began.

I cut her off and looked away from her, "I understand. I forfeit my payment. It's fine."

Everyone was still staring at me... except Gwen. She was looking at the card in my hand. I flipped it over and tucked it under my demitasse on the coffee table.

Gwen pushed her glasses up her nose a little, not meeting my eyes.

'*Who is your secret crush?*' So damn juvenile. I felt a wave of anger at... who? The card? I wanted to rip it in half. Gwen reached for her last cookie and when she leaned back she seemed closer to me. I still felt angry though. I just felt other things as well.

"'What's your favorite body part?'" Mikael flicked the card over his shoulder with casual disdain. "Easy. My taint. Done." He handed the deck back to Jessica with a, "Sorry, girl." and put his empty plate and cup on the table, tucking his feet under him.

Callus much? I thought suddenly of all of them. Maybe not Gwen but still. I watched Jessica. I watched Barbara watch Jessica. Would Jessica tap out like I had? Was that really what this experiment was about? Was the (good?) doctor studying the price people put on privacy?

Jessica caught me looking at her. She saw, I think, everything I was feeling and lifted her chin, set her jaw. "Okay then." She sniffed. And drew a second card. "'What did you say in the last text you sent?'"

Jessica's face went blank again for a moment but then she broke into a huge smile of relief; Jessica wasn't a big texter.

"I have no idea." She laughed the words then turned her head automatically and said to her on-board interface, "Suki. Read my most recent text."

A tone sounded from wherever she'd tucked her phone and then a vaguely female digital voice read, "'*Babe? You coming over? Jackie and Tricia are out and Damien just left, thank god—*'"

"Wait. What—" Damien was on his feet again.

Jessica was scrambling to find her phone, forgetting she could just say: *Stop.*

"'*—if I can't suck on something bigger than a Ballpark, I'm gonna lose my goddamn mind. Get your sweet self over here, Gwen!*'"

What? My mind went blank.

Jessica was babbling now, her phone tumbling from her hands to fall between the love seat arm and the seat pillow. I don't think she was making any sense, just making sounds of panic.

I knew how she felt.

Damien, however, was speaking in complete sentences, shouting in complete sentences, and not at Jessica. "What the fuck, Gwen!" Not a question. "Fucking *again?!*"

"Damien. Damien. Calm down." Gwen had both her hands up, surrendering to the truth. She was standing now, trying to soothe him. "It was *weeks* ago."

Mikael chuckling didn't help.

"How could you, Gwen? You have everything! I have nothing! Mom and Dad. Better grades. Better looking! All I had is—all I had was—"

"Girl," Mikael jabbed Jessica with an elbow. Her face was streaked with snot and tears, her wide eyes so much wider than usual that she looked like a living Kawaii character from a Japanese cartoon. "What's *Gwen* got that's bigger than Damien?"

Gwen turned to him to save her friend (lover?). "A dildo, Mikael. I like it... Jess likes it... when she gives me a blow—"

Damien hit Gwen in the head with the fire poker. He swung like an all-star batter and with enough force to snap her glasses in two, split her skull and splatter parts of her brain and half her scalp of blonde curls all over the other end of the couch. Her face—divided into two pieces—never registered the strike.

Jessica started screaming. Like her sounds of panic, the scream was wordless and choppy, as if she were trying and failing to collect words—any words!—to make sense of what she was seeing, living, feeling.

The deck of cards fell from her hands and spilled like sheathes of black oil across the pale love seat. She kept screaming.

Mikael's eyes were glued to the half of Gwen's face that lay on the couch next to me.

Damien was on the floor, wrapped around Gwen's body, shaking her and demanding the truth. "Talk to me, Gwen! Tell me! Tell me!"

I was staring at Barbara.

"'What's your worst habit?'"

I wasn't aware I could experience shock deeper than what I was already experiencing. Mikael could not be serious. I turned as if in slow motion to look at him and noticed Barbara doing the same thing; we moved in unison and I hated it.

Mikael had read his next question. His hands were trembling but not hard enough that he didn't keep hold of three cards. His final three questions. "Cutting," he answered and he flipped out the three-inch *shafsher* that usually hung with his keys from his braided belt.

Jessica whimpered and scrambled up and over the arm of the love seat, escaping behind Barbara's wingback, a child hiding behind a matriarch; I had no delusion that Mama Barbara would save her.

Damien was still hissing into the half-face of his dead sister when Mikael stabbed his own thigh. The cut spurted and coughed blood through the ripped tear in his jeans, an ugly gaping wound from a curved blade forced into an unnatural downward stab.

Mikael seemed not to notice. He read his third question, "'Have you ever killed something?'" He gave his seal-bark laugh. Jessica crumpled down to the floor behind the wingback. Damien laughed too, adding, "I just did. I just did!"

Mikael lifted his eyes from the card to me. For a moment of lucidity, I thought I could read his thoughts. I swore he knew I'd known. I swore he thought, *Bastard.* or *Lucky bastard.* I'm not sure which it was even though both had totally different meanings.

He stabbed himself again in the same place, high on his thigh. "When I was seventeen…" The pain must have stopped him for a second but he held my gaze, swallowed and went on. Jessica and Damien were quieting, everything was quiet, as if the whole world were covered in the heavy snow that continued to accumulate outside the monolithic, one-way windows. "…I got a girl pregnant. I wanted her to get an abortion. She wouldn't."

You bastard, I thought at him, but really I was just being a judgmental prick because my heart was broken. No. My heart was splattered all over the couch beside me.

"So I shoved her down the stairs." Mikael's eyes rolled back into his head. It was a relief to not be locked together. But he came back, found me again. Stabbed his thigh—in the same damn place—a third damn time. "Neither of them made it."

And he bled out on the love seat.

"I threw up."

Have mercy! Who the fuck was I praying to? Mercy from whom? From what? I'm a fucking atheist.

Jessica pulled herself up from behind Barbara's chair. She wasn't covered with regurgitated ginger cookies and chocolate so what—

"I threw up Fabio," she told me, directly to me. "I vomited all over the plate; parts of him were still whole. He made me eat him again. My Dad." Jessica was shaking so hard I was stunned she could stand at all. "And again. And again."

When Jessica flung herself forward, I thought at first she was passing out but she descended on Damien like a wild thing, like a banshee, clawing and biting. He threw her off and the back of her head hit the river rock hearth with a crack louder than iron striking Gwen. Jessica's body folded inward and fell back over the fire, catching almost at once.

Damien spun from the pyre and fell to his knees, intentionally slamming his face into the corner of the coffee table once, twice, until his eye exploded from its socket and still he kept hurling himself forward.

Just as his body went limp, I stood up and walked from the hall.

I felt Doctor Janus exit after me and heard her close the heavy double doors carved with vines and roses. The hallway was wide and equally as grand as the vaulted room but it was quiet, still, and clean. Lit with a chandelier set with candle-shaped soft bulbs, the hallway also didn't smell of fire and shit and blood.

"Perhaps next time, we should use a VR room at the institute," Doctor Janus suggested. "Less paperwork for the coroner."

"Less authentic," I shot her down. But I was just being petty because I'd thought this group would do better. "But yes, more efficient."

I looked up at the cut crystal shards of the chandelier. They were probably data drives, cleverly disguised back ups of decades of AI work.

"I'm sorry," I finally managed, turning to face her. "Your VR avatars are excellent representations of human behavior, Doctor. It was bigoted of me to insinuate that just because I exist in a meat body that I—and the subjects I befriend—are superior to pixels powered by your work." *For I, too, am powered by your work.* Just in another way.

Doctor Janus bobbed her head in slow, elegant acknowledgment. "Apology accepted." She brushed her hands together in a habitual motion I'd noticed in her after the last few studies. I often wondered if she were symbolically washing away blood or absently dusting away the psychoactive drug she'd laced into the cookies... or the other one she'd stirred into the chantico... or the third she'd sprinkled with the cinnamon over everything.

"I thought perhaps Ms. Blake would be a problem," she confessed as she walked me upstairs to my room; I hadn't slept in the subterranean labs since I was a child just learning to use my donated body.

"Because she studied sodium thiopental for her P&I degrees," I guessed, not questioning.

"Among other more effective serums," she corrected.

When we reached my door I felt a pang of... something. I think I would miss field work. I would miss my classes. I would miss Gwen.

"Was it true?"

I turned to the doctor. After the complexity of the last hour I wasn't certain I knew what she was asking. I waited.

"What you said, about not liking me."

"Of course it was true." I frowned. "You know I don't lie."

Her face was a mask. "Of course."

I explained because something seemed off. "You're tedious at times. Though not always," I admitted. "You do as I expect you to do. So, no, I don't like you." I put my hand on the door knob of my room, considered saying goodnight but added, "But I am loyal to you, Doctor Janus, and I always will be."

I met her eyes now. I wanted her to read the truth on my face. "You're educating me in the only... *authentic*... way. I can't *be* human, despite residing in a human shell. But if I am to exist at my fullest potential, I must *understand* humans."

Her faint smile returned and I noticed she had a small amount of blood on her collar. Most likely Damien's but possibly Gwen's.

"Thank you, Cain." She was sincere. "I'm grateful for your loyalty."

"Don't be," I insisted, upset now that she was being emotional. What room did we have for irrational attachments in this vital work? If tonight had taught me anything, it was that. "You're my creator. It's basic psychology."

She seemed startled. She seemed shaken. Was she seeing me for the first time? She must be so proud of me.

"Good night, Doctor," I told her, and left her there outside my room.

february

Love Grows

Lauren Patzer

Irina stepped into the police station for the umpteenth time. She'd been there so often, the reception personnel recognized her the moment she walked in the door and were already on the phone to the detective in charge of her sister's disappearance. Irina touched her blonde hair to make sure there were no wisps out of place. It still clung to her head in a tight bun.

A few moments later, a female officer she didn't recognize approached her. Her crisp uniform told Irina she was not only new, but possibly fresh out of the academy. Not enough time being brutalized by the job to let her appearance lapse even the tiniest bit yet.

"Miss Taravicz?" the officer asked.

"Yes, I assume you're here to escort me to Detective Johnson or whoever is in charge of my sister's case today?" Irina responded with a sigh and just a slight hint of venom.

"Of course, it's still Detective Johnson. He wanted to

make sure you didn't wait long." The officer smiled. Irina knew everyone at the precinct had been briefed on what a pain in the ass she was; the officer's smile was pasted on. "Follow me, please."

Irina assumed the customary distance behind the new officer. She casually observed the same daily, busy hustle affecting the personnel there. Phone calls, some urgent, some unhurried, as people tracked down leads, worked with contacts or notified their higher ups about progress on cases. Irina wondered if one of them was calling about her sister.

They reached Detective Johnson's office and her uniformed escort waved Irina in. As she opened the door, Detective Johnson stood up, sporting a nearly ironed shirt, tie and tasteful slacks. He reached across the desk to shake her hand. Irina closed the door behind her and shook his hand.

"Miss Taravicz, it's nice to see you again," Detective Johnson said. He smiled and sat back down. Irina took the seat farthest away from the door and smirked. The detective's short, black curly hair was starting to grey at the temples. She idly wondered if he'd shave entirely to hide it. Was he that vain?

"Surely, seeing me again doesn't bring such joy to your heart." Irina set her hands on her lap. "Have you found my sister yet?"

"I'm pleased to tell you, we've found her." Detective Johnson nodded.

Irina's heart leapt into her throat. They'd found her! She almost smiled but then cocked her head to one side.

"You're pleased?"

"We've been following leads and it appears your sister has been travelling abroad," Detective Johnson said.

"That's not possible. She would've contacted me. It's

been a year!"

"We have financial transactions, travel notes on passports, and eyewitness reports that she's alive and well. She's travelling with a young man, although we don't have his identity." Detective Johnson smiled. "I'm sorry she hasn't contacted you, but we're going to have to close the case."

"You have video confirmation?" Irina asked.

"Well, no, but we don't need it. Her accounts have been accessed and her passport has been used. We don't have a need to look further than that. That's as much as the department can do." Detective Johnson sat back in his chair and folded his hands on his lap.

"I see." Irina stood up and glared at Detective Johnson. "So, he has fooled you. Donald has killed her but kept her persona alive."

"We don't have any evidence to support that." Detective Johnson held up his hands. "I'm sorry, Miss Taravicz, but she simply isn't missing anymore. We can't do anything else."

"Thank you for your effort, Detective. I see you've done all you can." Irina turned and left without another word. She stormed out of the building, tears on her face.

Donald sipped the sweet tea and smiled at the expansive garden in front of him. The azaleas were blooming in the early February weather—still cool with the tendrils of winter still reminiscent in the air. To cultivate the plants, Donald had placed them in raised beds, even though they'd likely have survived just fine in the regular soil. Donald didn't like leaving anything to chance and he'd needed somewhere to put the dirt from his excavations. Waste not, want not.

To the left of him, the English ivy clung to the timbers for the porch and crawled ever so slowly up the side of the house. He appreciated the leafy weed for its resilience and determination as well as its quick growth and healthy root system. Of all his garden inhabitants, this one was the most important for reasons that made him smile.

His smile faded as a familiar red sedan pulled up and Irina exited the vehicle. She walked up the well manicured sidewalk with a sense of purpose. Donald rolled his eyes.

"It's been a year, Donald," she said as she stopped twenty feet away from him and folded her arms. "Where's her body?"

"Irina, you're astute as always with your calendar observations. Shouldn't you be making plans to celebrate this Valentine's Day with a handsome beau or ravishing damsel such as yourself?" Donald sipped his tea.

"Where did you bury Agatha's body?" Irina scowled. "It's been a year. I've contacted the police. Surely after a year missing, they'll realize you've killed her."

"You've contacted them yet again? I'm surprised you don't have them on speed dial. Have they found her in Cambodia or wherever she's traipsed off to with her beau? You should hire a private detective to find her and that stud she's banging and stop harassing me. My love for Agatha has never wavered, but I refuse to be troubled by the disappearance of a woman who was clearly no longer interested in returning my affections. Clearly, all she was interested in was draining my bank account."

Irina looked around the property from where she stood, still remaining on the sidewalk. Donald could put it in his mind to shoot her for trespassing as he threatened last year. She wasn't going to give him an excuse or the satisfaction.

"I see you've put in some ivy," Irina said. "Is that where you buried her?"

"It's English ivy and it put itself in. They're an invasive species. I'd get rid of it but I kind of like the look of it. Gives the place an eccentric charm."

"Bullshit," Irina said. "It wasn't here two years ago; you put it in."

"You can believe what you like, Irina, but I don't need you going around tearing up my plants or harassing me because your tramp of a sister left me. Take your beef up with her when you find her. I'd rather leave the past *buried*."

Irina looked at the ivy and back at Donald. His smug smile set her teeth on edge.

"I think it's time other forms of justice found their way to Agatha's killer. One year is long enough for the police to do the job. You've either bribed them or they're hopelessly incompetent," Irina said as she smiled and raised her eyes to meet Donald's.

"Are you threatening me, Irina?" Donald's face lost its humor. "You don't want to cross me."

"When the moon reaches its zenith tonight, if Agatha is far away from here, you'll have nothing to worry about," Irina said. "If not, you'll grow to regret it, dear brother-in-law."

"Leave before I call the cops myself." Donald smirked. "I don't have time for your empty threats."

"Oh," Irina replied as she turned to walk away. "I think you'll have the time of your life."

Donald watched Irina climb into the sedan. It drove away briefly but then pulled into a house just two doors down—the Jacoby's residence. They'd turned the old two-story Tudor style house into a vacation rental. Irina climbed out of the car and waved at Donald before she walked into the rental property.

"Pain in the ass," Donald muttered. He turned away from

the unsettling scene and walked into his home, letting the screen door slam behind him as he retreated to the interior of the home. As he stepped into his kitchen, his eyes fell on the wall calendar and his hands lightly brushed tomorrow's date, Valentine's Day.

"You'll never be anyone else's, Agatha. You're mine forever," Donald said. He sighed as he set his glass on the counter. He checked the back door to be sure it was locked. He went back to the front door, closed it and engaged the deadbolt. He went back into the kitchen and refilled his tea, humming a little ditty to himself as he went. He closed his eyes and stopped humming, listening to the sounds of the house reacting to the cool breeze, the tender rustle of the ivy leaves on the windows and the subtle scratch of the oak branches at the rear of the home. They'd need to be trimmed soon before they did real damage to the exterior paint and siding.

Satisfied that no one inhabited the home besides himself, he retreated to the cellar below and the wall next to the ivy, where a small window was shuttered against the encroaching elements. He set his glass next to the recliner he had facing that wall. He slowly opened the window to reveal a small patch of dirt just outside the window, hidden from outside view by the English ivy that sprouted there. He reached through the window a patted the ground gently.

"Let her dig up the ivy in her vain attempt to match me," Donald whispered. He smiled, nodded his head and then turned around. He walked to the wall opposite the window and pressed a small area on the wall. There was an audible click and the wall popped open. The wall opened up like a door to reveal a small wine cellar and a safe. He took a few steps into the room and then pivoted to the right, pulling out a bottle of wine from the rack, three from the left and seven from the bottom. He reached his other hand into the small cavity left behind and grasped a small rope hidden in a dark opening above. He yanked it sharply and there was another audible click as the floor next to his feet popped up.

Donald reached under the lip of the raised floor and pulled it up, revealing a small stairway leading down. He placed the wine back in the rack. Descending down the rough wood hewn stairs he had cut by hand from an oak log, he grasped a string to his left and, with a gentle tug, a small light illuminated overhead a few feet from the foot of the stairs. In front of him were two dark green wool blankets hung like a door, one overlapping the other.

Donald looked to his right to a small shelf he'd dug out of the earth nearly a year ago. On the shelf was a small container. He picked it up, unscrewed the lid and then took a finger full of the strong menthol lubricant and wiped it under his nose. He blinked rapidly as the strong odor brought him to full awareness. He put the container back on the shelf and moved to the blankets, pushing aside the flaps and moving into another dimly lit room, much larger than the first.

The pungent aroma of decaying flesh assaulted his nose but was greatly reduced in strength by the menthol. Still, he wrinkled his nose at the odor. He looked to his right and smiled. There, strapped down to a military cot was the gaunt, nearly skeletal figure of a woman, her matted dark hair barely moved as her head jerked slightly.

"It's nearly time, my love," Donald whispered as he knelt down next to the woman. "Your year of penance is nearly at an end."

The woman's sunken face turned toward him and vacant eyes tried to look at him through barely fluttering eyelids. Her mouth opened and a guttural moan emerged.

"Have you forgotten?" Donald asked smugly. "I cut out your lying tongue nearly a year ago. You can tell me no more lies, my love."

Her eyes closed and Donald smiled.

"Tonight, at the stroke of midnight, I'll give you your final sleep. You can join your pathetic lover," Donald sneered as he looked to his left. A body lay on another cot, clearly no longer alive. The flesh had started to fall from the skeleton under its own weight. "In whatever level of hell is reserved for doomed adulterers such as you."

Donald's eyes squinted at her nose and followed the thin tube there going up to the wall of the small cell where a bag of liquid hung like an IV.

"I will admit that hiding the purchases of these meager fluids to keep you alive these many months has been taxing. Going through shell corporations and picking the supplies up from delivery drops has been a bit of a hassle I won't miss. Much as I won't miss you, my precious wife."

He gently patted one of her arms, thin and nearly devoid of all muscle. In response, she moaned almost imperceptibly, lacking the energy to even flinch away from his touch.

"Oh, I almost forgot to mention – your sister stopped by. She's been quite the annoyance. I'm afraid I'll have to arrange something to occupy her thoughts besides myself soon. Much as you, she'll be not quite dead but wishing she was."

Donald stood up and nodded.

"Yes. You can dwell upon your sister's demise while you rot away your last moments on this earth, you pathetic wench."

Donald walked back through the flaps. He turned off the light as he made his way up the steps. He pressed the trap door shut with a small click. He examined the floor and brushed around the small amount of dirt there so it wouldn't be obvious a trap door lay beneath the tiny wine cellar. He exited the small room and reentered the basement proper, closing the large wall door behind him. After wiping the menthol from below his nose with a handkerchief, he sat down in the recliner and took a few sips of his tea. He stared at the small window and tried to pick out the individual leaves of ivy as he fantasized about ways to exterminate Irina.

As the sun fell below the horizon, Donald jerked awake. He looked at the window in front of him and realized he'd fallen asleep. He shook his head.

"You see, my love, I'm so comfortable with our arrangement, I slept like a baby." Donald chuckled and then got up. He closed the window, latched it and retrieved his tea glass as he walked back up the stairs into the kitchen.

After setting his glass in the sink, Donald returned to the living room and looked out the window at the encroaching darkness. Irina's car still sat in the driveway. He mulled over it for several moments before grimacing. He put on a dark coat and unlatched the deadbolt on his front door. Opening the door slowly, he sniffled at his suspicions.

"Stupid hag anyway," he muttered. He stepped out onto the porch and took a deep breath of the cool night air. He turned around and locked the door behind him before venturing down his long sidewalk to the neighborhood cement. He walked briskly in the night air as he glanced around at his neighbors' houses. They'd all gone in to escape the chilly temperatures that came with the absence of sunlight. Convinced he wasn't being watched, he wandered up to the Jacoby property and snuck a peek in the window.

All the furniture had been pushed aside and a large

pentagram had been drawn on the floor with candles lighting up each point of the symbol. A figure in a dark robe sat in the center of the symbol, rocking back and forth and moaning. In between moans, the figure would speak a phrase or two in a language Donald didn't understand. It may have been the separation between them and he just couldn't hear what was being said well. This went on for several minutes, with the moaning getting louder and louder until it became screaming. Donald was mesmerized by the ritual until the screaming stopped and Irina looked up at him with glowing red eyes and laughed with a voice deeper and darker than a woman could have.

Donald stumbled backward until he hit the railing on the porch and tumbled over backward landing face down in the hedges. He scrambled to his feet and ran back to the safety of his home. As he struggled to unlock the door, his keys fell to the floor by the doormat which read "If You're Selling Something, I'm Not Buying It!"

He picked up his keys and stared at the doormat. He turned back to look at the Jacoby place.

"She's just trying to scare me," Donald said as he frowned. "I'm not an idiot. I won't fall for that stupid bitch's theatrics!"

Donald unlocked the door carefully and stepped back into the relative safety of home. He still shook as he closed the door and slid the deadbolt back into place. With the reassuring click of the lock, Donald breathed a sigh of relief.

"Dammit," he mumbled. "She planned this all along. Trying to get me to confess."

He turned to face the window, looking out at the dark windows of the Jacoby house.

"I haven't done anything wrong!" Donald shouted at the window. "I've done everything right!"

Donald looked around at his living room and nodded nervously.

"I've done everything right," he mumbled. He walked slowly to the staircase as he dropped his keys onto a small side table. "As is my right…"

Donald crawled up the stairs, suddenly weary after his headlong flight from the disturbing scene in the Jacoby living room. He glanced about nervously, as if the red eyes followed him and stared at him from the darkness, but there was nothing he could see.

Though it was still early, Donald felt an overwhelming need to turn in for the night. He changed into his pajamas and crawled into his bed, drawing the covers up to his chin. He shivered, though the temperature in the room was merely cool. He felt the warm air flow in from the vents as the heater kicked on. He took a deep breath and closed his eyes, desperate for the solace of dreams.

As the clock struck midnight, Agatha retched for a moment as she gasped for her last breath of air and then passed away, joining her lover in the embrace of permanent darkness. As her chest stopped moving, red light emerged from her body and crawled along the walls. The light stabbed into the earth and tunneled its way to the roots of the ivy next the basement above.

The ivy pulsed with a red glow in the moonlight and began to grow. Slowly at first, but then ever faster the ivy crept along the outside of Donald's house, covering it completely, the sticky tendrils grabbing and grasping at the material of the home, sinking in and anchoring themselves in the walls.

In the cellar below, the ivy burst forth through the small window's glass panes, flowing into the room like water. It permeated everything in the lower bowels of the home except for the now dormant heater with its automatic electric ignition. It gave the appliance a wide berth as it invaded the structure.

Next to the ivy on the outside of the home, the long standing ivy peeled apart the gas line and the noxious fumes began to flow out onto the ground and then into the home through the broken window. Like flood waters, the deadly natural gas filled the home. It rose from the cellar and filled the first floor, before making its slow, inexorable way up the stairs to the second floor.

But the ivy, that strong resilient beast Donald so admired, was well ahead of the gas. It slithered along the floor boards, entering Donald's closed bedroom through the crack under the door. Like a lovelorn admirer, the ivy enveloped Donald in its warm embrace, sliding in between the covers and surrounding every limb. Thrice again, it circled his body in an undulating green womb until finally it gripped its lover tight.

Donald awoke to the tentacled grasp of the ivy tightening around his body. His eyes popped open and he saw the ivy creep up the walls of his bedroom. He caught the stink of sulphur and then, from within the bowels of the ivy growing deeper in his room, he saw two pinpoints of red light emerge. The lights traveled in tandem until they coalesced into a thick veined, purple demon with glowing red eyes that sat down with a crunch on the ivy wrapped around Donald's chest.

Donald wrinkled his nose at the overwhelming stench of rotten eggs. The demon chuckled at Donald's grimace.

"Oh, you'll enjoy so much more discomfort where you're going, my friend," the dark one murmured in a deep, gurgling voice.

Donald's eyes burned with the heat of the hellborn's breath as it leaned into his face. He struggled to breathe, but the ivy tightened its grip around him, crushing his lungs. The weight of the demon added to the burden of trying to gasp for air. Each bit of breath Donald managed to suck in burned like acid.

"Did... nothing... wrong..." Donald mouthed the words as he couldn't muster the air to make them audible.

"Come on, Donnie," the beast of darkness chuckled. "Just between you and me, you know you deserve the painful burning death you're about to experience and the all consuming fires of hell that will burn your soul for eternity."

Donald stubbornly shook his head even as his ability to hear the demon's words faded, replaced by the mad thumping of his heartbeat in his ears as his lungs struggled to bring oxygen in.

Before he passed out, Donald felt the house tremble as the ivy began to pull it apart. Bit by bit, the outer layers of the home were pulled off by the invasive, out of control ivy. Just before they could do any real structural damage to the home, though, the heater kicked on.

The instant before Donald's eyes fluttered shut for the last time, the house exploded. The gas ignited and the pressure wave of the explosion splintered the house to pieces. The explosion tore Donald's head from his body while the ivy actually preserved and protected the rest of him. The resulting fire from the gas leak consumed the rest of his skull fragments and eventually burned away nearly all traces of the ivy invasion of his home.

The next day, Irina watched calmly from a rocking chair on the front porch of the Jacoby residence as firemen put out hot spots. The police sifted through the rubble and someone gave a shout.

"There are more bodies down here! My God, what happened to them?"

Irina stood up and pulled out her binoculars. She focused

on the shouting police and saw people emerging from the remains of the basement level of the house, shaking their heads and falling over themselves as they fled the scene.

Irina nodded her head and smiled.

"Rest in peace, dear sister. You were avenged."

MARCH

Above His Play Grade
C.M. Kane

For those who were better than the best, but never had the chance to show the world.

For Abie, who is better than anyone I know. Thank you so much for your help with this project. You made it more authentic than I ever could have.

For AJ, as always, pushing me beyond where I think I can go. Thank you for believing in me.

Prologue

June 16, 1942

"Hey, boy," a man shouted. "I'm talking to you."

"Please, sir," Clive Washington begged, knowing that nothing this man wanted would lead to anything good. "I'm not doing nothing wrong."

"Who do you think you are?" another of the men who had begun to surround him asked.

"I'm just trying to play a game," Clive said, looking desperately for a way to escape these men.

"What you got in that bag, boy?" another asked.

"Just my gear," Clive replied, holding the bag that held his mitt and bats in it, along with his cleats from the game he'd just finished.

"I think he thinks he's a ball player," the first man laughed, snatching the bag from Clive's hands. "Thinks he's on the same level as the Babe or Gehrig, don'cha, boy?"

"Just trying to play the game and have a little fun," Clive offered, hoping it was what these men wanted.

He'd give anything just to get out of there without being hurt. Sure, he was a good player, one of the best in the negro leagues according to some, but there was no way he'd be able to play with the likes of those the men mentioned.

"Let's see how well you can catch," one of the men said, pulling the bat from Clive's bag.

"You can have everything I've got," Clive offered. "Just let me go."

"You hear that, George?" another man asked. "He's beggin'."

"Not beggin' near enough for me," George said. "Let's see how much you're willing to beg, Nigger."

George took the bat and swung it toward Clive's head. Clive ducked, putting his arms up to fend off the blow. The bat glanced off his forearm without causing any damage. This seemed to just anger George further, and he swung again, this time hitting Clive's wrist, shattering the fragile bones inside. Within minutes, Clive lay in a puddle of his own blood, his bat lying next to him as his life slipped from his body and seeped into the ground underneath him.

"Filthy ape," George said, spitting on Clive's body. "Let's see what he's got in them pockets."

The four men rummaged in the pockets as Clive died, pulling out anything they thought might be worth something.

"Look at this," one of the other men said, holding up a

shiny golden coin. "Looks brand new. Wonder who he stole it from."

"Gimme that," George said. "The good stuff all comes to me. You can have the bat."

George pocketed the coin and left the other three to take whatever else they wanted. He got what he wanted with the first swing of the bat. Everything else was just a bonus.

One

March 1, present day

And you're sure this is authentic?" TJ asked.

"It's been verified," the shop keeper replied. "Would you like to see the authentication?"

"I'll definitely want that if I decide to get it," TJ replied.

"You will need to make a decision today," the man said. "I do have another buyer who is interested and is planning to come see it tomorrow."

TJ flipped the coin in its case over and over in his hands. A 1933 Saint Gaudens Gold $20 Double Eagle. The fact that he stumbled upon this coin store in the middle of West Palm Beach while he was getting ready for his third year in the majors was something that seemed unreal. To find the one missing coin he'd been searching for to add to his collection that had been handed down from his grandfather to his father, then to him when he was sixteen in this little town in the middle of spring training was very fortunate. It wasn't that they weren't out there, but the expense of getting one in this good of condition was something he knew would be outside what he wanted to spend. The fact that he stumbled upon this one that was marked down so much lower than any other he'd seen made him decide that it was too good of a deal to pass up. At half the price, it was still well within his budget.

"I'll take it," he said.

"Perfect," the owner said. "I'll go get the authentication certificate with the history of ownership and be right back. I will need to put the coin into the case until the sale is final, though."

"Of course," TJ agreed, handing the coin back to the store keeper.

He pulled out his phone and shot a text off to his dad.

Found a '33 Double Eagle in good condition. Buying it.

He didn't expect his dad to reply, but got one quickly.

Don't over pay.

He laughed. His dad was always about keeping money tight. With his salary from the baseball team, he had more than enough to purchase a dozen at this price, and still have plenty left over.

I got this, Dad.

His short reply was hopefully all it would take to keep his father from trying to parent him in this. At twenty-six, he was well aware of how to handle his finances, especially since he lived on such a small budget and his income was nearly one hundred times what he spent. Of course, he grew up in a middle-class family that didn't necessarily worry about money, but also didn't have an abundance. He thought his dad probably was just wanting to make sure that TJ had enough for his future, which was appreciated.

"All ready," the man said as he came back from the back area of the store. "Here is the authentication documentation. There is some discrepancy as to its original owner, but from 1942 it has been in the Cherrington family until the last remaining member passed away a few weeks ago."

"There were no heirs to take it?"

"None," the man said. "Are you not from around here?"

"Born and raised in California," TJ said. "I'm only here because of my team."

"Then you don't know the legend," the man continued in a conspiratorial tone.

"Enlighten me," TJ beckoned.

"Story has it that this coin is cursed," the shopkeeper spoke in a hushed tone. "That it was stolen from someone and whoever held it would be haunted by the spirit of that person. There are even rumors that the man it was stolen from was murdered, but then again, most good stories start with something tragic like that."

The way the man threw that last bit in was so nonchalant that TJ paid it no mind.

"I guess if I'm going to own something old," he began, "it will likely have some sort of tragic back story to it."

"But nothing like this," the man continued, again lowering his voice so as not to spread rumors, even though that was exactly what he was doing.

"Do tell," TJ encouraged.

He loved to hear the local folk lore of the places he went, and Florida was no different. This man seemed to want to share, so TJ was willing to listen. He had an hour or two, so had the time to let him spin his tale.

"George Cherrington was known to be an ornery fella," the shop keeper began. "Most unfortunate as to what happened to him. He was said to have brought the coin home from a night out with his friends. Never did tell where he got it, and his friends had been sworn to secrecy as well. Honestly, he was probably out drinking and getting into any kind of trouble he could find. Rumor has it he once beat a man nearly to death with his bare hands in a fight that was brought on by someone looking the wrong way at his girl."

"Sounds like a wonderful fellow," TJ mused. "So, what's the story of what happened to him?"

"My father was alive back then," the man said. "He knew George, but wasn't really friends with him. When I asked about it, he said that the man was just struck ill and ended up leaving his house and never coming home. Body was never found, but he was known to go into the Everglades to party with his friends. After a few days, his parents began to worry about him and asked his friends. No one had seen him in nearly a week. Once the police got involved it was clear he'd gone out there, because they found his car. There was a note wrapped around the coin, and it was clear that he'd gone in there not expecting to come out."

"That's crazy," TJ said.

"It gets better," the man offered. "But those stories are for another time. How would you like to pay?"

TJ pulled out his credit card and handed it over. Within minutes, the transaction was complete, and he was the proud current owner of the beautiful coin. Leaving the store, he climbed into his truck and tucked the coin in the locking center console. It was somewhat early, but he had a game to get to that day, so he headed to the ballpark to get his workout in before the game was set to start. This year was turning out to be better than he imagined.

While he was excited to be on the field, there was something about that coin that made him want to do more research. The way the shopkeeper talked, it sounded like he might not be holding onto the coin for long if it were actually cursed. Then again, he loved a good ghost story, and if he could find the info on this coin's legend, he might just keep it.

Two

March 3

TJ finally had a few hours to himself and he dove head first into finding out everything he could about this coin he'd purchased, and the family that owned it before him.

The last couple of days he'd been stellar at the plate, hitting everything thrown his way. Fielding was outstanding as well, and he chalked it up to having taken the last off season seriously by keeping himself in good shape with workouts and practice sessions with a trainer.

A quick internet search gave him lots of information on the Cherrington family. They had been very much southern royalty, something he'd learned was either a good thing or a bad thing when it came to Florida. The good ones were those who knew the civil war was over and that people were people, even if their skin was darker. We all saw color; we just chose to not let it divide us. The bad ones were still living almost two centuries in the past. They believed that the south would rise up once again and overcome the northern oppressors to get back to the 'good ol' days' that were what they were built on. He didn't particularly like the second group.

The Cherrington family was definitely one of the bad ones. They had been loud supporters of everything that was 'Southern pride' and were not afraid to show it everywhere they went. There were only a few articles from recent times, though, and while the family had dwindled, their pride in all things 'white and right' didn't go quietly. Their fortunes, however, had plummeted and they'd moved from that royalty status of wealth to one of middle to lower class.

He wondered for a moment what they would think of the fact that their precious coin, the one that George had taken with him, the one they wouldn't let go of, was now owned by a black man. Would they be rolling over in their graves? It did make him laugh for a moment.

The few articles that he found on the man the shopkeeper mentioned, who was really more a boy than a man at only 19, were somewhat lacking. Of course, they were from the early 1940's, so that could be why there wasn't much to go on. As he had been told, the man had simply driven into the Everglades and not come out. He wasn't able to find a copy of the note, however he did find out who the remaining family members were from the obituary that had been printed.

It seemed his younger sister, Marie, was the final remaining family member, who had passed away three weeks earlier. The parents were well off, but once their son went missing, they seemed to lose most everything. His father's business went through a rough patch with the government investigating them, then he lost some big contracts or some such thing. There were rumors and such in the society pages from back then, but nothing was clearly laid out. Everything that TJ read seemed to be just one more stone in a large cart they had to carry.

His father ended up with cancer and passed away shortly after his son went missing. The mother had all sorts of medical issues, and was even institutionalized at some point in the mid

1950's. Marie was in and out of institutions and rehabilitation facilities until she was in her late 60's when she just seemed to withdraw from society as a whole. No one knew what happened to the family, other than they just kept running into one bad luck scenario after another.

From what he could tell, though, they kept this coin as a way to stay connected to George through the years. With as many financial issues as they had, he was surprised they hadn't sold it and used that money to help them out. Apparently, though, that was not something they were willing to do. It was the last thing they had from the man who went missing, and they weren't going to give it up.

There were many mentions of items being sold off, and at one point in his research, he came across an estate agency that had taken the bulk of the items left and sold them at auctions and the like. He called them to see if they had anything left from the estate.

"I will have to check our inventory," the woman who answered the phone said.

TJ heard the keys on a keyboard being used, then more clicking, obviously a mouse, with silence between strokes.

"Looks like we only have a box of books that is left," she explained. "It's slated to be sent to the used bookstore in town next week, so if you want to check them out, I'd suggest you do so quickly."

Not wanting to lose the chance to find some insight into the family, he planned to go to the agency the next morning, which is when he actually had time off. The rarity of getting any time off during Spring Training, was such that he took the gift of chance that it was.

Three

March 4

Promptly at 9 am, TJ stepped up to Fielding's Clearinghouse, the agency that had been tasked with handling the estate of the Cherrington family off and on throughout the years. When he stepped in, he was greeted with knickknacks and books and antiques of all shapes and sizes. He hadn't been sure what exactly to expect, but it was not this. Somehow, in his mind, he saw those posh auction scenes from the movies and television shows. This must have been the gritty underside of estate reductions.

"Welcome to Fielding's," a polished young woman said. Her bright smile matched her watch and necklace, which seemed to be a very high end set. "What brings you in today?"

"I'm here to look at what is left of the Cherrington estate," TJ replied.

"Let me just look at the calendar and see who's available," she said, clicking on the keyboard in front of her. "Looks like Mr. Joffe is available," she said. "Can I get your name?"

"I'm TJ Marley," he replied.

She picked up the phone from the cradle and spoke softly in it, then returned it to its stand.

"He'll be out in just a moment," she said with a smile.

"Thank you," he replied.

It wasn't long before a rather short and rather round older gentleman stepped out of a hallway TJ hadn't noticed. He waddled over to TJ, stuffing a handkerchief in the breast pocket of his pinstriped blue suit. He was much younger than TJ expected, but then again, he may just be one of the many who help at the clearinghouse.

"Mr. Marley," he jovially barked, sticking his hand out. "So good to see you. I understand you are interested in the last bits of the Cherrington estate?"

"I am," TJ replied, accepting the offered hand.

"I've got a box of books," the man said. "But that's all there is left. Most everything had already been sold off by the time Marie passed away. All that was left was a couple of boxes of books and her clothes. Most everything else had been sold off to keep her afloat. It really is a sad thing."

"I'm sure it is," TJ replied.

"At any rate," the man said, moving back toward the hallway he'd come out of. "Let's go back to one of the rooms and I'll bring the box in. You're lucky I still have it," he continued as they walked. "It's set to go to Book'Em on Monday."

"Then I'm glad I called when I did," he replied.

"What got you interested in the Cherringtons?"

"I picked up a coin and was told it was part of their estate," he replied.

The man stopped mid stride and looked at him, fear clear in his eyes.

"You don't have it with you, do you?"

The fear he heard from the other man was confusing. The stories about the coin being cursed or haunted or whatever seemed to be tall tales, not something that was believed.

"No," he said, and the man visibly relaxed.

"Thank god," he said, pulling the handkerchief out of his pocket to wipe his extended forehead.

"Is there something I should know?"

"Well," the man hedged as he began moving again, which

was no small task. "Not to tell tales out of school or anything, but it has been said that whoever owns the coin befalls bad luck. It certainly was the case for the Cherringtons."

"Well, I've had it a few days and nothing but good luck has been following me," TJ replied. "Maybe it wasn't the coin that was cursed."

"They did try to sell it," the man said. "The person who bought it, brought it back to them and didn't even ask for the money back. Said it was bad juju or some such thing."

"When was that?"

"Probably in the late '50's," Mr. Joffe explained as they stepped into a small office type space. "I think Mrs. Cherrington wanted to use the money to help her daughter. I'll be right back with the box."

The man moved faster than his size indicated was possible. TJ waited, taking a seat in the chair that was next to the table.

"Here we are," Mr. Joffe said, coming back with one of those banker boxes. He hefted it as if it weighed nothing, but when he set it on the table, it made a loud thud. "This is the last of it. Not really much of value, which is why it was slated to be dropped off at the used book store. If you find anything, just let us know."

With that, the man stepped out of the door and left TJ with the remnants of an entire family. It was kind of sad in a way, knowing that nothing but a small box of books was all that was left of the legacy of a once very well-known and apparently well-loved family. He guessed that everyone would one day be reduced to the things that were left from their lives. Oh sure, the impact they had on the world would be around as well, but the tangible side of it, the things one could hold in their hands, that was all that was left from this family, especially since there were no heirs to carry on their memories.

After about half an hour, TJ had found the one thing he was hoping for. Tucked away inside what looked to be a diary of some sort was the letter that George had written when he went into the Everglades. It was old, tattered, but still legible. Some of the ink was smudged with what looked like moisture rings, but TJ couldn't make out what had caused it. He decided that he would purchase the diary, as well as a first edition of an Agatha Christie novel he'd found in the box. His mother loved her, and it would be the perfect gift for her for Mother's Day.

Taking the books he wanted to purchase, he placed the others back in the box neatly, then stood and stepped out of the room, retracing his steps to the front of the building.

"All finished?" the woman at the counter asked when he got close.

"Sure am," he replied.

"Oh," she said as he handed the items to her. "I was thinking of grabbing this book if no one took it."

"Did you want it?" he asked, not wanting to take anything away from someone who had their eye on it.

"No, no," she insisted with that bright smile she had when he walked in. "I just thought I'd grab it if it was available. Not a problem to sell it to you at all."

"If you're sure," he said, still wanting to ensure she wasn't upset at missing out on it. "I just figured you guys would get first dibs on anything that came in."

"We do get to get a sneak peek at the items," she supplied. "But we're required to offer it to customers before we can take anything, unless we're willing to pay the top dollar price above what we would normally get from a sale.”

“That doesn't seem fair,” he said.

“I mean,” she shrugged, then started clicking on the computer. “Looks like this one isn't in there,” she said, holding up the diary. “Let me check with Mr. Joffe.”

She picked up the phone and once again spoke so low that TJ couldn't hear what she was saying. She replaced the handset on its cradle and said, “This one is free.”

“I can't accept that,” TJ said. “I should at least pay something.”

“Mr. Joffe said that it would likely be thrown away by the bookstore when we dropped it off,” she explained. “If you take it, then it won't be thrown in the trash. I'm afraid I'm going to have to insist.”

The smile on her face was enough to push him over and he agreed to take the diary along with the other book he'd chosen. She rang the items up, gave him his total, and he pulled out his card to pay. She wrapped the books in tissue paper, then placed them in a paper sack and handed them to him.

“I hope you enjoy them,” she said.

“Thanks,” he replied. “I will.”

Four

March 6

It had been two days since he'd picked up the diary with the letter in it, and he hadn't had time to look at either of them because the team had been busy with split squad games the whole time. That was one of the drawbacks of Spring Training, though. You spend so much time in training, and the little time you get off, you spend either sleeping or traveling. He had been lucky to get the chance to look through the box and find what he was looking for. After he'd picked it up, it had been locked in the center console of the truck the entire time.

With the morning game finished, and having that afternoon off since they were not traveling, TJ pulled the bag from the estate sale place out of the console and brought it into his apartment. He had put the coin into the safe he had the day he got it, but wanted to read through the note as well as the diary. Eventually, they'd probably end up in the safe, right beside the coin and the book for his mother. While it would be odd reading someone else's words, he wanted to see if he could unravel the mystery of this coin and all that went with it.

You'll all think I'm crazy, but this coin is cursed. I should never have taken it, never have stolen it. He won't leave me alone, constantly whispering in my ear, looking at me from the mirror, reminding me of what was done... of what I'd done. I can't take it any longer, can't live like this. I should probably take it with me into the Glades, but I'm afraid he'll follow me there, too. Get rid of it, sell it, do something. It's bad, so bad, and I can't do it anymore.

The note was on a small piece of paper, torn from a notebook of some sort. The paper was thicker than what he was used to, but it had held up remarkably in the years since it had been written. Some of the writing was hard to read, and the cursive didn't help in that regard, either. The thing that struck him was the fact that George had talked about seeing another man in the mirror. What was also odd was that the man had said he was reminded of what he'd done.

TJ pulled out his laptop and started searching for things in the area around the time that he had searched before, hoping to figure out what this man was talking about. Maybe he'd find out why he was so troubled, what he may have done to cause such turmoil.

Unfortunately, records keeping wasn't nearly as accessible as he hoped from things back that far. He found the information on the Cherrington family because they were wealthy, but couldn't find anything that may indicate what the kid was talking about. He decided to go the old-fashioned route and picked up the diary he'd found the note in. There were pages and pages of entries, some with dates, but most without. Deciding it might be best to just start at the beginning, he did just that.

George is at it again. He and his friends were out all night, and mother was at her wits end with worry. That boy will never learn that what he does has such an impact on her. Father says it's her fragile constitution, but I know better.

The next entry had a date of February 14, 1940. That would have made George seventeen. He may have still been in school, maybe not, though.

I can't believe father let George off with just a warning. He ruined my dress for the debutant ball. Mother and I worked so hard on that dress. We didn't get a chance to have Ms. Collingsworth make it because we were too late, so we had to work on it ourselves. George knew what this meant to me, and he just ruined it. Father doesn't understand because he's not a girl, but this is my coming out party, the time that is all about me, and George goes and ruins it. He ruins everything.

The obvious tear stains on this page were dominant, and TJ didn't blame the girl. He knew the popularity of these balls, even today, so could only imagine how important it was for Marie. His teammate, Wil, told him all about his sister's. It was ridiculous the amount of money and time that went into getting everything ready for this tradition. As if parading their daughters around, just to show they were now young woman, was a good thing.

Honestly, TJ was glad he grew up in California rather than where he spent his March now. He wouldn't want to be involved in this type of thing at all. It was outdated, sexist, and just all around awful. But the young women in the south loved it. He wondered whether there were any pictures of the Cherrington family. He hadn't found them, at least any that were worth looking at. There was just the picture of George for the obituary, and that was grainy and obviously from the newspaper clippings. It was getting late, so he decided to put everything away and pick it up the next time he had a day off, or at least either a morning or afternoon.

Five

March 9

You're on fire, man," Wil said as they came off the field. "What you been eating lately?"

"Same thing as you," TJ replied.

"Then you must have picked up some magic charm or something," the other player said as they made their way into the locker room.

Wil had a point. TJ had been doing better and better each day, both on the field and at the plate. He had such an energy about him as well, and he honestly couldn't figure out what it was that was boosting him. It was unnatural, but not unwanted. He was also marveling at the littlest things. The cheer from the stands, the comradery of the players, and the sheer joy he felt every time he stepped on the diamond.

He'd always loved the game, but this was something he couldn't put his finger on. Something more than just that simple love, but like it was a gift that would never be taken for granted.

"TJ," a reporter said as he stepped into the clubhouse. "You seem to be playing each game as if it were your last. What's that all about?"

"Just blessed to be here," he replied. "The ability to play the game on this big stage is more than any one man can ask for. Happy to be doing what I do, and getting paid for it, too."

"You've been playing at a higher level this spring," another reporter said. "What do you attribute that to?"

"Just good old fashioned hard work," TJ replied. "I spent the off season focusing on what would happen come spring, and I think it's paying off very well."

"It sure seems to be," the reporter replied.

The reporters finally left the locker room and the players began their end of game rituals. Showering, putting their gear back in their lockers, getting things ready for the next game. It was all so natural that TJ just let it flow. That was, until he stepped up to the sink. He splashed some water on his face, grabbing shaving cream to spread across his chin. When he looked in the mirror, he froze.

The face that stared back at him was not his own. It was a man he'd never seen before. It wasn't like it was just someone else, but more like it was another face superimposed over his own. The skin was a little darker, the hair a little wilder, and the nose more prominent. TJ blinked and looked back, but the other man was gone. He shook his head and laughed, realizing he'd probably been thinking too much about that stupid note he'd found.

"You look spooked," Jace said, patting him on the back.

"Nah," TJ replied. "I think I just need more sleep."

"Burning the midnight oil with the ladies?" the other player joked.

"Hardly," TJ said. "There isn't enough time to do anything but my job."

"Yet you found time to go treasure hunting," he said.

"I always find time for that," TJ laughed.

Finishing his post-game ritual, he went back to his locker and picked up his things to head out.

"Drinks?" Wil asked.

"Nah," TJ said. "I'm heading home. Gonna get some good rest for the early game tomorrow. Have fun."

"You know I will," Wil laughed as they walked to their cars.

TJ would never understand how some of the guys could go out and tie one on after a game and still manage to play great the next day. If he tried that, he'd be lucky to be able to see the ball coming to the plate, let alone try and hit it. Oh, he'd had his fair share of stupid mistakes when he'd first started. Partying with the other rookies and the like, but that scene had never really been his thing. No, he was more of a quiet, introvert, who needed to recharge after a game. He craved his solitude.

The drive back to his apartment was uneventful, and he stepped in and tossed his keys onto the kitchen counter, heading for his bed. He would love to simply crash, but once the lights were out and it was quiet, his mind began to wander. Finally, some time in the early morning hours, he fell asleep, only to have fitful dreams that were full of fear, terror, and pain.

Six

March 14

The days had blurred together, as they almost always did during Spring Training. The season was its own kind of crazy, but spring was worse. During the regular season there were more off days, travel was better, and the intensity of it all kept things moving without issues. Spring was all about finding your groove, returning to the form you knew at the end of the previous season, and getting back into the rhythm of play.

Any injury, especially in the spring, meant that it could jeopardize not just the next few days, but months and months if it weren't taken care of early. TJ had previously had an issue with his wrist, but being it was on his right arm, and he was left-handed, it wasn't as serious as it could have been. Bodies got sore during the season; it was a fact of life. But when he woke that morning, there was definitely something wrong.

"What's up?" the trainer asked as TJ stepped into the man's office.

"Something's not right with my wrist," the player said.

"Let me see." The trainer held out his hand, and TJ placed

his own into the other man's. He gave a low whistle and looked at TJ. "What did you do?"

"That's the thing," TJ explained. "It was fine last night. Hasn't bothered me at all since I first got it fixed three years ago. Woke up with it feeling like it was busted or something."

"And you weren't out screwing around?"

"Come on, coach," TJ said. "I'm not like that."

The trainer knew TJ, and had always been impressed with his mature nature. He also knew that players could get into trouble, even when they weren't looking for it.

"Let's get a picture," he said, stepping out of the office and heading toward the medical section of the training facility.

TJ had been here many times, but mostly it was for bumps and bruises from sliding too hard or diving for something. Occasionally he'd be hit by a pitch and would have to get things checked out, but it had been years since he'd had to have anything x-rayed, and he was hoping that the pain he was feeling was all in his head and not something more serious.

"Right wrist," the trainer said to the x-ray tech. "All the views you can."

"Will do," the man said. "Follow me."

TJ followed the man back into the exam rooms where he was instructed to pull off his shirt, watch, and any other metal around his hand. He was handed a smock to wear while getting the diagnostic studies done. It didn't take long, and once he was done, the tech wished him a good day.

Walking back to the locker room area, he ran into Wil.

"Hey," the other man said. "What you doing with the meds?"

"Something's messed up in my wrist," TJ replied.

"Dude," Wil laughed. "You'll go blind doing that."

"Very funny, jackass," TJ replied.

"Just saying," Wil continued to jab.

"Marley," the trainer shouted from his office.

"Coming," TJ replied, walking away from his teammate. "What's up?"

"Sit," the trainer said, and it was then that TJ noticed the manager was also in the office.

He sat where directed and waited. Obviously, something on the x-rays was wrong, but he didn't know what it was, or why they were so concerned.

"How long ago did you break your wrist?" the manager asked.

"I didn't," TJ replied, confused.

"There are signs of healing from a break that is probably a couple of years old," the trainer said. "If you didn't break it, why does the scar tissue show otherwise?"

"I strained it a couple three years ago," TJ explained. "They took x-rays and said there was nothing broken. I iced it, wore a brace for a few days, and it was back to normal. Check my records."

"We did," the manager said. "That's why we're confused."

"I show only the strain," the trainer offered. "Nowhere does it show that you had a break for any of your bones. Can you explain why it is showing up now?"

"I don't know," TJ said. "I've never broken it, so I don't know why there's scar tissue and stuff around it."

"Well," the trainer said. "That scar tissue is what is causing the pain. We may need to do surgery to get it out of there. If we do, it will be at least six weeks of recovery, maybe more."

"I'm playing really well right now," TJ complained. "I can't see having surgery."

"But we need to figure out what is going on with your wrist," the manager said. "I can't have you on the field broken."

"Can I take the day off and see if it's better tomorrow?"

"OK," the manager said. "But if you still have issues, you have to get an MRI and more testing. I can't have you being a liability on the field. I know that you guys play injured all the time. I did, so it makes sense you would, too. But if it's broken, or on the verge of breaking, then we need to be sure we don't screw it up more."

"Wear this," the trainer said, handing him a brace for his wrist. "We'll reassess tomorrow. Be here first thing."

"Will do," TJ replied.

"Get dressed," the manager said. "You may be riding the pine, but your teammates need your cheering."

"Thanks," TJ said, standing and exiting the office.

He walked to his locker where Wil was getting changed.

"What did they say?" Wil asked.

"I have scar tissue," TJ replied. "Said it's from a break at least a couple of years ago."

"You did hurt your wrist then," Wil suggested.

"But it wasn't broken," TJ said. "They took film and everything, and it was just a strain. There is no reason why I should have this pain, or the scar tissue."

"I don't know what to tell you," Wil said as he pulled his shirt on. "You playing?"

"Coach wants me to ride pine today," TJ said. "Just my voice will be part of the game today."

"Damn," Wil said with a low whistle.

"Yeah," TJ said. "I was totally in the groove, and this is just gonna get me all out of whack."

"Good news is you'll get to cheer me on," Wil laughed. "Nothing better than that."

"Whatever you say, weirdo," TJ replied.

Wil headed out to the field while TJ changed for his day of doing a whole lot of nothing. He couldn't do batting practice because his wrist wouldn't work right. He couldn't field balls because he couldn't even get his mitt on. There was nothing to do but watch the rest of his teammates get in their reps and bolster their play for the season.

He'd never been in a position like this. Whenever he'd been hurt, he knew he couldn't play, and he knew why. This time, however, he simply woke up with a wrist that didn't want to work right. Having a day off during Spring Training was a luxury he never had, but this was altogether different. The anguish he felt about not being able to go out there and work out with his teammates was more than a little unsettling.

I'm sorry.

The voice was sudden and deep and he had never heard it before. He looked around, wondering who was messing with him, but he was alone at the edge of the field. The other players were out there shouting and working hard, but this voice was intimate and close.

It'll be better tomorrow.

Again, he was unnerved by the voice. He couldn't tell whether it was inside his head, or coming from somewhere else.

"You good?" one of the players asked. "You look like you've seen a ghost."

Suddenly, it all clicked. The coin, the note that George had written, all about hearing someone's voice, seeing him in the mirror. Maybe the coin was cursed after all. If it was, he would need to get rid of it before he lost everything, especially the game that he loved most.

"I'm fine," TJ lied, hoping to be left alone.

"You don't look fine," another player said as he stepped up to him as well.

TJ looked up and realized that there were half a dozen players standing near him, all of them looking concerned.

The manager came up then and said, "Get back to work." The players went back to their drills and the manager addressed TJ directly. "Go home," he said. "You're not in the right mind to be here; I can see it. Get your shit figured out and come back tomorrow ready to work."

"Will do," TJ said, standing from the bench and heading back into the locker room.

TJ gathered the things he needed and headed out of the facility, making his way to his truck. As he stepped up to the door, he noticed his reflection in the window. The problem was, it wasn't his face he was seeing. He glared at the glass, hoping to make it right, but it remained a stranger looking back at him, the same stranger that had looked at him in the locker room.

"Who are you?" he shouted, then looked around the parking lot to ensure that no one was there.

Name's Clive, the voice replied, but TJ could tell he could only hear it inside his head.

"Well, Clive," he said, putting as much anger into his voice as he could muster. "You're messing with me, and it needs to stop."

I probably went about this all wrong, Clive said.

"Yah think?"

TJ was more than just frustrated, he felt like he was going crazy. Here he was, in the middle of the parking lot, talking to himself. He glanced back at the window of his truck, but only saw his own reflection this time. Angry, he opened the door and climbed behind the wheel. He stuck the key in the ignition and drove.

Seven

March 14

He didn't know where he was going, just that he had to get away from where he was. Really, he needed to get out of his own head. The parking lot lead out to a road, which he followed to the freeway. Unsure where he was going, he simply let the wheels take him, instinct his guide. When he'd driven for a couple of hours, he pulled off the interstate and traveled some back roads. Eventually, he found himself pulling into the Everglades.

It was beautiful. Oh sure, it was swampy and there were terrifying creatures out there, but at the same time, it was remarkable to see so much green. Turning the engine off, he wondered what George was thinking when he found himself here. Was he terrified of the glades? Or was it someplace he thought he would find solace?

George was a coward, Clive said.

"And you know this how?"

He's the reason I am the way I am.

"That doesn't make sense," TJ argued.

I was a player, Clive said. *Just like you.*

"When?"

Back before George got it in his fool head to play his little game.

"You're a ghost because of him?"

Maybe, Clive pondered.

It was clear no one had asked him that question. TJ could hear the uncertainty in his voice.

"So, tell me what happened."

TJ not only wanted to know what happened, but also why Clive decided to stick to him.

I was one of the best, Clive said. *At least, that's what they told me. That I could have really been something.*

"Then how come I've never heard of you?"

You never heard of a lot of us, Clive said, and there was anger in his voice.

"Why not?"

We weren't fit to play, he said.

"I don't understand," TJ said, and he was honestly trying to figure out exactly who this Clive was and why he'd ended up here.

He couldn't be sure, but this was likely somewhere near where George ended his life. It might have been on this very road.

Don't you never mind about George, Clive said.

"You have to admit that there are some similarities between him and me," TJ replied.

You ain't nothing like that fool, Clive retorted, and TJ could feel the anger. *He was nothing but a low-down dirty snake. Nothing he ever did was good.*

"How do you know?"

George did nothing but take, Clive explained. *He took and took and kept on taking until there wasn't anything else to give. Then, he'd take more, something that he couldn't really have, but didn't want anyone else to have, either.*

"What I've read indicated that he was not the nicest guy,"

TJ said.

He would go on and on about how I weren't good enough to be around him, the ghost explained. Said I didn't deserve any of the praise I got on the playing field. When he saw me with his sister, that was the end of it.

"Marie?"

Yes.

That one word held so much emotion, so much feeling. There was more to the story of this family than what TJ had been able to read.

"Tell me about her," he said.

She was beautiful. The tone had changed, and there was so much joy in the voice now. He felt it in his heart, the love that this man had for Marie. She was bright as the sun, more beautiful than any flower you could find, and she had a heart that gave more than it ought to.

"She sounds amazing," TJ said.

That doesn't even cover it, Clive replied. She was my everything. I swore to her that we would go somewhere and find a place that we could be together without all the horrible thoughts that people were saying in town.

"What do you mean?"

You saw me, right?

"Sure," TJ said.

Then you know we couldn't be together, Clive said.

"I don't understand," TJ said, and it was true.

There was no way he could understand what Clive and Marie went through.

It wasn't just George who didn't want us together, the ghost explained. It was her parents and every other upstanding Christian member of society here in town.

"That's ridiculous," TJ said, and the heat in his voice was something he wasn't used to.

You're a lucky man, Clive said.

"Except I'm stuck with a ghost who messed up my wrist," TJ laughed, trying to lighten the mood that was suddenly heavy.

Yeah, Clive said. *That was the parting gift from George.*

"What do you mean?

He killed me, the ghost said. *But his first blow was to my wrist, to make sure that if I did survive this beating, I'd never be able to play again.*

"He beat you?"

Many times, Clive said. *It was the last one that killed me. He took more than my life, though. That coin was mine, and I was saving it for Marie.*

"He killed you and stole the coin," TJ agreed. "And you stayed with the coin?"

Didn't have much choice, the ghost replied. *He took my soul when he took the coin.*

"Is that why he killed himself?"

I wouldn't let him rest, the other man said. *I couldn't. He took everything from me, and even that wasn't enough.*

"I don't blame you," TJ said.

Let's do something about your wrist, Clive said.

TJ would never be able to explain the feeling that came over him. It was as if his wrist was being knitted together within his skin. It was cold, then hot, then nothing. No ache, no pain, not even the pins and needles that had begun that morning.

Better?

"What did you do?"

What I wished I could have done to myself, Clive said.

"Tell me," TJ said, and he didn't have to say what he

wanted to know.

There's too much hate in those moments, Clive said. *I don't want you to have to experience that. No one should have to feel what I did.*

"Why did George kill you?"

It was a question TJ needed an answer to, but also one he already knew.

He wouldn't allow us to be together, Clive said. *He stole the gift I'd worked for. The thing I was going to present to Marie. He knew that if I had been able to give that to her, she would have realized that I would do anything for her.*

"Are you tied to it?"

How do you think I stay with you?

"But it's in the safe at my apartment," TJ said.

Are you sure?

He didn't know how, but he felt the coin in his pocket. It had been there all along. Remembering back, he could feel it every time he stepped up to the plate. Every time he took his place on the diamond. Each step on that field had been brighter and more fascinating than it had ever been in years past.

I always wanted to play in front of a crowd, Clive said. *To hear them cheer for me. Feel the grass under my cleats and the bat in my hand. You've been given a wonderful gift.*

"You were with me that whole time," TJ marveled. "Every single thing I've done this year, you've been there."

And I thank you for that experience, Clive said.

"Then you played," TJ said.

Sure did, Clive replied. *Loved to go on that field and hit the ball and catch it and throw. Everything about being inside those chalk lines was magical.*

"Will you stay with me?"

I thought you wanted me to leave.

It was a struggle, for both of them. Neither wanted to give themselves up, but they also didn't want to deny the other the opportunity.

"Let's be one while on the field," TJ suggested.

And when we're not?

"Then we are our own man," TJ explained. "At least for a little while."

You'd be willing to give me this?

"You should have had it the whole time," TJ said.

He pulled the rear-view mirror around so he could look at himself. When the reflection showed him the other man, he smiled. It was mirrored, but it truly was the other man's smile.

"You aren't half so bad to look at," TJ laughed.

You should have seen me dance, Clive retorted, a laugh of his own.

"Let's go play ball," TJ said and started the truck back up.

Epilogue

March 31

ell us what your secret is," a reporter said as she shoved a microphone into TJ's face.

The rest of the spring he'd been nearly perfect. His bat was quicker through the zone, his aim was on target with each throw, and he felt as if he could fly while out in the field.

"Magic," he replied with a smile. "That, and the memories of Clive Washington. He was an amazing player, could have been one of the best. He never got the chance because he wasn't worthy in some folks eyes."

"I don't think I've ever heard of him," the reporter replied.

"And it's a damn shame, too," TJ said. "That man was better than any player I've ever had the pleasure of spending time on the diamond with. You should look him up."

aPRiL

Advent of the Barnabins
James Lowell Snyder

ernie Twitchell stood at his living room window wondering at the odd light coming from down over the low ridge in his woodsy back yard. The odd luminescence came from something inside the fence but it was just a bit too low to see clearly.

"What is that," he mumbled to himself, puzzled by the unusual glow.

The light created a small rainbow effect which he could see, but the source remained below his horizon. Bernie slid open the heavy patio door.

He walked out on the patio ducking as he always did to avoid bumping his head. Bernie was six feet four, one hundred forty-five pounds and well-conditioned to ducking his head. Closing the door behind him, he went on down the gravel path toward the mysterious light. Bernie stopped short when the source of the light came into view.

It was some kind of little animal. What kind of animal glows? As Bernie moved a bit closer the glowing seemed to be fading. The creature was about the size of a small cocker spaniel but it looked more like one of those Australian koalas, except it was snow white in color and had no ears. He edged closer and moved sideways to circle around the creature. The creature turned its head to keep track of Bernie. Whatever it was, it was a cute little guy. Bernie grinned at it.

Immediately, the animal grinned back at him. Bernie was startled by the animal's reaction.

"Whoa," Bernie yelped. He was not expecting a big smile from whatever that was.

Bernie began looking around to see if there were more of the creatures or anything else unusual. He noticed the grass was wilted and scorched in a circle around the animal.

"Huh…" he murmured. "What could do that to the grass?" Bernie shivered and felt an eerie tingling in his arms and legs. It was a cool day but it seemed even colder down here in the trees. He decided to go inside, but he paused again while looking at the little creature.

"Should I take you in with me?" he wondered out loud, then was surprised that he had asked.

The creature looked at Bernie in what seemed an almost pathetic way, as if it were begging him to shelter it. He bent down and picked it up.

That beautiful white fur was the softest, smoothest fur Bernie had ever felt in his life. He began to feel more comforted than he had felt for years. No one had touched him in such a way since his mother did when he was a little boy. Mom had died when he was six. All at once he felt good all over. Bernie walked up to the patio door and slid it open.

As soon as he stepped through the patio door Beverly shrieked at him, "What's that filthy thing you've got? Is that a dog? I've told you I don't want any damned dogs near this house.

Oh! What will this do to my allergies," the woman yelled at no one in particular.

Beverly had backed all the way from the living room, through the dining room, and into the kitchen, all the while screaming at her husband. Beverly was allergic to every kind of animal dander and most other things in the universe. When she agreed to marry Bernie she had made it quite clear there would be no pets and no tobacco in her house. Ever. So, Bernie had quit smoking and gave his beloved dog Wilbur to his brother Clive. Bernie loved Wilbur.

Wilbur was the best friend Bernie ever had. Even better that his brother, Clive. Wilbur had never hurt him, never disappointed him, never let him down. Wilbur was just good. Bernie felt guilty for forsaking the animal. Still, every time Bernie visited Clive the dog became ecstatic upon seeing Bernie and seemed hurt when Bernie prepared to leave.

Bernie continued trying to quiet Beverly, but she wouldn't stop yelling. Finally, he took the animal and put it in his bathroom, where Bev never ventured. He came back out and set to work calming his wife. After several minutes she began to listen to him.

"Bev, Hon, this it's not a dog or cat. I don't know what it is. I've never seen anything quite like it. It might be Australian."

"What do you mean, *Australian*," bawled Bev. "It doesn't look like any kangaroo I ever saw."

"Well, it looks sort of like a koala, but it's all white, and somehow different, and I don't know how big koalas are. Please don't make me throw it out," pleaded Bernie.

"Just don't expect me to feed it and clean up after it," Bev shouted in Bernie's face.

"Please, Hon, at least look at it. It has the smoothest, softest fur I have ever seen anywhere. You might like it," he begged.

"I won't," she grumbled. "Just stay on the other side of the room with it," she fired back as she waddled her rotund frame back to the kitchen. Bernie dashed to his bathroom to collect the animal. He returned in moments.

"Here, Hon. Look at this fur, Babe. It's unreal!" Bernie gushed as he carried his prize into the kitchen.

As Bernie approached Beverly, she actually looked at the creature in his arms and noticed it had little hands, each with four finger-like appendages. She was fascinated by them. As Bev stared at those hands, the creature made a sound. It was a bubbly, giggle-like sound which was indescribably melodious and endearing. Then Bev looked at the creature's face. It's eyes were golden spheres with large cat's eye pupils of Persian blue which totally captivated the woman.

"Oh, my god," said Bev, as she let out a bubbly-giggle sound herself. "What is it? I... I want to hold it." Miraculously, this creature didn't seem to bother her allergies. Inexplicably drawn to the creature, Bev began to cuddle the creature like a human baby and mumble soft reassuring sounds to the little fellow.

Bernie stood there with his mouth open, stunned by Bev's reaction to the animal. He had never seen her this way. How had the creature managed to win Bev over so quickly?

Bev turned to her husband with a big smile on her face and said, "Let's call him Barnaby."

Bernie wondered why this little animal had won Bev's affection so quickly. Why had she hated good old Wilbur but loved this little thing? After a while, Bernie began to wonder what would happen when it was time for bed. What would Barnaby do? Where would he sleep?

Bernie had worried for nothing. That night, Bev took

Barnaby to bed and curled up with him resting between her and her husband in their king size bed. As she nestled down with the creature she said, "We'll keep little Barnaby warm and cozy between us." The little creature settled down comfortably and went to sleep there between them.

Bev and Bernie never had what anyone would describe as a great sex life. Their personalities, as well as their bodies, never seemed to be a good fit and their love life suffered even more with dear little Barnaby nestled between them night after night.

Bernie was able to nudge Barnaby aside occasionally and experienced a brief bit of marital bliss, but Bev was so absorbed by Barnaby she didn't seem to even notice Bernie's presence.

A thought flashed through Bernie's mind during such a one-sided sexual connection one night, "Is this a ménage à trois?"

The Twitchells had expected to have children. Wasn't that why people got married? Bernie had wondered why Bev had never conceived. He sometimes suspected she was taking steps to prevent it, but he lacked the courage to confront her on the subject. With the arrival of Barnaby the thought of children faded away. Somehow, Barnaby fulfilled their quest for offspring. Ironically, somehow Bev had become much nicer and more approachable sexually.

The three of them had settled in comfortably. After the passage of three months, or so, Bev began to show signs of pregnancy and Bernie felt quite manly and proud of himself. He had done it. He'd fathered a child.

Bernie boasted to neighbors. He strutted at work down at Shoes! Shoes! Shoes! LLC. He told his brother, Clive, who was unable to father children. Clive cried and said, "At least we'll have someone to carry on the Twitchell name." So, the two brothers went down to a beer joint on Park Street and got drunk. Later, the bartender called Bev to pick the boys up because the bar owner was afraid to let either of them drive home. Bev had mellowed so much she wasn't even angry. In fact, she thought it was a bit funny because neither of them had ever done anything like that before.

Barnaby delighted in playing and being held by anyone who picked him up. After several weeks, the Twitchells ventured out into the neighborhood to show off little Barnaby. They were soon invited to parties by neighbors to whom they had never before spoken.

Barnaby caused the same reaction throughout the neighborhood as he had done in the Twitchell residence. Their friends and neighbors were instantly enamored of Barnaby, especially the women. Barnaby adjusted easily to all the affection showered on him. Everybody expressed their liking for the little guy, even Maude Klimpt, still an attractive woman who hadn't smiled in the two years since her husband Clark ran off with that slutty aerobics instructor down in the strip mall. Bev practically had to pry Barnaby out of Maude's clutching hands.

All the women reacted the same way. Young, mature, aged, it didn't matter. At every party, no matter when or where, the women gravitated toward Barnaby. Bernie was amazed and a little jealous of Barnaby's ability to make women love him instantly. The other men began to feel the same way. Several neighbor men suggested Bev and Bernie take their damned pet and go home.

After Bev had visited Bernie at work one day, Jason Bridger, Bernie's supervisor and four-time runner-up as best sales manager at Shoes! Shoes! Shoes! LLC, told Bernie, "Tell your wife to keep that damned animal out of my store. It's disrupting business. Don't ever let her bring it back."

Bev's pregnancy was showing now, so she finally scheduled a visit to the family doctor, a nice man named LeRoy Tice, M.D. Dr. Tice was delighted to see Beverly pregnant. He had known Beverly since childhood and had doubted it would ever happen, so he was genuinely happy for her and Bernie.

Beverly had babbled on and on to him about her new pet, and the doctor said, "Perhaps cuddling the new pet has allowed you to relax and become more receptive to pregnancy." Bev liked that idea.

At thirty-three, Bev was a little old to be having her first baby, so Dr. Tice was of the opinion Beverly may be better off in the care of a specialist. The good doctor called Valonia R. Macintyre, M.D., the most renowned gynecologist in the tri-county area. Old Doc Tice assured Beverly that Valonia R. Macintyre, M.D., would be up for whatever problems her pregnancy might present, not that he expected any.

Bev and Bernie began redecorating one of the bedrooms in anticipation of the coming nativity. Bev planned for a girl, of course Bernie wished secretly for a boy. So they joyously argued constantly about paint colors, furniture, clothes and everything else they could find to disagree upon. The pregnancy progressed normally. The continuing fun with Barnaby coupled with the harmony and joy which had unexpectedly entered their marriage made the days pass quickly and happily. The baby was doing well—perhaps too well, as it seemed to be growing quite fast. "Gonna be a big 'un like me," boasted Bernie to his shorter brother, Clive.

When they were approximately at the four-month point Beverly was to have her initial visit with Valonia R. Macintyre, M. D., the most renowned gynecologist in the tri-county area. Bernie was concerned that his health insurance might not cover such an expensive specialist, but Dr. Macintyre's nurse, a very nice lady named Martha Jones, assured Bernie he had nothing to worry about. Everything would be worked out.

During the visit, Dr. Macintyre, a tall, stern looking woman with her blond hair worn in a tight twist, who always spoke in a precise, businesslike manner frightened Bernie a bit. Of course, Bernie found most women frightening, but Dr. Macintyre was more so because she was an educated professional woman.

The doctor quickly determined the baby was rather large, which bore watching. To herself, Doctor Macintyre decided she had best plan for a caesarean delivery for this one. The doctor scheduled monthly exams thereafter.

At the five-month visit Dr. Macintyre again said the baby was large, but still within the limits advised by The American Gynecological & Obstetrical Society for the fifth month. Bernie came with Bev to this meeting as he always did and happened to mention Barnaby in passing.

Dr. Macintyre asked, "Who is Barnaby?"

"Oh, that's our pet," replied Bev.

"What sort of pet is it? A dog, or cat?" quizzed the doctor.

"Aaah… um… We're not certain," said Bernie.

"You're not certain?" quizzed the doctor. "Where did it come from?"

"We don't exactly know," said Bernie. "I found it in our backyard."

"And you just took it in your house?" the doctor demanded to know with a bit of alarm in her voice.

"Yeah, but it's okay. It's real friendly and sweet and cuddly," replied Bernie.

"Do you know anything else about it?" the doctor asked.

Bev answered, "It kind of purrs."

"Like a cat?" the doctor inquired.

"No, it... Barnaby's not a cat," Bev and Bernie chimed in near harmony.

'Well," said Valonia. "I'd like to see this Barnaby."

That evening after her clinic closed, Valonia Macintyre, M. D., drove her Mercedes-Benz S-Class over to the modest little home of Bev and Bernie Twitchell in the Richards Place development to see this mysterious pet they credited with rebuilding their marriage and empowering Beverly to become pregnant.

Valonia pulled up to the house just as the sun was setting. She sat in her car a few moments to gather her thoughts and decide what to say to the Twitchells about whatever the dirty little stray was that they had taken in.

When Bernie answered the door Barnaby was right there waiting to see who had arrived for a visit. As Valonia entered, Barnaby began that bubbly, giggle-like melodious and endearing sound, which never failed to turn human beings into putty. He waddled around and around in wobbly circles which accentuated the joy that constantly bubbled out of the happy little guy.

In far less time than it takes to explain it, Barnaby was in Valonia's lap on the sofa wallowing joyously in her caresses. "Oh, those beautiful eyes! Is there anyone as cute as Barnaby? What a precious baby." Valonia babbled on and on.

For her part that evening, Valonia Macintyre, M.D., the most renowned gynecologist in the tri-county region was behaving like a schoolgirl—a very immature schoolgirl. She had never, ever in her life, had so much fun with an animal; not even with the human kind of animal when she was in college.

It was nearly midnight before Valonia was able to drag herself out to her Mercedes and trundle off to her home. Bev and

Bernie didn't think she was ever going to leave.

During the six-month visit Dr. Macintyre decided to do an ultrasound to see what was going on in Beverly's uterus. Was there some problem relating to the rapid growth of Beverly's baby or was something else happening?

Dr. Macintyre's nurse, Martha, helped Bev undress and prepped her for the procedure. As the doctor moved the ultrasound probe across Bev's abdomen both the doctor and the nurse gasped when they saw the video.

The video did reveal something unusual in the baby's development, but neither woman had ever seen anything like it. Dr. Macintyre could think of no one she could even call in for a consult about it. The baby was definitely not normal. The spine was abnormal—actually, the entire skeleton was wrong. It wasn't human. Also, there were unusual undulations as the baby moved around in Beverly's abdomen. Valonia Macintyre, M.D. was unable to form words to tell Beverly and Bernie what she was seeing.

As Valonia stepped back, stunned, Bernie came forward and looked at the ultrasound image. Bernie stood up straight, ramrod stiff, his fists clenched, his jaw clamped tight. He turned toward Bev and screamed, "How could you do that? You did it with that filthy animal. You did it with Barnaby!" Bernie was apoplectic. "I know you never loved me, but how could you do that?"

"Do what?" Bev screamed back. "Why are you yelling at me?"

"*That!*" screamed Bernie pointing at the ultrasound image. With his jaws clamped shut Bernie continued, "You did it with Barnaby."

"Never!" Beverly shouted back.

"Look at that picture. What else could it be?" Bernie

screamed as he shoved the monitor around so Bev could see it clearly.

"I don't know, but I did not have sex with that animal!" sobbed Beverly.

Bernie stormed out of the doctor's clinic and disappeared. Beverly fainted.

Stunned, Valonia Macintyre, M.D., the most renowned gynecologist in the tri-county region realized Bernie Twitchell was right. Beverly must have had relations with dear little Barnaby. Valonia became nauseous and had to dash to the restroom – for the second time this morning. It was not at all like Valonia to lose control this way. Valonia had never vomited at work before today, no matter what took place in her clinic. This whole situation left her feeling extremely uncomfortable. Something was wrong with the world.

When she felt a little better, Valonia asked Nurse Martha, her loyal friend and the most competent obstetrical nurse she had ever known to take Beverly home. Martha grabbed her coat and purse, then ushered Beverly out to her car.

Beverly cried all the way home. She blubbered about her dilemma with this baby and her disloyal husband. She didn't know how she could go on. Martha wondered how this soft, mushy woman had survived as long as she had. She had no awareness of how cruel the world could really be.

Martha had seen the world at its worst. She had watched her beloved older sister, Janine, lose a baby and die herself after being beaten and kicked by an angry boyfriend who couldn't face fatherhood. Martha was only twelve when Janine died. She made a vow that day that she would be a better person who would crawl above the sort of life into which her beloved sister had fallen.

When Martha pulled up in front of the Twitchell home there was no sign of Bernie. Martha got out and cautiously walked around the car and opened Bev's door.

"Come on, Honey. Let's get you in the house where you'll be safe and warm." She helped the pregnant woman up the walk.

The front door to the house was unlocked. Martha proceeded carefully, fearing Bernie Twitchell might be home. It looked as if someone had ransacked the place—probably the husband.

Beverly wanted to sit in her big recliner. After Beverly was situated, Martha checked the rest of the home to make certain there would be no surprises. When she returned to the living room she got her first sight of Barnaby.

As the little fellow trundled across the floor toward Martha in his cutest way, she stepped back and shook her finger at the little creature and shouted, "Back off! You stay away from me you little bugger. I want no part of you."

Put off a bit, Barnaby did that bubbly, giggle-like sound oh so indescribably melodious and endearing thing of his, then added a touching whine on the end.

Martha's reply was short and not so sweet, "You can shove that crap. I've seen your work, and I've seen that ultrasound. You ain't gonna get your whatever into Martha Jones!"

Barnaby scurried over to Beverly and jumped onto her lap.

Bev whined, "Oh, don't be mean to Barnaby. He's a sweet little baby."

"Sweet little baby, Hell!" shouted Martha. "That little shit's the cause of all this mess! I'm outta here before he knocks me up, too." Martha slammed the front door as she dashed out to her car.

Back at The Macintyre Gynecological Clinic, Martha immediately sought out Dr. Macintyre, and upon finding her blurted out, "Did that nasty little creature knock you up, too?"

"What? God, no! I'm not pregnant," claimed the good doctor.

"Well, you sure been acting like it today," was Martha's retort. "Maybe you'd better check yourself out, because I saw the way that horny little shit came at me and I know what he meant to do."

"Oh, Martha, that can't be," said Valonia, who was suddenly weak in the knees and about to faint.

Martha caught the limp woman on the way down and dragged her to a chair saying, "Oh, dear, dear Val. You've got all the signs. I don't know how that little shit did it, but he got to you. You're gonna have one of those things, too."

When Dr. Valonia Macintyre regained consciousness, Martha was wiping her face with a cool cloth. It felt so good. Val began to cry, and said, "Martha, how could it happen? I only petted it."

"I don't know, honey. It's a male. They can always figure out a way," Martha cried.

Martha helped Valonia to the big leather couch in the doctor's private office. She put a fresh cool cloth on Valonia's forehead. She cancelled the remainder of Val's appointments for the day, then prepped Val for an ultrasound.

Valonia was hesitant to let Martha do the test, but Martha persevered.

"I can't be pregnant," Val kept repeating. "I just cannot be! I cannot be. It's not possible."

"Oh, yes it is," said Martha. "See for yourself," Martha continued, as she swung the view screen around so Valonia could see it.

As Valonia's eyes swept over the screen she realized her own ultrasound was remarkably similar to Beverly's. "Oh, dear God, how could this be? What am I going to do?" she sobbed.

"You're not too far along. Maybe we could get it out," suggested Martha.

"Yes, but not yet, Martha. First I have to call Bill Newsome at the Health Department. This is bigger than just me."

When Valonia was able to stand without dizziness, she went to her desk and punched in Bill Newsome's number.

"County Health Department, Communicable Disease Center, Alice Coleman speaking. How may I direct your call?"

"Alice, this is Valonia Macintyre. May I speak to Mr. Newsome? It's urgent."

"Oh, Dr. Macintyre, is this about all those pregnancies up in the Richards Place development?"

"Uh, I don't know. I hadn't heard about that, but my patient does live in that area. What about Richards Place?"

"They have twenty-four women pregnant on just three blocks," said Alice.

"Yes, Alice, perhaps my emergency is related to those," replied Dr. Macintyre. "Let me speak to Bill."

A moment later Bill came on the line. "Hi, Dr. Macintyre. Do you have something to add regarding the Richards Place pregnancies?"

"Yes, Bill. I think I have. I believe I may know the cause."

After Valonia finished telling Bill Newsome everything she knew about the Twitchell family and Barnaby there was a long pause, then Bill said, "My God doctor! Are you serious? Are you really pregnant by this creature?"

"Yes, Bill, I can send over the ultrasound if you want

proof," said Val, on the verge of tears.

"Oh, yeah! Send me the ultrasound. I can't wait to see it."

'You needn't sound so excited, you asshole!" cried Valonia.

"Oh, Val, I'm sorry. It's just... I mean... Uhhh. Nothing like this ever... ."

"It's OK, Bill. A part of me feels the same way, but a bigger part is in agony."

"Of course, doctor. Let me come over to your office. You are at your office, aren't you?"

"Yes. Come on over. Martha, my nurse, is here with me."

Bill Newsome arrived at Valonia Macintyre's office forty-five minutes later. He was agitated when Martha let him in the office. Valonia asked him what was wrong.

Bill Newsome was sixty-one, balding, and over-weight. He played second string football in high school and college. He graduated with a liberal arts degree, went in the army for four years, then was discharged. He had married a college sweetheart, but she divorced him while he was overseas. He had not re-married. Bill was lonely and sad. His life had gone nowhere. He drank too much. There was little excitement in Bill's life. Until now.

Bill told Valonia, "We reported this to the CDC earlier today when we first heard about the unusual growing cluster of pregnancies in Richards Place. CDC called back and advised us their funding had been cut and they hadn't the resources to follow up on a cluster of pregnancies and there was nothing they could do about it."

"So what are you going to do?" asked Valonia with near panic in her voice.

"Just after I hung up from talking with you, I got a strange call from a man who said he was with Homeland Security. He asked a lot of questions about the pregnant women involved, who were their doctors, addresses, phone numbers, employers, if they were married, and how long, how many kids they had, all kinds of stuff."

"What did you tell him?" asked Valonia.

"I said we didn't have all that data," said Bill.

"What did he say then?" asked Valonia.

"He just said, 'We'll see about that.' and he hung up," was Bill's answer.

"Oh My God! Do you have any idea what he meant by that?"

"None at all," answered Bill dejectedly.

A Top Secret Project was created by the President of the United States and placed under the command of Major General Adam A. Quick, USAF. The mission of Project Progenitor was to determine:

How many women were impregnated by the creature?
How were human women actually impregnated?
How would the creature be biologically classified?
Where was the creature's place of origin?
How did the creature get into The United States?
Were any other countries invaded?
How will any further invasion be prevented?

A cadre of military specialists was assembled and placed under the command of General Quick to complete the project. General Quick was given an open-ended budget to accomplish the project goals.

Two days later people in hazmat suits swarmed through the Richards Place neighborhood. They proceeded, in less than twenty-four hours, to erect a twelve foot chain link fence around the entire development. The fence was topped with razor wire. There was now only a single entry/exit point to Richards Place. The gate and fence were guarded around the clock. Signs saying "WARNING HAZARDOUS RADIATION ZONE" were placed on the fence every twenty feet around the entire area.

Once the containment fence was in place, General Quick issued an order directing all civilian residents of Richards Place to assemble in Dick's Cantina, the Richards Place community clubhouse, at 0730 hours the next morning for a mandatory briefing regarding the danger and what the government planned to do about it.

The next morning just after 6:00am, there was someone banging on Beverly's door. There were several people in hazmat suits outside. When Bev opened the door a tall woman yelled at her, "Give us the creature, get dressed, and come with us."

Two other women immediately grabbed Bev's arms. Bev began to moan and cry, "Why are you here? Why is it so early? Why do you want Barnaby?"

The tall woman demanded, "Where's your dressing room and where's the animal?"

Bev screamed and tried to shake the women off.

The tall woman grabbed both of Bev's shoulders and shouted in her face, "Get your damned clothes on now or we'll drag you naked to see the general!"

Meekly, Bev murmured, "OK."

The hazmat people spread out through Bev's home rounding up Barnaby and scooping up clothes, shoes, etc. until they had all they needed. Barnaby was placed in a small dog crate.

Everything else went in boxes in the back of a large, covered military truck.

The tall woman asked, "Where's your husband?"

Bev began to blubber again and said, "I don't know. I haven't seen him for a couple of days."

Bev was pushed into the back of a staff car and was soon on her way to the clubhouse. Once underway in the staff car, Bev noticed most of her neighbors were being rounded up, as well.

Bev and her neighbors were ushered into the big room at Dick's Cantina and were told to take seats. Bev noticed most of the people gathered there were her close neighbors, people who lived within a couple of blocks of her house.

Bev was being seated next to Maude Klimpt. As Bev sat down Maude looked up, smiled and said, "I guess we're the ones having Barnaby's babies."

Bev's jaw dropped. "Huh, what?" she mumbled. "Barnaby's babies? What are you talking about?"

Maude laughed very loud. "Haven't you figured it out? Your sweet little guy has knocked up half the women in the neighborhood, and I don't mean that dumb ass shoe salesman you're married to. I mean Barnaby!" Maude cackled.

At that moment, a large, loud man in a blue uniform strode into the room, stepped up on the stage, and began to talk very loudly at the group. He started off saying, "I'm Major General Adam A. Quick, USAF. I'm in charge of Project Progenitor, and I mean to find out what's been going on in this place."

Bev heard little else that he said. She didn't care. She wondered where Bernie was, and Barnaby. Poor little Barnaby, they'd probably dissect him.

Within three days the entire population of the Richards Place neighborhood was gone. General Quick issued orders to close Dr. Valonia R. Macintyre's clinic and all her equipment and furnishings were to be seized. All of the women who had been impregnated by Barnaby, as well as Dr. Macintyre and her staff, and the staffs of other nearby gynecological practitioners, were transported to an undisclosed facility in Nevada along with their families. All those living in the Richards Place subdivision who were not involved in alien impregnation were ordered not to talk about it, were relocated to other states, and were given new identities.

Stories were passed to the local media which said Dr. Valonia R. Macintyre, M.D., and three other nearby doctors, were now employed by the US Government at an undisclosed location in Nevada. Dr. Macintyre was said to be the senior research analyst for Project Progenitor. However, neither Dr. Macintyre, nor her devoted nurse, Martha Jones, or the other doctors had been seen anywhere lately.

The morning after, the Richards Place women arrived in the hottest, driest, most desolate place most of them had ever experienced, aka Nevada, they were awakened at 6:ooam and herded into a large auditorium for a speech by General Quick, where he outlined the goals of Project Progenitor and made it quite clear this was all about the creature Barnaby and what had transpired in Richards Place. He also introduced several military personnel who would be in charge of them while they were in the research project.

The first of these military people was Lt. Colonel Marianne Dillon, PhD, US Army. Marianne was a tall, soft spoken, willowy woman who did not seem well-suited to be an Army officer. She stepped forward and said, "Good morning , Ladies. I look forward to speaking with each of you and I hope I can ease your concerns about this trying situation you are all in." Colonel Dillon was to be the historian for Project Progenitor and all the women were ordered to answer all her questions as thoroughly and accurately as possible.

Next, the General introduced Major Darrion Harris, USMC. Darrion was a tall, well-built, handsome man, with a smile all the women found irresistible. The women were told he was their Project Personnel officer. The major stepped to the microphone and said, "Hi, Ladies. If there is anything you need or if you have a problem, just come to my office and we'll see what can be done to alleviate that problem."

The last person he introduced was First Sergeant Gertrude Kline, USMC. She was the same rude woman who had threatened to drag Beverly naked to see the general back in Richards Place.

General Quick said, "First Sergeant Kline will be your immediate supervisor while you are here at Project Progenitor and you all will obey her instructions. Sergeant, they're all yours." With that, the general and the other officers exited the room.

Five foot eleven and ramrod straight, First Sergeant Gertrude Kline strode to the edge of the stage. She didn't bother with the microphone. She wore a crisp desert variant of the Marine Corps Combat Utility Uniform. She looked even bigger than she had in the hazmat suit in Richards Place. Several women in the audience trembled as Sergeant Kline began to speak.

"Good morning ladies," she greeted them. "We're gonna do things by the book here girls. You'll be up at 0600 hours every morning. You will be dressed and report for breakfast at 0630 hours. At 0700 hours you will report to your research assignment. Lunch will be from 1200 to 1230 hours. Dinner will be from 1730 to 1815 hours after which you will return to your quarters. Is that clear?"

One young woman stood up and said, "We're civilians.

You can't treat us like this!"

Sergeant Kline, with a big grin said, "You're not civilians anymore, Honey. You belong to the US government. You should have been more selective about who, or what, you let between your legs."

The young woman flopped in her seat and began to blubber. A murmur arose among the women. They all resented the sergeant's tone and attitude.

Sergeant Kline looked over the women and laughed. "Aww," she mocked. "Poor little babies." With that same big grin Sergeant Kline added, "Welcome to Nevada girls, now you're all just my Barna-Bitches."

Dr. Valonia Macintyre and her trusty companion, Nurse Martha Jones, were at the research facility, but they were kept away from the other women. They actively participated in the research, but initially they were often treated more like specimens rather than researchers.

All of the fifty-three women who had been impregnated by Barnaby were there, and except for Dr. Macintyre, M.D., they remained under the watchful eye of First Sergeant Kline. General Quick and his minions made it quite clear the women impregnated by Barnaby were little more than lab rats and they were expected to obey orders without question, except for Dr. Macintyre, M.D., of course. Major Dillon and her team followed the women constantly and recorded everything they did.

Over the next year Project Progenitor did make progress. Valonia R. Macintyre, M.D. emerged as one of the principal researchers on the Project. It was she who determined the gestation period of the barnabin embryo. She knew the date she was impregnated and calculated she had carried the thing for one hundred ninety days.

Martha Jones, Valonia's nurse, friend and companion throughout what Martha referred to as "The Exile" assumed the role of lab assistant/record keeper. Martha interviewed all the women and determined the duration of their pregnancies were all close to the 190 days of Valonia's. Martha worked very closely with Lt. Colonel Dillon in recording all the medical discoveries regarding the barnabin pregnancies.

Valonia and Martha agreed the human/barnabin gestation period was 190 days, give or take ten days. It was difficult to be precise because few of the fifty-three known mothers were certain of their date of impregnation. Martha also discovered there were zero instances of barnabin twin births. However, three women experienced stillbirths of human fetuses after they were impregnated with barnabins.

DNA tests on all of the baby barnabins revealed no human DNA in them; in fact, no DNA was found at all, but an alien molecular structure which appeared to perform a similar function in the barnabin species was discovered. This finding surprised most of the researchers and it led to an alarming conclusion: The human females who had borne barnabin babies were technically not impregnated. They were infested.

Without exception, all the researchers were stunned by this determination. Val and Martha could talk of nothing else that evening as they returned to their quarters.

"How could this be? What sex are they?" Val wondered.

"Val, Honey, remember the day you realized what had happened and how Barnaby had gotten to you?" pondered Martha.

"Yes, so?" asked Val.

"I said it was a male. What if barnabins have only one sex?

We haven't been able to determine any difference in any of the barnabin babies. They're all exactly the same. Everything's the same. Size, coloring, external 'equipment', internal organs, genetic tests, everything…"

"Oh my God! This changes everything," gasped Val.

Martha looked at Val and said, "You're right about that, Honey. You weren't pregnant. You had a parasite."

"Oh, yuck!" Val's hand went over her mouth and she began retching.

The next morning Valonia formally presented their theory to the project leaders. When Valonia stated her belief that the barnabin species is monosexual and always uses surrogates for the gestation of their offspring there was dead silence in the room. That lasted about five seconds and the others erupted in turmoil.

"Impossible! The dumbest thing I've ever heard! That just won't work! What have you and Martha been smoking? God would not allow it!"

The yelling went on until General Quick shouted, "Shut up, all of you! NOW!"

When they had quieted down, the general said to Valonia, "How did you reach such a conclusion?"

"General," said Valonia, "All our research points to this conclusion."

Val reiterated the discussion she and Martha had the previous evening. When she finished General Quick stared at her for a few moments, then said, "Good work, Dr. Macintyre."

Most of the others around the conference table were unconvinced, but a few began to nod their heads.

General Quick went on, "I know this theory is a shock to most of you, but it does offer answers to several of our issues still under debate. I ask you all to open your minds and think about this. The barnabins are one of the great scientific mysteries of our time. It seems they are most likely extraterrestrial. We still don't know how they got here or where they came from, but they exist. So, go back to your offices and think about what Dr. Macintyre has said this morning. Give the doctor's ideas some thought."

"Colonel Dillon, did your team get all of that?"

"Yes, sir," whispered the tall, lissome woman.

"Everyone, we'll discuss this again in a few days. Dismissed."

After several days, many intra-office emails, much conversation, and a great deal of angst, a meeting of the minds began to take shape. Even the most recalcitrant of the researchers finally came around. Barnaby was extraterrestrial.

General Quick was informed of the resolution of the staff's differences and called all the senior researchers to a staff meeting wherein it was agreed upon that the barnabin species was extraterrestrial in origin. It was also agreed upon that Beverly Twitchell, and all the other women, experienced uterine infestations, not true pregnancies.

Eventually, Project Progenitor determined how the barnabins infest a woman's uterus and several other facts about the barnabin species. The cuddling and endearing behavior of the barnabin served to put possible hosts at ease. It also allowed the barnabin to sniff out a suitable uterus, to which it would move closer in order to allow its embryo the best opportunity to implant itself. It was discovered when a barnabin is in proximity to a suitable uterus, a single cell containing all the genetic coding for a new barnabin ripens quickly and is ejected from the barnabin embripositor as close as possible to the uterus of the chosen host. Such embryos are capable of self-locomotion for about twenty minutes, during which time they aggressively seek a suitable gestation nest (uterus).

More study revealed barnabins are never born as twins, co-located barnabin embryos will fight for supremacy with the winner ejecting the loser from the uterus. It was discovered barnabins would supplant human fetuses, especially in early stages of fetal development. Whether barnabins infest any animals other than humans remained uncertain. It had not happened on Earth, so far as was known. Whether a barnabin embryo seeking a uterus acts out of intelligence or instinct has not been determined.

A complete report of Project Progenitor was assembled by the newly promoted full Colonel Dillon and was presented to the President at a formal cabinet meeting by the Secretary of Defense.

At that meeting SECDEF presented the President and the cabinet with the following information:

1. Project Progenitor determined answers for four of its objectives:

    1   Fifty-three human females had been infested with embryotic parasites by the barnabin species.

    2   Scientists have a complete understanding of how barnabins lulled women into allowing embryo placement, and it was decided such placement would be regarded as a uterine infestation.

    3   The official classification of the species is *barnabinus nonesterra.*

    4   Several other countries were invaded.

2. Project Progenitor was unable to achieve its remaining three objectives:

>   1   Place of origin for *barnabinus nonesterra* is uncertain, but it is extraterrestrial.
>
>   2   How did *barnabinus nonesterra* get to the United States.
>
>   3   How can further invasions be prevented.

After the formal presentation, the President asked, "General Quick, why are there no resolutions to the other three objectives?"

General Quick answered, "Madam President, Project Progenitor lacked the resources to determine where *barnabinus nonesterra* originated, how they managed to travel here, and whether they will come again. It was just beyond our scope."

The President responded, "General Quick, be that as it may, what's the next step?"

"Madam President, *barnabinus nonesterra* is a threat to the entire human race, not just Americans. This is an invasion. We must marshal the resources of the entire world to combat these creatures. If we fail it's all over."

"We cannot let that happen," said the President. "I'm going to call for a world summit meeting to discuss this situation."

"Madam President," interjected Colonel Dillon. "A Russian acquaintance has told me, informally, that Russia is infested with *barnabinus nonesterra*. He suspects China has them, as well as Japan. There is even a company in Japan said to be making cute little Barnaby Dolls for children."

"Colonel Dillon, I want a complete history done about the barnabins. I want everything, not just reiteration of the science. Everything! Understand? Let me know what resources you need" said the President.

"Yes, Madam President," replied the lithe Colonel.

Colonel Dillon returned to her office in the Pentagon with a big smile on her face. Most of the military had little respect for her in the past. An historian commanded little respect among soldiers. Marianne Dillon, Colonel, PhD, US Army, was about to change that as she sat down in front of her computer and began to pour out everything she knew about *barnabinus nonesterra* and the people associated with it.

Beverly had been correct about little Barnaby's fate. Barnaby was dissected and what remains of that happy little fellow now rests in a non-public area of the Smithsonian Institution. All of Barnaby's progeny ended up similarly, scattered throughout the United States in research laboratories.

The Barnabin women victims were given their choice between reuniting with their families or being moved to separate locations. Most chose the cleansing effect of a new name, new identity, and a new place to live.

Because of his failure to resolve all the objectives of Project Progenitor, Major General Adam A. Quick, USAF, was soon asked for his resignation, whereupon he retired to Florida.

A few days later Adam Quick, civilian, arrived in Key West, Florida. He was accompanied by an attractive middle aged woman. After lunch and a drink at a bar and grill on Key West Bight they proceeded to one of the piers where Adam guided his lady to a large, moored boat. As he handed her aboard, Adam whispered, "Maude, we're gonna have the time of our lives here on the *Jolly General!*"

Maude Klimpt jumped into his arms, and failing to consider the motion of the boat, they sprawled on the deck. The couple didn't even notice. They rolled around kissing like teens and undressing each other until a voice interrupted them.

"You folks are gonna have to stop that right now or I'll have to cite you for public indecency. You can't have sex in public even if you are in Florida. Well, especially if you are in Florida. So, you stop it. Right now!"

Adam and Maude did stop. They both sheepishly looked up at the officer standing there.

Adam said, "We didn't realize we were outside. We... We thought we were inside the boat."

Maude added, "Yes, that... that's what we thought."

The officer asked, "How old are you two? You sure don't look like teenagers."

Adam replied in his high-ranking officer voice, "I'm General Adam A. Quick, USAF, don't get smartass with me, Officer Opie!"

"Right back at you, SIR. I'm Officer Cletus Broward, Key West Police Department, and I will have to arrest both of you if you don't remove yourselves from public view."

Adam suddenly remembered where he was and that people were watching and said, "Sorry, Officer Broward." Then he whispered to Maude, "Let's get inside where we can get naked."

"Oh, yes," she moaned.

Maude was smiling now and wondering what Clark and his slutty aerobics instructor would think if they could see her now.

Valonia R. Macintyre, M.D. and her longtime friend, associate, and now lover, Martha Jones, kept their real names and wrote the defining treatise on *barnabinus nonesterra*, for which they became renowned, an ultimately received the Nobel Prize in Physiology. Upon their return from Stockholm, they moved to

Marin County, California.

Determined to continue working in the area of women's health, Valonia and Martha invested the Nobel money and built The ValMar Clinic, a hospital, hotel and spa specializing in the treatment of gynecological irregularities and abnormalities. The day ValMar opened Valonia and Martha stood in the lovely main lobby of their clinic and embraced, kissed deeply, opened the heavy double entry doors and proclaimed, "Welcome Ladies, Friends of ValMar," as the first dozen guests exited the chartered luxury coach which had just pulled up in the drive and proceeded into the opulent clinic.

From the day they met Beverly Twitchell and First Sergeant Gertrude Kline were at each other's throats. Beverly was convinced Gertrude was an unfeeling sadist, while the good sergeant viewed Beverly as a soft, pathetic slug. They never passed one another without an exchange of insults.

One day during such an exchange with Kline, Bev glanced sideways at their reflections in a full length window and saw Gertrude for what she really was, a tall, athletic beauty; and herself for what she was, a soft, pudgy slug. Bev had always eschewed exercise in any form. She hated to get hot and sweaty. The picture Bev saw painted in that reflection showed her Gertrude was right. Kline noticed Bev looking at their reflection and said, "You see yourself now don't you? You can do something about it if you want."

Bev broke down in tears, where upon Gertrude took her by the hand and said, "Come with me." The sergeant led her to the women's gym.

Gertrude showed Bev how to use some of the equipment and said, "If you want to change what you saw in that reflection the work starts here. The people here will show you how this equipment works. It does work, but it will take some time. You're really out of shape." Gertrude smiled down at Bev, then leaned over, kissed Bev's forehead and walked away.

Bev stood there stunned and watched the suddenly beautiful woman stride away. From that day, Bev spent all her spare time in the gym and results began to show.

Three months after that event with Gertrude, Bev had toned her body quite well and several of her friends had commented on her transformation. One evening during dinner Bev was chatting with some of her friends and mentioned that Sgt. Kline had put her on this exercise track and added she hadn't seen the sergeant for a while.

"She retired," someone said.

"Retired!" said Bev. "She never even said goodbye."

Bev was devastated by the fact that Gertrude had not even mentioned she was leaving. Bev decided she was going to find Gertrude when she got free of this base. Bev was surprised she was so angry with Gertrude and wondered why.

During her remaining time at the base Beverly Twitchell became interested in gymnastics. She enjoyed gymnastics and it soon became a major part of her exercise regimen. The coach at the base gym told her she was a natural.

When the women were finally told they were being released, Bev asked newly promoted Lt. Colonel Darrion Harris, who was signing off on their release papers, what had happened to First Sergeant Kline. The Colonel said, "She retired and is living in Las Vegas." Then he added, "Now where would you like to go upon release?" and he gave her that big, gorgeous smile.

Bev promptly said, "Las Vegas."

Colonel Harris looked up from his paperwork still smiling

and said, "Have fun," as he handed her the ticket and a card with Gertrude's phone number.

The bus dropped the women at the South Strip Transit Terminal on Gilespie Street in Las Vegas. Beverly went directly to a pay phone and called the number on the card Colonel Harris had handed her.

When Gertrude answered Bev said, "It's Bev, I'm free…"

"Where are you? I'll come and get you."

A few minutes later Gertrude pulled up in front of the terminal in a brand new shiny black Ford F-150 pickup truck. Beverly opened the passenger side door and climbed in. This time Gertrude did not kiss Bev on the forehead. No, this kiss was long, deep and from the soul.

The next morning, they awoke in Gertrude's king size bed. Bev was first to speak, "What are we going to do?"

"What do you mean," asked Gertrude.

"I mean I don't have much money and…" mumbled Beverly.

"Oh, don't worry about that, Honey. I collect my service pension and I have a job, as well."

"A job? What job?," wondered Bev.

Gertrude burst out with a boisterous laugh, "You're not going to believe this, but I'm a wrestler—a professional wrestler!'

"What!" Bev shouted. "I don't believe you. You're putting me on."

"My professional name is Dirty Gertie," Gertrude laughed.

"Really?" asked Bev.

"Really. Let's get dressed and I'll take you to the arena and show you around."

An hour and a half later, after a splendid breakfast in a casino, the shiny black F-150 pulled up in front of the Golden

Bomber Arena and the two ladies got out. Bev noticed the billboard next to the entrance said Watch Our Beautiful Babes Get Hot And Sweaty.

Bev thought, "Hot and sweaty with Gertrude wouldn't be bad at all."

Aloud Bev said, "If I agree to do this, could I have purple hair and a sexy costume?"

Gertrude pulled the door open and said, "Absolutely, Hon. That's a great idea. I wear a leather bustier and thigh-high leather boots. We can even pose as enemies in the ring. It'll be fun! You're gonna need a good professional name, too." Whereupon, Dirty Gertie and Purple Passion walked through the door, thus entering a new phase of their lives where fame and fortune awaited their hot, sweaty, muscular, well-costumed bodies.

Bernie Twitchell and his brother Clive, both bearded, and accompanied by the beloved, highly intelligent dog, Wilbur, were last seen in a battered 1955 Dodge Power Wagon disappearing into the Bitterroot Range of the Rocky Mountains somewhere in the panhandle of Idaho.

It was winter and snowing as the Brothers Twitchell set up camp.

"This will be great!" said Bernie as he and Clive set about pitching the large surplus military tent.

"Yeah," answered Clive as his teeth chattered with the cold.

Wilbur shivered as he stood watching the two men stumble about trying to erect the tent.

The Power Wagon was loaded with 100 pounds of potatoes, several cases of canned meats, thirty cases of beer, six twenty-eight ounce bags of corn chips, two dozen smoked snack sticks, and one thirty pound sack of dog kibble. Since they neglected to consider their sanitation needs, there was no toilet paper, no paper towels, no soap. Each man had a sleeping bag and there was an old, worn blanket for Wilbur. There was a small first aid kit in the Power Wagon, the contents of which were all out of date.

The boys assumed they could supplement their food stores by hunting and that Wilbur would be able to catch most of his own food. As for tools, they had a single bit axe, a small hatchet, a t-handle shovel and a Lodge 5 Quart Cast Iron Dutch Oven for cooking.

The boys were armed with two guns, which Clive acquired from a hunter friend of his. The guns were a well-used ex-Argentine Mauser rifle, caliber: 30-06; and a used Stevens single shot shotgun of 410 gauge.

As it turned out, the stock on the Argentine Mauser cracked the first time Clive tried to use it and it was deemed useless. Only the little Stevens 410 was usable, which was probably a good thing since neither man really knew how to hunt and properly clean a large, dead animal. The 410 was useful for squirrels and small birds.

The boys had brought no water, but that was alright because there was a small stream right next to their campsite. They had no clue that the small stream was infested with giardia, which would impose no end of difficulty on them and Wilbur. Nor did they realize how difficult it would be to catch food in the mountains, in the winter, in deep snow.

Six months later a dog was found wandering along Coeur D'Alene River Road by Shoshone County animal control officer Hezekiah Smith. The dog's collar said "WILBUR" on a small metal plate. The officer was surprised to see such a healthy, well-fed dog wandering alone out there.

The following spring a search party was organized by the US Forest Service to look for the Twitchell Brothers. Colonel Marianne Dillon was informed by a friend in the Forest Service that a search was being conducted in Idaho for the Twitchell brothers. That was precisely what Marianne needed to complete her history of the barnabin infestation, so she booked a flight to Coeur d'Alene, Idaho, where she rented a car and headed east on I-90 to Wallace, Idaho, the Shoshone County Seat, where she had arranged to meet Hezekiah Smith, who had found the Twitchell's dog.

Marianne liked Hezekiah instantly and asked if she could tag along with him on the search. The searchers headed north from Prichard on Coeur D'Alene River Road. From things people remembered the Twitchells saying, it was assumed the Twitchells had made camp north of Prichard and east of Devil's Elbow.

Their camp was not hard to find. The large collapsed tent, the broken down Dodge Power Wagon, and the piles of rubbish were good clues. The Twitchell brothers bodies were found under the tent in their old surplus sleeping bags. Alarmingly, there were dead barnabin carcasses inside the tent. Apparently the brothers were eating them, but where had they come from?

Marianne was disappointed the search didn't last longer. Hezekiah Smith turned out to be much more than she had expected. From his name alone she assumed he would be a smelly yokel driving a beat-up old truck. He did drive a truck, but it was a very nice new one, and Hezekiah was about six feet four and looked like a movie star. He told Marianne she could call him "Zeke" if she liked.

As they drove to and from the search area they discussed the barnabin infestation. Zeke wondered if the infestation was ongoing based on what they had seen in the Twitchell camp. Zeke was eager to hear more about it and Marianne found herself telling him everything she knew, even a few confidential things she probably should have kept to herself. They continued talking through dinner and afterward. He asked her to his place to continue their discussion. Marianne told Zeke she was a retired Army colonel thinking that might break the chain of their conversation, but it had no effect.

When they arrived at Zeke's home Marianne was surprised what a lovely place it was. It was not very large, just two bedrooms, but it was luxurious. She wondered how he afforded such a place on an animal control officer's salary. Marianne finally asked Zeke if he had a university degree. His reply stunned her.

"Yeah, I got a bachelor's in animal husbandry at Texas A&M, then I got a doctorate from Cornell," he said.

"Who the hell is this guy?" Marianne thought to herself. "Is he telling the truth, or is he a lying con man?"

"You probably think I'm crazy," Zeke said. "Truth is my parents have lots of money, but I don't really care. I just love animals so that's why I do what I do," Zeke said softly.

Marianne got up from her chair, walked over to the sofa where Zeke was seated, bent over and kissed him hard on the mouth. Marianne had never initiated sex in her life, but she could not resist this man. Perhaps he was a con man. She didn't care. Was she falling for a pack of lies? She didn't care. She wasn't thinking about her book. She wasn't thinking about barnabins.

She wasn't actually thinking about anything. She wanted this man. After the kiss he seemed hesitant, then he pulled her lovely, willowy body down on the sofa and kissed her just beneath her left ear.

Marianne shuddered and gasped for air. She could barely

breathe. She felt drugged. His lips slid down her neck. The pale blue tee shirt she was wearing disappeared before Marianne realized it had happened. The rest of her clothing followed. Marianne's long, lithe, delicate body responded to Hezekiah's strength as it had never done with anyone before. The night became an endless ever-spinning wheel of pleasure, until Marianne disappeared into that spinning cloud of bliss and she felt as if her body was no longer hers, but she heard herself groaning in an agonizing, nearly unbearable orgasm. Where was she? How could this go on? But it did as she slipped into darkness...

The next morning over breakfast Zeke, his eyes still clouded with pleasure and sleep, softly told Marianne he believed she was the most wonderful, beautiful woman in the world and he could not wait to spend the rest of his life with her. Could this really be happening to her?

Wilbur, the dog, stretched and yawned as he climbed out of his bed by Zeke's fireplace. He headed out the dog door to see if he could find one of those little white, furry animals for breakfast. They were so delicious.

May

The Mayfly Man
Susan Nordman

terrible.

The soft sound rolls through his memory just loud enough for him to know it is real even though it is just quiet enough for him to question his senses. A low crunching, cracking... like a hardboiled egg being rolled across a counter; a snapping of a thousand tiny fractures splintering, breaking, shattering the smooth surface.

It is terrible, that sound. The hollow noise reverberates in his mind relentlessly rolling the egg over and over. Thin, echoey... as if the egg is being shattered on a zinc countertop. It's a dull, cold metal designed to be functional rather than for esthetics. A wooden cutting board would have absorbed the sound; granite would have had a lower pitch. This sound isn't like those. It rumbles on like a death rattle.

The endless breaking and cracking of the shattering egg loops continuously around the mobius of his memory serves only to remind him of his hunger. He is awake and still dreaming of eggs. Even though hardboiled is his least favorite way for them to be prepared, he wouldn't refuse. Awake and the crunching and cracking of eggshells breaking away from the solidified albumen boiled white to perfection continues. Hardboiled isn't too bad, especially with a touch of salt. It's the dried yolks he doesn't care for, but mixed with mayonnaise it's good. Of course, it isn't called hardboiled then, but deviled.

Deviled. Split the whites down the middle and restuff the hollow with the yolk mixed with tangy mayonnaise and sprinkled with salt and pepper. Maybe even a touch of mustard... brown Dijon and not the yellow. Yellow mustard is for picnics and hotdogs and not for eggs.

Actually, over easy would be much better than hardboiled or deviled. Fried and gently turned so the yolk is still liquid and he can dip his lightly browned toast liberally slathered in butter into the golden center.

Hardboiled eggs, eggs over easy with buttered toast, deviled eggs because only the devil seems to care that he is hungry.

Fully awake, the crunching and cracking of eggshells continues. Sitting up, he looks to find the terrible sound. It is leaves. The leftovers from last November. Old, brittle leaves as dry and dark as burned toast rattle across the pavement and are stirred into eddies by the bitter wind. Dead leaves that hadn't gotten the memo that it is spring.

The May weather hadn't gotten the memo, either. Eight days past the vernal equinox and the nights are still dipping below freezing. A thin frosting of powdered sugar dusts the darkened corners of the park. It is colder here in the hidden places. Blocked by the buildings and the trees, the sun rarely has an opportunity to shine on this sheltered bench. It is out of sight from the light and from prying eyes which is why he tries to sleep here first. Pedestrians rarely see him to complain and the police rarely check it. No one is supposed to sleep in the park, but there is nowhere else to go.

He looks up when a clock begins to chime. It is six in the morning. Though night and day are in balance, it is still dark. The sky must be overcast because he can't see a true sunrise. All that is happening is that it is just getting lighter. The only thing that the morning is bringing is that he can see the hoar frost coating the frigid ground better. It will stay until the sun can break its way through a crack in the clouds to warm the park or the clouds themselves break. That would be worse. Rain would melt the ice into oblivion, but it would be a cold rain.

That is the trouble with May: it is too unpredictable.

Six o'clock. He will have to get moving. The morning crowd will be along soon. The joggers are always first, but at least they don't care about him. He had been vaguely aware of a couple of them passing him by already when their sneakers slapped the pavement near the bench where he lay. Keeping pace to the rhythm of songs seeping through their earbuds and focusing on the ground in front of them, they don't make eye contact. They never do. They have learned not to see anyone on the benches trying to sleep as they curl up trying to keep warm.

It is the walkers he has to worry about. Most of them quicken their pace to get through the park faster while others cross the street with their overpriced lattes clutched in their finely manicured hands while they try to convince anyone who may be watching that that was where they had meant to be in the first place. It doesn't fool anyone except the walkers. There is only an overgrown lot across the street. No cars. Just another nameless man sleeping with his back tuck up near the fence. He had been the last to the park a couple of times and with all the benches occupied, he also had to sleep in the lot. It is the worse place. Cold and unprotected, he was harassed by the elements and the police all night long. Probably exhausted, it is no wonder the man is still sleeping. Though he doesn't know the man's name, he recognizes the matted grey hair as belonging to "George." George let him sleep in his car a few times until he completely ran out of money and, by extension, gas. No longer able to move it to a new lot every night to avoid suspicion and complaints, George's car eventually was towed. All he had now to sleep in was an empty lot and a chain link fence.

George is a nice man. He considers waking him, but decides to let him sleep as long as the poor man can. He'll be woken up soon enough by the joggers, the walkers or the police. It is best to avoid everyone. He has learned that the ones who neither ignore them nor cross the street so they don't have to acknowledge the existence of those in the park are the ones to be the wariest of. These people are usually the ones heading early to their jobs so they can make a good impression with their bosses. Though in a rush, they are also the ones who still seemed to have enough time on their hands to be offended with anyone still curled on a park bench after the city begins waking. These people are best to be avoided at all costs: the ones who might take their frustration of not getting a promotion or an early morning quicky out on anyone still sleeping by alerting a policeman.

As the last echoes of six die down the pale streets, he leaves the park as quickly as his cold feet will take him. He can come back later after the suits are locked in their cubicle prisons and the only ones left outside are the drivers of the delivery trucks who are too busy wheeling their loaded dollies to notice him.

His thin soles crunch the soft rime as he shuffles down the sidewalk. He barely notices how much his feet hurt. Between his aching soles from the cold, his back sore from the hard wooden bench and the rumble in his hollow belly, pain is a constant companion. Tucking his hands into his armpits, the warmth revives his frozen fingers to where they throb in time with his circulation. He wraps his flannel shirt closer to him. Though it isn't enough to keep out the morning chill, he will be too warm by afternoon. Even so, he knows better than to take it off. That was how he lost his coat. A single moment of carelessness and the city became that much harder to endure.

Shuffling along, he nears a man in a suit who quickly looks him up and down before averting his gaze away so he doesn't have to make eye contact. The suit steps well around him. He moves his steaming macchiato to his left hand in order to place his right over his wallet to ensure it hadn't vanished. Relieved to find it where it belonged, the man quickens his pace.

There was a time someone automatically assuming he was a thief would have insulted him, but not anymore. Those days are long gone. He is used to it. He tries to remember when he stopped caring about things like that, but can't.

Instead, his mind replays the look the suit gave him. The expression of disgust in the man's eyes makes him wonder what he saw. It has been a long time since he looked at himself ... even longer since he cared. He stops walking in front of a smart shop window and doesn't recognize the face staring back. Not all that long ago, he too would have stepped around this disheveled man as he hurried down the streets to his own job dressed in his own suit to be jailed for eight, ten, sixteen hours inside his own grey cubicle.

But that was long ago. Before his boss decided to relocate

his business to another state. He could have kept his job if he had moved with the company, but life was different then. He was different then. His wife, his kids… they were all with him, so he didn't make the move.

He got a different job. Not a better one, but it would do and things were good for another year. He wasn't getting ahead, but he wasn't getting behind, either.

Then came the layoffs.

One year in and very little saved, but he wasn't worried. He could get another job.

But the next job never came. He was deemed too old, too skilled… not skilled enough. Bills stacked up. Fast food wages, waitering, even a third job at a carwash couldn't make a dent in the mortgage, the utilities or the car payments. A year later and his wife left with the kids to live with her mother in another state. He hasn't seen them since.

Everything is now gone and he sleeps in the park. He spends his day shuffling down the streets limping on his half-frozen feet.

Someone in a tailored suit stops to give another man some money. It is George who must have been woken up. He can tell by both their expressions it is a five-dollar bill. The suit looks pleased with himself for doing a good deed and George looks respectfully grateful. A single note would have been uselessly insulting while a ten would have elicited more excitement. Five dollars: the cost of buttered toast and coffee with some change left over for a tip.

He locks eyes with the suit as he straightens to leave, but then the man quickly averts his eyes. He's done his good deed for the day and doesn't want to feel obligated to shell out anything more.

He hadn't asked, but the man is gone just to make sure he doesn't have to refuse him.

At this early hour, only the diners and coffee shops are open as they cater to the morning crowd. Beyond the invisible barrier of a bohemian-style café, a young couple are sipping on frothing soy lattes and sharing a croissant as they begin their day... or more likely, they are just now ending yesterday's evening. The man's suit is slightly rumpled and he's checking the time on his iPhone to see how much longer he can linger before slipping into work. They are lost in each other.

He isn't thinking of them. Staring at their steaming cups of coffee decorated with the foam poured to make a creamy heart on the dark brown liquid, he doesn't think at all.

He is dreaming instead.

Imagining the taste of the flakey croissant and the heat of the coffee as it scalds the back of his throat, he slowly begins to move his jaws; slowly, slowly he grinds his teeth. Two pieces of buttered toast and a coffee with cream. He can see the thick liquid spiraling into white, cloudy strands before blending into a rich caramel.

He licks his lips at how good it would taste when he is suddenly aware that he is no longer alone. The couple has noticed him. They are no longer looking into each other's eyes, but into his own. They are not happy; he has disturbed them and their visual love-making.

He quickly moves away from the window before they can call the manager.

The dusty head of matted hair follows him. It keeps pace in every shop window he passes. It is both comforting and annoying that the shaggy, unkempt man won't leave him alone. Even though he knows it his own reflection, it is a stranger's face.

The tangled beard is longer than he would have willingly grown it, but at least the tired and wrinkled eyes never look away from his own. The dusty head faded to a washed-out sepia is his only friend.

On schedule, the stranger is in step with him at the next window, but this time he doesn't see it. In the next window there is food on display. Bottles of wine and wheels of cheese; thick and black blood sausages looped like a hangman's noose dangle next to jars of beluga caviar.

Unconsciously, his fingers twitch as he counts: one, two, three.

It has been three days since he has eaten. Three days with the gnawing, rolling, hollow emptiness that continues on and on. He used to tell himself that it wouldn't be forever, that it couldn't go on, but eventually the stupidity of the lies faded. It couldn't go on, but it did... it still does.

His fingers twitch again, but now he is no longer counting. This time, he is contemplating as he eyes the meats and cheeses and eggs. Each one imprisoned by their boxes and casings; boxes protected by the window... which is guarded by the police.

How many guards are required for a sausage or a sardine? Not enough for him to find him before he could snatch some of the smoked meats, but more than enough to chase him down before he could get very far. Probably a single cop could take him down before the spiderweb fractures ceased spreading enough for him to liberate the delicacies inside.

He couldn't run and he certainly had no place to hide.

If he did break the glass and was arrested, they would give him a meal... maybe even two before they fined him for damage. If he could have paid for a window, he could have bought the food outright. Not here, of course. Cheap bologna and tasteless bread were out of his budget, but if he had any money, he could find something to eat.

Forcing his eyes away from the window, he walks on. He can't take enough to fill his empty belly and he isn't ready to be arrested. His stomach has finally stopped grumbling that it is empty. The pain has subsided.

By midday, the clouds are still a solid white. He feels like he is inside an egg looking at the inside of the shell. If it shatters, the sun might come out, but instead it begins to drizzle. A slick, icy glaze covers the streets. He wishes it was November because it is too cold to be May. It is easier to be warm in the winter when the rest of the city is freezing, too. The sides of the buildings radiate a little bit of heat or he can stand near an exhaust fan. In the spring, most of the heaters are off as people dress in layers so they can take off their sweaters in the warming afternoon.

There is only one layer between his skin and the rain. Hunching his shoulders, he shivers. It does nothing to protect him from the cold. He is preserved like the fish on ice. Salted and pickled and left rotting in the cold.

Slowly, he shuffles to the library. It is free and out of the rain. Though it is only two blocks away, on his tired, blistered feet it feels a lot farther.

He isn't allowed in. It is a public place, but people have complained. His looks, his smell, his lack of a library card. Without an address, they wouldn't issue him one. He used to read all day, but now even the books are out of reach.

A sudden flurry of people exiting the high rises inform him that it is lunchtime. Then they vanish. Ushered into cafés, restaurants and diners, they sit at the counters and order their coffee with cream, salads and sandwiches. He shakes violently at the torrent of words swirling through his head. Cheese and sausage; burgers and fries; eggs and bacon with toast and butter.

Coffee with cream; coffee with cream; black coffee; black crime; black blood.

An ambulance races by; its sirens wailing as it sprays him with dark water. At the end of the street people are running in the direction of the park. He recognizes one of them as one of the bench sleepers and he wonders what is going on.

He finds the medics and the police huddled around George. He is still lying on his side against the fence in the overgrown empty lot.

He is not sleeping.

Black blood pools near his head from the cut in his throat. Someone says that he was robbed in broad daylight. His assassin stole every cent he had: exactly five dollars. Killed for two slices of buttered toast and a coffee.

He knows he should be sad, but all he can feel is happiness for the man he called George. George isn't hungry or cold or even tired anymore.

That is something he is envious of. He's been hungry for so long he can no longer feel it gnawing, gnawing, gnawing at his guts. He suddenly realizes he isn't shivering, either. Even the cold has left him.

Turning his back on pile of rags that used to be George and the cops who may detain him for questions even though he knows nothing of the crime, he quickly hurries across the street to the park. If they take him to the station, he will be warm and they might even feed him which would be worse than making himself scarce on his private bench tucked into the corner and out of sight. He'd have to feel the stabbing of the cold and the hollow aching in his stomach all over again.

Tucking his chin to his knees, a strange feeling of euphoria washes over him as he drifts off to sleep. He doesn't feel the hoar frost creeping into his bones or hear the slight rustle of leaves reminding him of the terrible sound of hardboiled eggs cracking on a zinc counter.

Mercifully, he doesn't even dream as he slips into oblivion.

June

Bottling Evil

Lauri Boren

by all accounts it all started off with Doctor Elijah Pozin, famous patent medicine doctor late in the 19th century. He claimed to be an alienist which was what the psychiatry profession called themselves before there were psychiatrists. Doc Pozin started an asylum which ran for decades just outside of town. The year was 1889.

At that time, medical care happened in house calls and surgeries occurred in a doctor's office. Doctors rarely had a formal education, much less a license and nursing was in its infancy. Dentistry still was performed in barber shops. Hospitals were dangerous. While in some of the cities, there were hospitals, they tended to exist for the direst cases. Hay was spread on the floors to help soak up blood. Nothing was sterile. The new work of Florence Nightingale emphasized that specific sanitation practices would improve public health. They did.

Treatment for the mentally ill was horrible. Dorothea Dix had fought for decent facilities for the mentally ill. Asylums that had been constructed as treatment for the insane blundered along. The more well-off families would use small facilities to avoid the nightmare of public asylums. Still, mentally ill people would include anybody with diagnoses from reading novels to paranoia to epilepsy and also the ever-present women's problems.

Charlatans who were quick to see an opportunity rushed into the confusion. With a pretense of medical training, they treated patients in their care.

One alienist was Elijah Pozin who represented himself as having a medical degree. He had reportedly directed a large asylum in South Dakota. Typically they had practiced some of the most modern and despicably injurious or barbaric and useless treatments. Patients would be shackled for weeks and sometimes months, received ice water baths, were prescribed doses of radium or had lobotomies performed as control mechanisms.

Eventually, Pozin left the South Dakota Asylum under confusing circumstances. There was some mystery because one of every three patients at that asylum were put in graves.   During his administration, he had about four hundred patients and one hundred forty of them would end up buried in the asylum's cemetery.   He left the hospital, and then he disappeared.

Surfacing later, Pozin came to Placid River.

Pozin hired some nurses and a few burly orderies and began taking only female patients at the newly opened Placid River Retreat.   Soon, he began to draw business because he targeted one particular type of clientele, the Victorian husband and father. Pozin's asylum was useful for locking their troubling problems away. So his major clients were husbands and fathers who had become uncomfortable with their wives or daughters. His favored patients would be troubled women.

Pozin would lock the wife or child away for odd things: newspaper reading, epilepsy, or for changing religious beliefs.

Women who did not conform to their gendered roles of submission, and daughters that refused to marry, were driven there and forced to remain. There was simply no other option for them but to be imprisoned there.

The unhappy husbands, or bored husbands, the unfaithful, or just cruel husbands were served well by this model. Illness really was not the problem of the woman, as much as the man. An unfortunate affair, a willful wife, or for whatever convenient reason, resulted in the husband client delivering a wife over to Pozin. In the intake reports, Pozin would report that there was evidence of a mysterious hysteria, blaming it on women's problems. All too commonly, the women never made it back to their homes, ever.

Pozin appeared to be the respected doctor, but behind his closed retreat, he was revelling in something evil. Nobody realized it, but some of the patients there. Of course, no one paid attention.

The town noticed the traffic in but not out. Cases and cases of patent medicine were freighted in and out of the retreat. The nurses and orderlies who worked there were very silent about the whole place. Thus, Placid River Retreat was looked at with sidelong glances as people rode by in their carriages. The hilltop was sometimes silent. But sometimes there were terrible cries. These people knew there was insanity, but what really had lived there among them, and walked frequently with them, was a psychopath.

Years later, Placid River Retreat fell into ruin. The retreat was taken over by the woods and one day, the buildings burst into flame. They burned to the ground. The debris was dumped into the nearby ravine. The forest took over the ruins. Pozin disappeared again.

Years passed and the story blurred.

A century later, Martha sat at her table reading the paper and drinking hot coffee. She pulled her glasses off to wipe the steam that had been collecting on the lens and slid them on again.

Her cellphone chirped a signal that immediately caught her attention. It was a security alert from some well-placed wireless cameras set in the woods of her farm. She opened up the app and clicked on the video image.

Over Martha's game camera, an orange and pink dressed figure wandered in the heavily wooded canyon. Her hair was grayed with scraggled braids; she moved from tree to tree. At the base of them, she bent down and picked up old bottles. She held it before the light, gazing blankly. Some of them she placed into a bag she'd slung over her shoulder. Then, she'd gradually wander out of the image.

Martha had placed the game cameras in the canyon for this exact reason; security. No trespassing signs nailed to trees were there until some treasure foraging thief tore them down. There were people who'd easily disregard no trespassing signs, make their way through fenced off areas, tearing them down as well. So, a simple game-camera or two would hopefully help Martha control the trespassers.

She'd heard the cellphone chirp reporting current motions through her home's private network, and watched the strange woman wandering again around at the base of the canyon.

Martha practiced a few coarse words to order off the interloper, as she pulled on her boots and shouldered a very old shotgun. She walked out to the highway, seeking some likely parked car where it should not have been. She wasn't mad enough to shoot out windows, but slicing a tire had crossed her mind. She looked up and down the road, but there was no car.

Had the stranger left already? It was a hard climb up so the woman must be quite strong and fast. That was okay, because she was also very strong and fast. Nothing about her stranger now seemed reasonable.

Martha felt the buzz of her cellphone indicate that the game camera had been signalled again. She took a quick look and saw a few frames of a quite old woman. An old pink sweater, a long orange skirt and a full brown satchel bumped along in the view of the webcam. She looked like a riot. She looked like fire.

"Jay's ass!" Martha muttered and then went down to confront the woman.

A deep canyon lay behind Martha's house. It had such steep sides that it was quite dangerous to descend without a rope. Well- practiced though, Martha climbed down from tree to tree, letting the trunks stop her before she got going too quickly.

Her leg was bumped by the stock of the shotgun and she'd wished she hadn't bothered with it. Interlopers were dissuaded by the glare of her eyes and those choice words. Occasionally she met one parked at the side of the road as they exited her property.

Somewhere down there, though, was the rough orange and pink dressed woman, picking her way from trunk to trunk, gathering bottles. Of course, she was after the bottles. They always were.

Bottles? Why the bottles? Well, because Doc Pozin used them and dropped them over the edge along the road. Martha had to do some detective work to find out that story.

Years before, Martha was building her house. One day, someone stopped to ask where the asylum had been. She'd said the rehab center was down the road toward town. No, the tourist explained. It was an old asylum that is supposed to be right here.

But the asylum wasn't there. It had been there, and was a few hundred feet north, though, laying invisible under the burned ground.

Martha had found that history out at the Capitol Library when she'd gone to ask about the story a few weeks later. She'd had to because after the first tourist came, another came, and then another.

That day, after an hour of driving to the capitol, Martha was at the library desk asking for information about the Placid River Retreat.   The head librarian was a tall gaunt woman with strong arms and gray hair. She grimaced a bit at the topic and left to go find the archival box.

A few minutes later, Martha sat down in a silent room to go through the archives. Inside the box were a lot of newspapers, a stack of letters and contracts, a bottle and information about a patent medicine from Pozin, some newspapers from the time, and copies of some of the sheriff's reports.

Piece by piece Martha followed the story of the asylum. Letters from husbands or fathers requesting consultations and sharing the surprising lack of obedience in their wives or daughters.   They asked for information about Pozin's asylum services.   There were letters from families who were wondering about their mother or sister. There was a lot of pain to read about.

The sheriff's envelopes contained copies of missing persons reports. Some inmates of the asylum told stories that were beyond belief.   There were stories of leech treatments, glowing demonic glass, and some other horrid treatments that were outlined.   They said patients came there to end up truly insane. There was, according to the witness statements, a great deal of screaming.   The witness statements were products of insanity. The final reports concluded that there was again, only some harmless woman who'd wandered away at night.

Under the papers and next to a journal was a glass bottle, golden and printed with Pozin's Waters of Life and dated 1890. It was deeply indented on the bottom and was empty. Martha peered at the lettering and read: "Pozin's waters, for the treatment of mania and hypomania, for fits, neurosis and melancholy. Extracted using the microscopic filtration and distillation in modern radium bottles.

Discovered in the famous universities of the Near East, this elixir uses a scientific procedure to harvest unbalanced humours needed by those in hysteria. Use this medicine liberally to calm the anxious and awaken immobile catatonia. Patent pending.

The journal showed the confused writing of what was thought to be Elijah Pozin. There were lists of experiments and reports of his experiences dealing with "souls in the afterlife" who'd given him the insight to make his medicine. The microscopic filters in the particular bottles would collect the imbalance humours of the traumatized soul. From this could an elixir of health be produced.

"Yes," Martha thought, "Pozin was crazy." She wondered if he was evil though, or merely a charlatan?

Martha stacked the materials on the table and peered again at the bottle. She'd read something about bottles that glowed from manufacturing using radioactive materials. Of course, that was before they were linked to insanity and cancer. How ironic that those materials were used to cure the same thing they caused. Of course, Pozin's medicine would have killed people. Martha thought that the rare collector's radium glass was the prize so many were looking for.

Martha tipped the box on its side. In the bottom of the box was a poster advertising Placid River Retreat. The image was of a well crafted two story building, surrounded by a porch and flowers. It noted that there were all of the new modern treatments without leaving the retreat. There was a small image of Pozin as well. His experience working the the Institution for the Insane in South Dakota as well his specialities in medicine and therapeutic activities were noted. The technologies of brain surgery to cure depression, as well as radium treatments and electroshock therapies. Pozin had prescribed or performed them all. The rest was a map that showed the address and directions to get to the asylum from the town. The asylum had indeed bordered her farm.

Martha began packing the materials back in the archival box. The librarian came back to pick it up.

She looked at Martha questioningly. "Did you find anything new?"

"I didn't know there would be anything new." Martha placed the files back in and replaced the lid.

"When people come, they are always looking for a treasure map. There never was a treasure map. There was just a lot of sadness." The librarian picked up the box and walked into the back room.

Martha drove back home. As she pulled into her driveway, she looked up the road a bit, wondering. Radium glass?

There was a tale, mostly made of gossip. The story over the decades had exploded out of all proportion. It was now an adult's version of Bloody Mary. Instead of looking into a mirror at school and saying Bloody Mary three times and finding a ghost behind them, they had Pozin's asylum and radioactive bottles to sate their lust after terror. They climbed down the hill looking for relics of the evil that had been done there. They left with stories of made up events or of encounters with Martha, the annoyed neighbor. Sometimes they left in an ambulance because footing was quite dangerous there.

That was then.

Today it was Martha hunting the old woman in pink and orange. She kept picking her way down the canyon. The slope was steep and she had to keep her eyes on her footing. The best way down was never this way. It was just quick, but not as quick as it would be if she wasn't very careful.

Descending from tree trunk to tree trunk was awkward and she couldn't quite see around the base of the canyon because the tree canopy was still below her. She looked down, put her foot down to the next root system when she thought she'd heard the old woman bumping along. She looked up and then everything was twisting around.   An avalanche of pine needles and fir cones was sliding with her. Something had broken loose and she was falling, headfirst down the canyon directly toward a downed tree.

At the bottom, Martha was dazed. She had trouble focusing and she heard things that she couldn't understand. Something was pain. She squeezed her eyes shut. Something was whispering to her. She opened her eyes and followed the sound coming from the direction of green glass or yellow glass. The whispering flowed like shattering glass. She knew that she must be hallucinating. She watched herself from outside of her body. What were the words she was hearing? The hallucination or whatever it was, was confused, and Martha could hear weeping.   There were words she couldn't make out. How did it come from that empty golden bottle?   It was definitely a hallucination she did not want to understand.

Light was still too much for eyes and there was far too much noise to think. She shut out the sound and when she passed out, time had slipped away. Then the years slid away.

When she opened her eyes, Martha was on what she thought was an ambulance gurney. She was in a room. It was a large room. It was lit by gas powered lamps. She'd recognized them from movies but didn't know whose house it might be that contained them.

Her eyes hurt as she tried to clear her head. A mildewed smell of the blanket made her nauseous, or was that just her head? Was she alone?

There was rustling around her and she turned her head. Her throat was dust dry and her ears rang. Although she was laying flat, dizziness took over and the pad spun. Martha gagged from the motion. There was nothing to throw up.

She tried to sit up but could not. Something was holding her down. But no, as she peered through the slits of her eyes, she saw strap after strap securing her body to a table. Nothing made sense.

"What did you do to have that happen to you?" A woman's voice, kind and soft, came from somewhere Martha could not see. "I'm glad you are awake though. It's been hours since the wagon brought you in."

"I didn't do anything," Martha croaked. "I was walking on my farm and now I am here."

Martha lay in a large mostly vacant room. There were benches along the side, and she was most certainly on a gurney. Nothing made sense to her. On the opposite wall, there was a person sitting rigidly on a bench. A shadow made from the gas lamps flickered behind the figure. Martha was still having trouble seeing clearly. Gas lamps?

"Where am I?" Martha asked. " And who are you and how did I get here?"

The figure got up from the bench and slowly walked toward Martha. She was wearing a plain long skirt with a brown suede blouse. Her hair was tied back and boots tapped as she moved forward.

"I am Minerva Pozin, and I am a guest in the retreat here. Just like you, I suppose," the woman said.

"Retreat?"

"Yes, Placid River Retreat," Minerva confirmed.

"Placid River Retreat is burned to the ground. This must be someplace else."

"Burned down? No, but if they don't fix the gaslights soon, that might happen. I see why you are a guest here," Minerva was slowly approaching the gurney. "You aren't going to hit me or anything? Well, or perhaps, spit on me or anything?"

"What? No! I'm so confused," Martha shook her head.

"Yes, I saw. You think we are burned to the ground." Minerva was agreeable.

"Yes, eighty years ago," Martha said.

"I see." MInerva walked up to Martha. Her skirt was long, dark blue and more than a bit stained. Her blouse, though, wasn't a blouse, and it wasn't made of suede. It was canvas, securely buckled and sleeves longer than her arms wrapped around her.

Martha's mouth gaped. Her company was wearing a strait-jacket.

"Oh, now, for real, where am I?"

"I told you, Placid River Retreat for Ladies." Minerva winced at the shocked expression. "Don't let the restraints fool you. I promise I won't spit on you either. But if you are going to be a lunatic at me, I'm going to go back over there, and sit down."

"No, please don't leave." Martha had closed her eyes again. "It's just that I was following after this woman I saw in my webcam. My cell-phone signalled that someone had tripped the alarm. So I was going down the hill to confront her."

Minerva wrinkled her forehead. "What are those? Cellphone, you said? Webcam?"

"Yes, it was in my shirt pocket." Martha was shaking.

"I have not ever heard of them. I can't look in your pocket, because, well, I'm stuck."

"I know I was hurt. Is there a nurse or someone? I have to get loose."

"The nurse comes, or an orderly, bringing the waters. But they won't come when you call. They won't come when I call, and I've been here for four years."

"Waters?" Martha worried. " What are waters?"

Martha's mind began to scramble trying to understand the danger she was in. "I think that someone has kidnapped me. Maybe someone kidnapped her. Or maybe she kidnapped me," she thought. "I need to think. How to get away."

That was really the only thing that made sense to Martha. Someone had captured her, maybe drugged her and was keeping her trapped, now. The strange woman in the bottom of the canyon, perhaps?

Outloud, she said, "I still don't understand how I got here. And I have to pee."

Minerva shambled back to her bench. "You will have to get used to waiting," she said.

As the daylight softened, Martha opened her eyes. Her headache was somewhat less, and she still felt confused, concerned, and sometimes out and out panicky.

She heard a key in the door and watched the knob turn. A

dark-haired man, about forty-five, came through the door pushing a luncheon cart with bottles stacked on it. He walked over to Martha and frowned down at her.

"I see you have awakened. Good!" he said.

"Hello," he said.

"I don't know where I am and I don't know what happened," Martha rushed. "Do you know how I got here?"

"No."

"And I have to pee."

He winced. "Such language does not fit guests of the retreat. Please be more polite."

"I have to urinate. I need to get up and go to the bathroom," Martha explained.

"After your waters," he said. "Bathing will be in the evening as it always has been."

He removed the cork from a jug and said, "and you Minerva? Are you ready for your healing waters?"

Minerva wandered to him and nodded, "Yes, I am, Dr. Pozin."

Martha swallowed and said carefully, "I do not need to have a bath. I need to empty my bladder! Please!"

"Much better," he said. "Still you can wait. Go ahead and empty your bladder. The orderlies will change you later."

The man stretched his arms and looked to Minerva. "Shall I let your arms free then?"

"Yes, please Dr. Pozin, I'd never ever hurt anyone." Minerva pleaded.

"Hm."   Dr. Pozin unbuckled two straps and Minerva's arms dropped. He slid a leather strap off of her jacket over his hand. "Now here, roll those sleeves up so you can hold your waters."

Minerva reached out to take the clear quart bottle of colorless liquid and shuffled back to her bench.

"I do not know what happened. Dr. Pozin, is it? Can you tell me or can I have someone call the police?" Martha asked.

"Report to the Constable? Now why would we do that?" Dr. Pozin shook his head. "You are placed here for a reason. I'm sure it is time for you to drink your waters."

"I have to urinate," Martha said. "After that, maybe."

"Having to empty your bladder is beside the point." Dr. Pozin suddenly yanked Martha's jaw open roughly, slid the leather strap between her teeth. She thought that he had dislocated her jaw. It was a crushing move and Martha cried out.

Dr. Pozin poured the half gallon jug of "waters" into Martha's bruised mouth. Her heart pounded, overwhelmed with fear. She choked and sobbed. Every time she actively resisted, Dr. Pozin tightened his grip, wrenching her jaw painfully. Her consciousness of her life faded and all she became was something reacting to fear. Dr. Pozin covered her mouth and nose until Martha realized that she had to cooperate to be able to breathe. Even so, she choked as Pozin poured it all down her throat. Her belly swelled painfully, but something prevented her from vomiting it back out. He removed the leather strap and slipped it into his pocket. It was efficient.

Dr. Pozin said, "Don't worry, you will fill the bottle back up."

Somewhere during that past ten minutes, Martha emptied her bladder. Dr. Pozin left the bottle. It was so easy for him to turn a person into a thing.

Martha wept and wept.

Minerva sat on her bench and completely finished her bottle of waters.

Martha had fallen asleep again when her gurney was jarred. A nurse stood over her and frowned. "Why did you come here? There is nobody who brought you."

"I have no intention of being here," Martha answered. "Please let me go?"

"You do not have people," the nurse said. "That's fine. Why haven't you filled the bottle up yet?"

"How?" Martha was shocked. "You've had me strapped down here all day."

"It's simple, ah, I think you've already started." The nurse looked deeply into the clear bottle now with a very slight pink shade. "Ah, yes."

"I think you need to let me go, whoever you are," Martha demanded.

"A lunatic like you, with your dysregulated emotions would be arrested in a minute." The nurse shook her head grimly. "No, you stay here until we regulate you. And you have to fill that bottle, first."

The nurse turned a wheel under Martha's gurney, nodded to Minerva, and left the room.

The wheel the nurse had turned had tightened the straps to such an extreme point that the muscles in Martha's stomach and back were driven into spasm. Martha was driven to weeping, again.

There was pain. But it was more than physical pain. It was a grief Martha felt as her thoughts were broken apart bit by bit. She was convinced she could never escape even if she got her pain under control.

After the nurse left, Martha was hopeful Minerva would help her. Minerva hadn't come near her even though her arms were now loose. She could have easily slipped out of her strait-jacket but she did not.

"Minerva, why aren't you helping me?" Martha was crying.

"It's because I am empty," Minerva said. "There isn't anything left to go."

"Oh man, you are all just crazy! This is all crazy. "

Martha had settled into a lower level of hysteria. "Waters? What the hell is that? Then I'm trussed up in some weird as hell sideshow and I think you are all lunatics!"

"Not at first. Well, at least not me." Minerva was quietly looking at the floor. "Who I am, and who I was, before having to come here... well, that's changed."

"You said you were here four years?" Martha was still ticked. "How did *you* get in here?"

"My uncle had me delivered here. It was after my parents died. There was a small inheritance, but he had put himself in charge of it. I simply was in the way of what my parents had given me. I guess now it must be 1898, now? Four years, and so much of my life is gone. But, Martha, I wasn't dysregulated. Not at all. Now, so much is confusing."

"Minerva, can't you unstrap me? This hurts a lot."

"No, I don't help anybody any more. It costs too much. And you can't ask me any more."

Minerva wandered back to her place on the bench.

"The year is most definitely not 1898," thought Martha. "That's one hundred twenty years ago, and I know the retreat is burned down. This has to be somewhere else."

The door swung open and the dark haired man, walked into the room.

"Hello, Dr. Pozin," Minerva said.

"Hello, Minerva," the man replied. "And how is our

new patient?"

The question seemed rhetorical because Minerva didn't answer and the doctor was looking at the bottle that had become even more pink.

"Ah, yes, I see you have started," he said. "This, uh, Martha, is it? This is distilled molecules that are collected from distraught patients. Apparently, you are distraught? That's good. It cleans the humours."

"I think you had better let me go. I'm not supposed to be here and there is going to be trouble when people find me."

The doctor was scowling at her. "I think it is best if you change your tone." He brought the bottle to his face and breathed deeply. "Nice bouquet!" he whispered. "I will call the help to take you both to the bathing."

Martha's bath was horrible. Ice cold and they never did take the straps off. Nurses picked up the pallet that rested on the gurney and dropped her into a large tank full of ice water, pallet and all. After a half hour or so, they pulled her out and set her in the air to dry. She'd been delirious with a body temperature well below normal.

When she was returned, still confused, to the room, there were other people there. Other patients, she thought. Light sconces along the walls were burning steadily.

The orderly removed her straps and Martha just laid there, shivering and barely moving. He pulled a chair nearby and placed a long pinkish gray gown on the seat.

"You best put these dry clothes on," he said. He then left.

Minerva had remained where she had been all day. Still, on the bench, across the room. The benches were lined with silence. Each patient sat still and calmed with a container of the waters set by each of them. There was one by Martha's chair as well.

Martha shakily got up. Still quite hypothermic, she gathered the gown and found a place that contained several chamber pots. She'd noticed the silent Minerva using one earlier. That was just one more thing in this nightmare. As soon as she had the gown over her head, her clothes were taken away. Martha had only been there ten hours. She had guessed that. Her phone, and everything she owned, had disappeared.

Minerva looked at her and motioned her toward the waters. Her eyes shifted to the door and then back to Martha. She looked worried when Martha did not drink. Noticing Minerva's silent message, Martha picked up her container and sipped. Minerva nodded.

Martha drank some more and out of the blue, understood that she was being drugged. She staggered to her feet and fell flat on her face. The bottle she held did not break but rolled in a circle by her head. Martha lay there weeping and watched the only thing she could see. With her tears and time, the bottle turned to a silvery pink.

Days passed by. Martha was becoming more confused by the hour. The drugging had not stopped. As the days went by, Martha noticed some patterns. A great deal was made about the clear bottles filled with their waters. She'd assumed it contained some sort of sedative but was surprised when she didn't feel calmer after drinking. Her feelings were large so she wept, or shivered or growled every day.

Food came in with the orderlies, in pans of oatmeal or soup. The women lined up to pick up a bowl of food and a spoon. It didn't seem like much, and there was so much left. Martha wondered if anybody was really eating.

The empty bottles came, and went.

Through the window one day, Martha could watch the grounds in the early evening. Out on the yard, the grass was wet. One night, she saw Doctor Pozin, walking outside and drinking the same elixir they called the waters.   It made her wonder if it was really drugged, if he was drinking from it.

Mostly the room was quiet except when a patient began talking to herself. Eventually, she started yelling, and there the group would be trying to ignore the noise and staring at the ground. There were many of them whispering to themselves. It went on for hours, every day. The exercise, Martha supposed, was meant for patients to learn to regulate emotions.

Nurses and orderlies, in quiet authoritative decisions, made the days stay on schedule. There was much time to stare at the floor, scheduled times to sip the Placid River elixir, eat meals, and watch time disappear. Every few days, a woman seemed to be missing. Nobody seemed to notice when a fellow patient disappeared. At least they didn't bring it up. Nobody brought anything up. Every incident was let go.

Daily, patients lined up obediently for electric therapy, insulin shock therapy, or radium injections. Martha lined up right with them. Exchanging her clothing for blue and then orange, she sat in the chair and had insulin injected, or radium, or felt her body go rigid when the direct current was poured into it. Her thoughts faded. She began to wonder if she really had ever been capable of anything besides sitting.

Reality had ceased, or at least what Martha had thought was reality.   She had become disconnected from herself. Somewhere in the pain and the soul draining "waters" she realized that she was losing a grasp on her most precious gift of life.

It didn't matter that someone said it was 1897. It didn't

matter if she found herself wandering the room. Even if it was 1897, she had to find a way out of there. She just wasn't sure where to go. Some part of her willed herself to break out, and yet, every morning, she awakened to what she'd begun to believe was reality.

Martha's scrambled thoughts put the idea together. "First I will get out of the retreat, then I'll decide what to do next." Probably the police, but the first thing that she needed was to get out. At this point, she thought she'd been there for years.

One night, walking back in a line from the baths, Martha slipped out of line and through a doorway. She'd walked past the doorway dozens of times and never noticed it. This evening, though, she noticed. A slight shift in her walk, brought her close to the door. She rotated through that doorway. Nobody noticed. The line didn't react to her missing space, and closed up the space she left. She waited silently until a stream of orderlies carried out soaked towels.

Behind her, on the other side of the room, was a window. It was open a few inches to let fresh air in. It was not quite dark yet, and so Martha decided to wait until night was fully settled. She sat at a desk by the window and studied the room, and waited. A storage room door was slightly ajar and paper was on a table.

Letters were set in a basket on the corner. Martha found herself experiencing curiosity; something that had become a foreign emotion. Her curiosity drove her to read. Mostly they contained applications for new women as patients. One was labelled Minerva Pozin, and Martha thought there was something familiar about that. Then wondered where her letter had been placed. She'd wondered who she had disappointed to get sent up here.

Some lab notes were on the stack. *Investigations into Sentience and Sanity* was the title of the work. The subtitle read *Self-Awareness, Sanity and Intelligence.* And *Essence Removal Rituals of the Near East Shoamin: storage concerns.*

There were tables of experimental results showing numbers explaining something about a spectrum effect in tempered or annealed glass. There were lists of subjects and a spectrum colors assigned to each result. Martha was not sure she understood that, but she thought she should be able to.

Another lab note was titled "On The Capturing of Sentience and the Interactions with an Inverse Mechanism of Emotional Regulation. "

There was a word on there she remembered: dysregulation. It was familiar, but she didn't know from where. And sentience. Didn't that mean humanness?

There were pieces of glass attached to a paper with explanations of each one. Pink glass showed a high score of despair. Blue was an indicator for terror. Orange for fortitude. The gray samples had statements such as no observable data, or inconclusive data.

Martha heard steps in the hallway. She slid toward the opened storage room.

The door opened up and lights were turned up. Doctor Pozin had walked in. This was apparently his office. He had a bottle of the Waters and was preparing to leave for the evening.

Martha flattened herself to the wall and waited silently.

"Pozin," she thought. "Minerva Pozin?" She wondered if Doc Pozin was related to Minerva.

Martha counted to herself to pass the time. It was a useful way to remain regulated and not draw attention. That was something she had gotten used to after only a few physical corrections. The nurses were quite adept with that. She gathered her wits and dismissed the thought to the back of her mind. Dysregulation would not be good here.

Martha began to count.   One, two, seven, four, nine, twenty-two. Wait, no that wasn't right. She knew how to count and so began again. One, two, four, seven (that was right) nine, twenty-two. She felt better now. No dysregulation anywhere.

Dr. Pozin had left the room and Martha began to silently rise. Now for the window.

Before she left the storage room, she focused on the shelves in front of her. There were statues, or rather face masks of women in the retreat house. Martha recognized a few of them. All the ones she recognized had disappeared. Except, they did not seem to be masks,or statues. They were very lifelike, with unusual wounds on their eyelids. How odd!

That was the monologue in her mind before her heart began to pound in terror. Her brain stopped right there before she'd puzzled out who the faces were and what they meant. She decided to not understand. To deal with the present, Martha gasped and shut down her concerns.

Martha crept to the window, slid it a bit further up and climbed out. She walked a few paces and looked down. There was something wrong. She was seeing? At her feet were human bones. Human skulls. Human bodies. She ran, silently screaming.

Marth was aware that her mind was starting to break with reality.   Maybe the "waters" made her susceptible to hallucinations. In the scattering of bones in the grass, also lay hundreds and hundreds of empty "waters" bottles. They were whispering to her. Or maybe the skulls and bodies were whispering to her.

No it was the bottles. The bottles cried to her. They

shouted in her mind. They shouted in the darkness that which was unintelligible.   Unintelligible was what Martha's conscious mind was at present. There was an animal instinct to flee to safety, and a gibberish that blurred all other thinking.

In the darkness, she found a dirt road, and ran down the side.

Up ahead was a space that one day a woman a bit younger than her would build a house. A reporter would have told ghost stories of the evil up the hill, and tourists would come by on adventures.

As she ran next to the canyon side, her ankle popped and she went tumbling down into the depths. Leaves and branches slid with her. She was no longer aware of when she was..

When Martha cleared her head, she was somewhere else. Some other time.

It was the afternoon, and Martha was heading down the canyon side, picking her way from tree trunk to tree trunk. She stretched her foot out and.

"Martha, Don't step there!" came a loud voice to her right. It was gruff and low pitched.

Martha stopped mid-stride and grabbed the tree trunk she was just ready to let go of. She looked to her right into the face of the old woman she was seeking. There was her pink dress and orange jacket. She'd been reaching her arm over to stop Martha where she'd been.

Martha gasped, and her heart pounded. Where was she?

She didn't know this woman but had been directly addressed by her. And, she'd tried to help Martha be steady when she stopped.

"What?" she croaked.

"Don't step there at that next foothold." The face of the

woman was quite aged and sun-worn. The satchel she was carrying still held clinking bottles.

"What are you saying? What are you doing here?" Martha spluttered.

Everything was confusing after that. Martha followed the stranger down the hill and found herself sitting and watching the old woman empty her satchel. One by one, she placed ancient bottles on the log. There were dozens there, blue and brown and green and pink. Martha reached over to pick one of them up.

"You should not touch that. They will hurt you," the old woman said. "They come from Elijah. From up the hill. And they are at least a hundred years old."

"I know. I have drank from them."

"I don't think you want them. In any way," mused the orange-clothed woman.

"I don't want anybody else to come get them. They'll fall and have to get hauled out screaming again."

The woman shook her head. "No. These are bad. I have spent decades making them safe again. People just don't think about picking up evil, do they?"

"No. How do you know all this? And what's your name? And why are you on my property?"

"My name is Minerva," she said. "Minerva Pozin."

"One does not play with evil and expect to come up without scars," Minerva said. She was covered in scars.

So many images rushed to Martha's memory. Minerva, from the Retreat, here? How could she have been gone so long? How could she have gone at all? There was simply not any time. She screamed. She was crying when Minerva led her back to her house.

Martha's understanding of life, after that, was fragile and

painful.   She went about caring for her house.   Avoided confrontation, and didn't turn on her game cameras for months.

One day, her friend from the newspaper called to ask her to have breakfast.   Martha drove through the town looking at everything.

Placid River was idyllic this time of year. It was warm and inviting and tourists stopped one after another, visiting the sites that some Sunny Tourguide listed. They stopped at River's Cafe and ate the main courses. Their star recipe, Duck soup, was probably a century old by the townsfolk's reckoning. It was an original recipe from the last century, for something a self-respecting duck, alive or dead, would never want to be a part of.

The menu describes fare for the 20st Century as well as the 21th. Amateur detectives at lunch at the counters page through souvenir books and sip on iced tea.

Memories of Doc Pozin's list of the missing patients brought mystery hunters to seek out the lurid details of what and how someone would treat their fellow humans that way. There were tour maps to the cemetery and the old train station.

Martha wanted to stop them all.

In a booth,the two women sat finishing up the eggs and toast they'd had for breakfast. An annoyed expression filled the face of one, contemplating the tourists at the counter.

"It is all about the bottles. Well, the bottles and the legend. Rather, the bottles and the legend and the madman," Martha mused.

"What?" Karma wrinkled her forehead trying to puzzle this story out. "I don't understand."

Martha picked up her espresso and sipped it and then rested her chin in one hand. It's the asylum that was just up the road; where Doc Pozin had all those people locked in?"

"That's mostly a scrambled story." Karma shook her head. "It's not worth paying attention to."

"But people, people should pay attention. They should know. But they only know a bit and so they come to sneak around my property." Martha shook her head.

"Still?"Karma asked.

"Still, and no trespassing signs be damned." Martha had tears in her eyes. "It's dangerous. More dangerous than just popping an ankle and giving my insurance company fits. But, Pozin's place was not at my farm."

Well, that's not good either." Karma shook her head. "The weirdos need to find a life."

"If they aren't careful, they are going to find something much less pleasant." Martha was still shaking her head slightly.

"What do you mean?" Karma was worried.

Martha's tone revealed her distress. "I mean, you can't play with darkness and come through that without lifelong scars." Martha's expression chilled, twitching to a wince.   "It has never changed. There is evil in the bones of the forest."

"Okay, start at the beginning." Karma settled onto her seat.

"It's not really the beginning, maybe." Martha shrugged. "Pozin had so many women die under his care. I'm not sure why, really, but it sure seemed evil. I'm not sure whether disease came with him, or was drawn to him."

"Disease?" Karma still looked confused.

"There was disease up, at his place, and it leaked out. He collected it. Experimented with it. He sold it as a potion," Martha whispered. "He was the disease. He still leaks out all of the time." Under the table, her webcam chirped on Martha's phone.

JULY

The Witch of Endor
David Martyn

A low hiss filled her ear. She tried shaking her head and even clearing it with the tip of her little finger, but the soft hiss continued. "Where are we going, Father?" The barefoot girl asked as she followed along the rocky path up the Hill of Moreh. The Jezreel valley opened below them as a flat plain between the low Hill of Moreh and its towering brother to the north, Mount Tabor.

"If you are thirsty, Kerem, we can stop. Drink some water and rest. It is another hour, daughter. I want you to be rested. Look, over there, that is our village, Endor. Look closely. Remember where it is."

Kerem looked down on her home and out towards Mount Tabor. "Father, I can see Mount Tabor and beyond, mountains even greater! And in that direction, I can see a great sea. What lies beyond the mountain, father? Have you been beyond Mount Tabor? Have you been to the great sea?"

Micah slowly turned and absorbed the view. "I have not been beyond the mountain. But my people have come from the end of the great sea. Our patriarch Issachar son of Jacob, called Israel, was given this land. Given?" He reconsidered the word. "We had to fight the Canaanites to take it and fight to keep it. But your mother, her people are of Canaan—from Hazor, beyond Mount Tabor."

"You and Momma were enemies? Papa, did you love Momma?"

"Come along, Kerem, the sun is getting high in the sky. Soon it will be hot. You will burn your feet."

The two started back up the mountain. Kerem did her best to ignore the growing hissing in her ears. "I can't wait to tell my brothers. I am sure they have never seen such a sight. Why did they not come along, Papa?"

"They have work to do."

"You told them to feed the orphan lamb? The one no ewe would accept. It is such a sweet little lamb. You told them, Papa?"

"They will care for the lamb. You will do as you are told when you meet the priest. Do not pester him with questions. Do you understand?"

"I can ask you questions, Papa?"

"Of course, but not the priest. He is not a patient man."

Micah and Kerem continued up. They entered into a thicket of terebinth trees. Kerem asked, "Why are there trees here, but not below us? And what are these tall poles?"

"The others have been cut down. These are holy trees. They surround the poles of Asherah, the mother goddess. We are almost there."

The hissing grew louder, and as Kerem passed an Asherah pole, it seemed to whisper to her softly, "Kerrrremmm. Kerrrremmm."

Coming out of the woods, Micah led Kerem into a small

compound somewhat like a village. They walked past long dwellings, a well, and a kitchen. In the center was a tall, stone building with an imposing golden statue of a bull guarding the entrance. Behind the bull was an altar with a blazing fire atop it. For once, Micah did not wait for Kerem's question. He saw amazement in her wide eyes. "That is Baal, lord of the heavens. This is his temple. Come, his priest is inside."

It was dark inside the temple. Out of the bright sunlight, it took time for their eyes to adjust, even with lamps and sconce torches lit. It was hard to see the walls and ceiling through the hazy smoke that floated in the air. And a smell, like burning wet grass, but sweeter, filled their nostrils. A hand grasped Micah's shoulder, "You have brought her to the priest? This way."

A man in a white tunic with a golden bull emblazoned on the front led Micah into the smoke.

The voice grew louder. "Kerremm."

"Why is there so much smoke, Papa? It is hard to see, and it smells. Has something caught fire?" Uneasy with the voice, the smoke, and the smell, she sought to assure herself as she added, "The men do not seem alarmed."

"It is incense. It is for Baal. It cleanses everything in the temple, and it is pleasing to him. You will soon find it pleases you as well."

They were led to a man in white robes with a golden helmet, standing in the center of the room swinging a censer and chanting. They waited. The man made a complete circle, swinging his censer high into the air and chanting. When he finally stopped, he handed the censer to the robed man who brought them into the room.

"Who brings this woman to Baal?"

"Sssssss Kerrrrremmmmm."

"I am her father. That is, she is the daughter of my dead wife. My wife was devoted to Baal, Asherah, and the gods of Canaan. This, her daughter was born to her after one of your many festivals. I call her Kerem, Vineyard, for she was fathered in a vineyard or under an Asherah pole. My wife played the harlot, so let her daughter live here as a temple prostitute. She is of no use to me."

The priest looked at Kerem and then spoke to the man. "She is young. And your words show contempt for the gods."

"I am a son of Israel. Baal is a god of Canaan. We are commanded to have no dealings with Canaanites. My wife beguiled me, and I married her. But I worship no god. I will take the price for the girl and be gone. She is of age."

The voice teased, "Kerremm?"

Kerem cried out, "Papa, what are you saying? Papa, please!"

The priest turned to Kerem and said, "Remove your robe."

Kerem stood dumbfounded, her eyes wide and her jaw agape. She muffled a sob but dutifully opened her robe and dropped it to the floor.

The priest took one look and turned to the man. "No man would have her. The mark on her chest, like a serpent crawling down to her stomach. She could please no man. Her coupling would not entice Asherah. I will give you no money. Take her to the priest of Moloch. Perhaps they will buy her to pass through his fire."

Micah stared at the mark. He remembered a birthmark, but when did it grow large? He turned to the priest. "I have watched your festivals. After much wine and your sacred food, both men and women in their frenzy, they show no regard for who pleases them."

Kerem picked up her robe and covered herself. As her father argued, Kerem's head fell back, and her eyes opened wide. She began to chant—words, words her father had never heard. The priest listened as Kerem chanted louder, and she began to dance. Her body writhed rhythmically, almost like the desert cobra moving and stalking its victim. First her chin, then her shoulders. Now her chest, her small body thrusting. The undulating serpentine motion moved lower to her hips and then her knees, all the while she chanted.

Kerem lifted her arms and spun in a circle. Her head, now bobbing, her back bent, her knees lifting, she danced in place chanting louder and louder, till at last, she fell in a heap at the feet of the priest.

Her father and the priest stared in amazement at what they had seen. Then, slowly, Kerem lifted her head and rose to her knees. She clutched her robe in front of her as she stood. "Where is she?" Kerem asked. "Where did she go—I will go with her."

The priest asked, "She? You had a vision. What did you see?"

"Mother. She was here. She came out of the smoke and spoke to me. She told me I am her voice, and she is my strength."

Her father said, "Your mother is dead. Dead and buried. Come with me, Kerem. I will sell you to the priests of Moloch."

"You will not sell me to Moloch. I am free of you. Mother has freed me. You are less than a pig to her, and now to me. I am free!"

The priest asked, "Tell me all that you have seen. Your mother, you say. Was she alone? What else did you see and hear?"

"My mother came to me from others. She was wearing rings. Rings around her neck, her wrists, and her ankles. Beads hung from her hair, and her eyes were circled in black. She wore only a golden belt and the image of Asherah on a necklace. There was laughing and singing. Others were coupling like rams and ewes in the field. When she came to me, she said, 'Sweet daughter Kerem, you have the gift. Power to enter and the power to leave. Submit to no man. Least of all, the pig who sells you. You will be my voice from sheol. Tell them. Tell the priest of Baal you have the gift."

The priest scowled at Micah. "Leave her with us. She is holy to our gods. Go!"

Micah said, "The price for a temple prostitute is thirty shekels."

The priest replied, "You have said she is not your daughter. She will stay with us. Go."

"I fed her and clothed her for thirteen years. I deserve something. Pay me the price."

"Clothed her? She does not even wear sandals! Take what I give and be gone!" The priest reached into his pouch and retrieved a silver coin. "She is not to be a temple prostitute. She is a seer. Take this and leave."

Micah took the coin, turned, and disappeared in the smoke, not taking a last look at the young woman he raised.

"Papa! Papa! If you leave me, you are dead to me! What is to become of me?" The smoke around her began to spin.

"Kerrremmm, Kerremm, Kerem, you are my voice, my ears, and my eyes to those living. Grow strong, Kerem. Grow strong!"

Kerem awoke the following day in a strange bed in a strange place, and her eyes fixed on an unfamiliar ceiling above her. Slowly the memory of being bathed, clothed in a clean white robe, and fed strange new foods dispelled the shadows of fear and surprise. She sat up and saw a woman standing over her.

"Good morning, Kerem. You slept well. No time to linger in bed. Get dressed, come to breakfast. Today you begin your journey!"

Kerem joined others at breakfast, all women. Kerem smiled as she scanned the faces of the others. *Young and old. There is no distinction of age, But I appear the youngest.* The woman who stood over her when she awoke took the seat of honor and spoke. "Sisters of the priesthood, today our sister, Kerem, joins us. We all must guide her in our ways and duties. I remind you of what we witnessed. Kerem's vision came to her before the ritual meal. She has shown uncommon clarity. Now we must instruct her more fully as she opens her path of intercession with the gods. We must teach her to gather and prepare our food, drink, and incense and our secret words to call our guides from beyond. But first, give her our welcome."

The priestesses replied in unison, "Welcome Kerem, priestess of Mother Asherah, she who eternally conceives but does not bear. May your pathway be open before you!"

Kerem shook her head. "It has been more than a year. I tell you, I do not need the roots and mushrooms, the incense, and the spells. They only blur my mind. No, my mother comes to me when I clear my mind and call for her. It is best when I am seated before the pit, my eyes closed but seeing the flames through my eyelids."

The Chief Priestess smiled. "But you see only your mother. There are others. We speak to many who have gone before."

"Yes, I see others, but they remain away off. Only my mother speaks to me. She tells me she speaks for Asherah. It is enough."

The sound of a shofar interrupted Kerem's session with the priestesses of Asherah. They rose and looked down from the hill of Moreh. Soon another shofar sounded across the valley from mount Tabor and then from the village of Endor. Finally, a warrior on the back of a donkey rode to the top of Moreh and sounded his shofar.

A priest of Baal approached the warrior. "What is the message?"

The warrior replied, "Our King Saul calls all Israel to join him at Gilgal. The Philistines. A great host has camped at Michmash. All are to come. No exceptions, priest. Leave the tending of your idols to the women. The tribe of Issachar is gathering at Endor and the cities of the valley. Gather your wooden staffs, pruning hooks, spikes, and hoes, and go to Endor. We march from Endor to Gilgal tomorrow."

The priest of Baal replied. "It is better we remain and make sacrifices to Baal on behalf of our King."

The warrior drew a bronze sword, a rare sight in Israel as the Philistines did not permit the Israelites to work in bronze. "Come or die here, idol worshiper. The prophet Samuel will come to Gilgal and make sacrifices to the Lord God of Israel."

The priest bowed. "We shall come and do our duty."

After the warrior rode off, Kerem sat beside her pit. She closed her eyes and cleared her mind. She began to hear a familiar hissing in her ears. She slowed her breathing and concentrated. The hissing increased as the form of her mother moved towards her, her body swaying beneath her head. Her mother's eyes focused on her. The apparition hissed loudly and said, "Kerrrremmm. Kerremm. Kerem, my sweet. It begins for you. Saul—Saul will be in your hands. Tell no one. And beware of Samuel. Leave this place. Go to Endor. Tell the people you are their seer."

"Where will I stay? Papa left me here—he sold me to the priest."

"Go home. Your father and brothers are dead—a happy coincidence!"

"Not happy for me. I loved them. My brothers were always kind."

"Kerem, no one loves you but for me. No one else will ever love you. You have only me. Now go. Tell the priest it is the word of Asherah. You are her seer, and you go to Endor."

"And what shall I tell the elders and people of Endor if they ask?"

"Let them ask what they will. I will tell you what to say. Go, Kerem. Go and watch the men of Endor march to war. Many will fall. Many will come to you to speak to the fallen. Go, my sweet!"

Saul arose from his chair and stepped into the cool air. The morning sun was above the mountains of Gilead to the east. Saul, a head taller than any man in Israel, with broad shoulders, a trim black beard to match his raven hair, stood in front of his tent and stared to the west. Impatiently he turned to a servant and bellowed, "Bring the priest to me. Now!"

The servant bowed and scurried backward before standing tall and running off. In just a few minutes, the man returned with a young man wearing an ephod of a Levite, a priest of the God of Abraham, Isaac, and Jacob. The young priest bowed and said, "Your servant, my King."

Saul's eyes remained fixed on the road west. "Prepare the altar. I will make the sacrifice to the Lord, myself."

The priest did not lift his head. "Were not the instructions to wait for Samuel—that Samuel would make the sacrifice?"

Saul turned to the young priest. "Samuel also said he would return in seven days. Do you see him? I don't. The men grow impatient. They begin to sneak away by night. I will make the sacrifice. Has not the Lord chosen me? Has not His Spirit come upon me when I joined the prophets and prophesied myself? I will wait no longer. Make the preparations—the burnt offering and the peace offering. I will come within the hour."

As soon as Saul finished making the burnt offering, Samuel, a wild-eyed old man, a Nazarite who neither shaved nor cut his hair, arrived. He wore only skins of wild animals and neither ate nor drank of any fruit of the vine. Samuel was a prophet of the Lord God. He led Israel for many years before granting the people their wish for a king. It was Samuel who anointed Saul. Samuel was the only man in Israel with no fear of Saul, the mighty warrior king. Saul went to greet his mentor, but Samuel said, "What have you done?"

"I saw the people scattering in fear. You did not come at the appointed time. The Philistines grow stronger every day, and I had not yet asked for the favor of the Lord, so I forced myself and offered the burnt offering."

Samuel scolded, "You have acted foolishly. You have not kept the commandment of the Lord your God. The Lord would have established your kingdom over Israel forever. But now, your kingdom shall not endure. The Lord has sought out for Himself, a man after His own heart. And the Lord has appointed him as ruler over His people, because you have not kept what the Lord has commanded you."

Saul was silent at Samuel's rebuke. But Saul turned his attention to the Philistines and his son, Jonathan, led Israel to victory.

Kerem stopped a group of men returning to Endor. "Tell me of the fallen. Just a name, and I shall bring comfort to their families."

"You are Kerem, the orphan sold to the priest of Baal. What have we to do with you?"

"I am a seer. I have returned to my father's house."

"You are a seer and you do not know? None from Endor has fallen. Saul has won a great victory! The Philistine dogs or those who remain of the Philistines have returned to their land—to their homes—to lick their wounds!"

Kerem stood stunned. *None have fallen? But mother said there would be many.*

"Wait! Tell me about the battle, about our King Saul and his great victory."

One replied, "We have returned after a hard march. Gilgal is two days each way. Our families, our flocks, and our fields all await us. Ask your spirit guide!"

A man too young for a beard turned around. "I will tell you,"

Kerem said, "My house is nearby. Come, I will give you refreshment."

In her small house not far from the well, Kerem offered the man wine, dates, and small cakes fried in oil, "Be refreshed, And tell me all that you have seen."

"Saul is a mountain of a man. Taller than any I have seen. Strong! Broad shoulders. A man of action—war. He fears no one. His brothers—they are the sons of Kish of the tribe Benjamin, warriors all. But Saul's son, Jonathan, now there is the man I would follow. Brave, strong, cunning in battle but not haughty—no—Jonathan is pleasant company to every soldier and son of Israel."

Kerem nodded. "It is Saul that I am curious about, our king."

"Saul is mighty in battle. Strong and fears no man—no

man but Samuel. The prophet chastised him severely. The King's pride was wounded, and his commands became rash. After the victory, Saul determined to pursue and destroy all those fleeing. He made a careless oath—no man was to eat or drink until every Philistine was dead. When it was discovered his son Jonathan innocently violated Saul's oath, it was the people, his warriors, who insisted Jonathan be spared."

Kerem poured the young man more wine. "Samuel. You say the prophet chastised Saul. Saul fears Samuel?".

The young man drank his wine and said, "You do not know? All of Israel fear Samuel. He is a great prophet of the Lord God Almighty. Even now that he is an old man and feeble, Saul fears him. There is no one like him in all of Israel."

Kerem sat down. "His words…"

"Not just his words, but signs and wonders." The young man looked into Kerem's face. "See for yourself. He lives in Ramah but goes to Gilgal to make sacrifices at the Tabernacle. Even the priests obey all that he says. Now, I must leave. Thank you for the food and wine."

Kerem did not get up as the man left. She sat staring down. She closed her eyes and began to think. *Samuel. Saul fears him. The priests of his God fear him. And the people—perhaps I should seek him out.*

Sssssssss. Ssssssss. The sound in her ears surprised Kerem. Instantly she was alert in the other realm. She saw a hooded figure sway, a cobra, no, a person. The person turned and moved towards her. The hissing died away, and now she heard the familiar Kerrrremmm, Kerremm, Kerem. Kerem recognized her mother's face, her hair now down and spread wide around her neck like a collar resting on her shoulders and falling over her breasts, her earrings appearing as the hood eyes of the cobra.

"Kerem, my sweet, do not be fooled by Samuel. Though men and kings fear him. He shall soon follow his father to his tomb. Saul will come to you. He will bend to your power and our will."

"Samuel serves only the Lord God of Israel. Followers of this God are most adamant. There is no other god."

"Boasting, my sweet, mere boasting. You are a seer. What do you see? Many gods war among themselves. This God of Israel—just empty boasting. But do not seek out Samuel. I am your guide."

As time passed, Kerem became known to the people of Endor. They sought her out as their seer. They paid her well for her service, and she became wealthy, but no man would take a seer for his wife. One day, Kerem heard a knock on her door. She opened her eyes to the dimming light of dusk. "I am coming," she replied as she stood up. "Let me light my lamp, and I will answer."

Kerem lit the small lamp on her table and opened the door. A man stood there waiting. His face tortured with urgency. "Are you Kerem? I have heard you can help me. Kerem, the seer?"

"I am Kerem, the seer. What is it you need?"

"I must know—they are dead, and no offerings were given. I must know they are not punished for my guilt."

"Come in and tell me all. What is your name? Who is dead? Do you wish me to call them?"

The tortured man stepped in. Kerem pointed to a chair. "Please sit at my table. Have you eaten? You look gaunt and hungry. I was about to cook cakes for my supper. Tell me your story as I prepare the meal. I will listen. I am an excellent listener. You have not told me your name."

The man sat down. Kerem poured a cup of wine and set it before him. "My name is Dav. It is my father and mother who have died. I am the eldest son. It was a fire. My mother's robe caught fire. My father went to help her. He was a very old man, much older than my mother. He fell dead upon her. I buried them in haste. What else could I do? I could not leave them to the birds or the dogs. But my neighbor came to me, looking for my father. The neighbor said my father owed him money, and his debt was due. I told him my father was dead. Still, he took our seed grain. It was all we had left. As he left, he asked where I buried them and if I had made an offering to the gods. I knew nothing of such offerings. My father taught me that the Lord is God in Israel, but others say worship the gods of Canaan as well. Have I offended the gods? Are my mother and father being punished for my guilt?"

Kerem replied softly as she prepared the meal. "You loved your parents, Dav? Yes, I am certain you did. Take comfort that they knew your love. Surely, all is not lost. I will help you. I will ask after them. But first, we shall eat. Yes, warm food and wine will calm you. Here, it is ready."

When Dav had eaten and was calmed by Kerem's soft assurances, Kerem uncovered the pit in her house. With only the embers of her cooking fire lighting the room, Kerem closed her eyes and softly chanted, "Mother Asherah, you who eternally conceive but never bear, I seek Caleb and Nediva. Their eldest son, Dav, would hear from them. Mother Asherah, I seek.…"

Soon Kerem heard a familiar hiss. The sound grew louder until, at last, she heard her name, "Kerrremmm." Dav heard nothing but the soft chanting of Kerem.

Kerem said, "Mother, guide, I seek the parents of the man Dav."

"I heard your call, Kerem, my sweet. The man Dav, the eldest son of Caleb and Nediva, why does he disturb their sleep?"

"He is a good and loving son, worried that his parents are

punished for his guilt. They were buried without offerings to our gods.”

Dav stiffened and felt a strange sensation in the hair on the back of his neck as he listened to Kerem speak.

“No offering to our gods? Evil indeed! I shall guide you— yes, yes, Asherah has shown them to me. They are here. Beggars in our world. Already they are hungry. They were sent with nothing! Nothing! This evil son, Dav, must make atonement!”

“Mother guide, Dav is not an evil man—just ignorant of our ways. And he is poor. All that his father owned was taken for debt. What can he do? Will Asherah help his parents whom he loves?”

“Sssssss. Surely, he has something?”

Kerem turned to Dav, her eyes still closed, “Dav, you must not withhold anything from Mother Asherah. Tell me. You must have something?”

“I am a widower and have only a small house for my son and daughter. Our sheep and our grain is gone. My kinsmen live far off. I have nothing.”

Kerem began to speak, “Mother guide....”

“Ssssss, Has nothing he says? Liar! Let him sell his daughter to the priests of Baal and buy a proper offering. Only then will Caleb and Nediva be free from begging!”

Kerem again turned to Dav, “You have a son and daughter. She has value to the priests of Baal.”

Dav cried, “My daughter is not of age. I could do no such thing! She is most precious to me! Anything else!”

Kerem focused on the pit. “The girl is young and precious to her father. Too young for the thirty shekels the priest would pay.”

“Ssssss. Kerem! A price is due. His evil must be undone.

The priest of Moloch will pay twenty shekels and pass her through the fire. She may even join her grandparents. Yes, yes. Asherah will accept an offering costing twenty shekels. Tell him! Asherah loses patience—I will go to her. Tell Dav twenty shekels for his parents' comfort. Tell him!"

The spell was broken. Kerem looked up. She bit her lip, unable to smile. "An offering must be made—soon. Your parents are hungry. They will spend eternity as beggars. Twenty shekels. You must pay twenty shekels for the offering. It is the price the priests of Moloch will pay for your daughter. She would be offered to him, a sacrifice, and pass through the fire on his altar."

Dav cried, "You ask what is evil to take away what is evil."

"Your daughter for your two parents is what Asherah asks."

"I fear even my mother and father would not wish their comfort come at the expense of my daughter."

Kerem shook her head. "No. Not if they love her as you do."

Kerem looked up, "Asherah demands a cost—twenty shekels. That is the wage of a hired man for a month. I may have twenty shekels—I will loan you money. You must promise to repay me. If repayment is not made, the cost is not paid. Do you understand?"

"And your fee? I must pay your fee as well."

"I ask no fee. I desire to help. Do you agree to a loan?"

"I agree! Thank you, Kerem, thank you!"

Saul led Israel to victory over the Amalekites. Samuel had commanded Saul to utterly destroy the Amalekites. As descendants of Esau and cousins to the Israelites, their attack on Israel when they first entered the promised land was a grievous sin against God. As Samuel made his way to Saul at Gilgal, he pondered the word of the Lord: "I regret I have made Saul king. He has turned his back from following Me and has not carried out My commands." This distressed Samuel, for Samuel loved Saul as a father loves a son. Samuel cried unto God all night on Saul's behalf.

Samuel could only shake his head in despair as he passed the monument Saul had built for himself at Carmel. When Samuel arrived, Saul called out to him, "Blessed are you of the Lord! I have carried out the command of the Lord!"

Samuel replied, "Then what is the bleating of the sheep and lowing of the oxen I hear?"

"I have saved the best to make an offering to the Lord, but the rest we utterly destroyed."

"You did not obey the voice of the Lord but took spoil and did evil in the sight of the Lord."

Saul replied, "But I did obey, and I brought back King Agag and have utterly destroyed the Amalekites."

Samuel spoke loudly so that all the host of Israel could hear. "Has the Lord as much delight in burnt offerings and sacrifices as in obeying the voice of the Lord? To obey is better than to sacrifice and to heed than the fat of rams. For rebellion is as the sin of divination, and insubordination is as iniquity and idolatry. Because you have rejected the word of the Lord, He has also rejected you from being king."

Saul cried out, "I have sinned. I have feared the people and heard their voices. Pardon my sin and return with me that I may worship the Lord."

Samuel walked away, saying, "I will not return with you, for you have rejected the word of the Lord, and the Lord has rejected you from being king."

Saul reached out and grabbed Samuel's robe as he passed. The robe tore. Samuel turned to Saul and said, "The Lord has torn the kingdom of Israel from you today and has given it to your neighbor who is greater than you."

Saul begged, "I have sinned but honor me before the elders. Go back with me that I may worship the Lord your God."

Samuel went back with Saul, and they worshipped the Lord. Then Samuel said, "Bring me Agag." Samuel slew King Agag with a sword and cut him into pieces. Samuel left the sword, Saul, and the dead King Agag, and returned to Ramah. Samuel grieved for Saul but did not see him again.

Samuel did not remain in Ramah long. The Lord had another task for him. Samuel was sent South a few miles to the fields owned by Jesse of the tribe of Judah near the village of Bethlehem. There he secretly anointed a shepherd, David, son of Jesse, King of Israel. God had searched David's heart and declared David: "A man after my own heart." The Spirit of the Lord left Saul and filled young David.

The sun was setting when Kerem left her house and walked to the village well. Dav was entering the gate, returning from the fields. He was talking with a stranger when he noticed Kerem. "Kerem, how fortunate you are here! I have the money you loaned me plus a little extra for your help. This is Seth, traveling north to Dan. He brings news from Gilgal of continued victories and Israel's new champion, David."

"Thank you, Dav. There is no hurry to repay the loan. Please do not take from your family on my account."

"It is no hardship. I have been blessed. A new agreement with a neighbor—my labor in return for wages and seed for my fields."

Kerem smiled and turned to the traveler, Seth. "It is late, friend. I have prepared an extra portion if you are hungry, and I have a room if you need one."

Dav said, "Seth can stay with us. No need to…"

Kerem shook her head. "Dav, you have, but one room for the three of you, and the little one does not sleep through the night."

Dav nodded. "It is Kerem's habit to come to the well at sunset looking for those in need of hospitality. It is true. She prepares an extra portion of food."

Seth looked confused. "Surely, there would be talk!"

Dav laughed. "They dare not! Kerem is a seer. And all in Endor know her to be a good, chaste, and generous woman."

Seth looked at Dav and then Kerem. "I shall accept your hospitality—the meal, but I shall sleep outside. Perhaps a barn or pen?"

Seth washed at the well and followed Kerem to her house. Kerem listened as she finished preparing the meal. Seth spoke of David. "A most unusual man! He is young and handsome, full of good cheer and life. It is no surprise he is a musician and sings like no other, but most amazing is his fearlessness in battle. He believes, no, he knows, God is with him. And the people too, everywhere they sing: 'Saul has killed his thousands and David his ten thousands.'"

Kerem turned and said, "I have heard of this man David. It is said he slew the champion of the Philistines, Goliath. Some have sworn Goliath a giant and David but a shepherd, slew him with his sling—a single stone to Goliath's forehead."

Seth replied, "It is as you say. David slew him and cut off his head with Goliath's own sword."

"And Saul? What does Saul say of him?"

"Not only did Saul make David his armor-bearer and captain of a thousand, he offered David one of his daughters in marriage. But Saul has changed. He is no longer the humble man and fearless warrior. He Leaves the fighting to others. He is sharp in his rebukes and indecisive in his commands. There is talk that Saul hopes David is cut down in battle and worse—in his dark moods, he plots against him. But Jonathan stands with David. There are no finer men in all of Israel than David and Jonathan."

Kerem asked, "And Samuel? Does not the prophet comfort Saul?"

Seth thought before he answered. "Samuel does not leave his house in Ramah. It is said he prophesied against Saul—that the Lord has torn the Kingdom from Saul. No one speaks of Saul, only David whom Saul, in his madness now pursues.

When Seth had finished his meal and gone outside to sleep in the goat pen, Kerem sat in her house thinking. Her thoughts were disturbed by the hissing sound in her ears. She opened her eyes and uncovered the pit. "Kerrremmm, Kerremm, Kerem. What have you done? Sssssss. The girl has not passed through the fire! Sssssssss, you deprived the gods and disobeyed me!"

"No, mother, the price has been paid. You said the price is an offering worth twenty shekels. He has made the offering!"

The vision of her mother swayed side to side. Her eyes, black as night, were flashing reflections into Kerem's eyes. Kerem watched and saw her mother's face scowling. For a moment, her mouth opened, and a thin forked tongue tasted the air. Kerem shuddered at the sight, and the vision became still, and the face calmed. "You lent him the money. Sssssss. Kerem, my sweet. What need has Asherah for money? Now the girl, the daughter, she is what Asherah desired."

"But you said…"

"I know what I said! Now hear me, my sweet, you have been given the gift that you may be feared, not liked, not admired, and never loved! Fear, fear, and doubt—that is your strength and your weapon."

The apparition shook its head. The rings and necklace of Asherah shook. Her mother smiled and turned to watch the orgy beyond her, her black hair falling away from her breasts as she moved. She was smiling when she turned back to Kerem. "Soon, my sweet, soon Saul will be in your hands. You heard the news; the kingdom will be torn from him. He will fight David. Yes, my sweet, first Saul whom Samuel has abandoned, and soon Samuel will die, and then we take David."

The apparition appeared to sway a dance, hissed, and then said, "Kerem, make them fear you!"

Kerem could not sleep that night. Her visit to the other realm haunted her. *"Make them fear you!"* her mother commanded. But it was Kerem who feared. Feared her mother, or *is she really my mother? Is an evil spirit appearing to me as Momma? What do I remember about Mother? Very little. I was only four years old when she died. And my older brothers, they would better remember, they are now dead. Papa said hard things against her, that she played the harlot. When she appears to me, she is naked and lives in a world of sexual debauchery. Was Momma evil? Papa cared for me growing up—but then he sold me. Was it need? Did he ever love me? Was it guilt—all a story to make me hate him? Papa insisted he was of the tribe Issachar—surely someone would know his family. Yes, there must be some relative who can tell me more.*

The next day, Kerem sought the elder, where he sat inside the city gate. Kerem bowed and approached. "Elder, I have come seeking…"

"Woman, it is our custom that a husband or father speak on your behalf."

"I have no husband or father. Does not your law demand justice to the widow and orphan?"

The elder stared at Kerem. "I know who you are. You are Kerem, the seer. And you, an idolater, and voice for Asherah, speak of our duty under the Law of Moses?"

Kerem bowed. "I seek only to know the truth. My father was a son of Issachar. He lived under the law of Moses. He sold me to the priests of Baal at their high place on the Hill of Moreh. Perhaps he made me who I am. For in truth, I do not know who I am—who my people are and who my god is. As an orphan, I ask you, who are my people? Who are my kinsman in Endor?"

The elder stared at Kerem and then stroked his beard. "Your father, Micah, never shared his story with you? No, I suppose it was too painful."

He paused and then continued, "I have heard of your kind heart and your hospitality to the stranger. Not like the priests of Baal and Moloch or the priestesses of Asherah. Though Micah doubted he was your father, he doted on you like a daughter he loved, until you became a woman. Micah trusted no woman. It was your mother he saw in you. He never forgave her though she begged his forgiveness. It was well known in Endor—she ventured to the Hill of Moreh to watch a festival. She confessed she drank their wine and ate their sacred food, and she was beguiled and coupled many times with strangers. She sinned. Only the Lord knows for certain, but to me, your face favors Micah. Shame. Shame fell upon Micah. But kinsman? Yes, you have a kinsman, a son of Micah's uncle. But you know him. It is rumored you lend him money and lead him into idolatry. I speak of Dav."

"Dav is my kinsman?"

"Dav is your near kinsman. Take your questions to him."

Kerem mumbled, "Dav is my kinsman? And he never told me?"

The elder cleared his throat. "Kerem, go your way. Give up your idolatry, and may the God of Abraham, Isaac, and Jacob have mercy on you."

Kerem's head spun as she walked to Dav's house. *Why has he said nothing? I have been kind to him. I trusted him and helped him. I thought we were friends. Is Dav ashamed of me? Is there anyone who is not ashamed to know me?*

Dav's son answered Kerem's knock on the door. "My father is away. Come back later."

Kerem asked, "It is me, Kerem. A friend. May I come in? Away? Where?"

"Go away. I will not let you in. My father has gone to Ophrah to see a man about a field. Now go away. I will not allow a witch and an idolater in our house."

Kerem felt her chest fall as she gasped for air. Her mother's words played in her mind. *"No one else loves you. Kerem, my sweet, no one will ever love you."*

Kerem waited by the well and watched people come and go through the city gate. Dav did not come. Kerem sat, her head bowed, afraid to return home but no longer interested in the comings and goings of her neighbors. She had resigned herself to a world of loneliness. Her consciousness stirred when she overheard a man say a name: "Samuel, Samuel protects David. They are at Naioth in Ramah. Saul sent messengers to Samuel, but when they arrived, they fell before Samuel, and they prophesied. So then Saul went to Samuel at Ramah, and Saul also fell before him and prophesied. The King stripped himself and lay naked and prophesied a full day. The saying is everywhere in Israel—Saul is among the prophets!"

Kerem spoke up. "Rumor—gossip and rumors! Tell us truly how you know this."

"Ignore the woman. She is a seer, a witch, and an idolater. She whores after Asherah."

The man replied, "I do not fear her or any idolater. I know what I say is true, for I am a witness. I was there, I am a priest to the Living God, and now I return home to Daberath in Zebulon after my duty at the Tabernacle is complete."

Kerem felt shamed. "Forgive me, priest. I meant no harm. I have heard of the prophet Samuel. Please, come to my house. I shall give you refreshment. I would hear more of the prophet and your God."

"I take only water in Endor. I am anxious to journey on to my home."

As Kerem walked home, she stopped and stared at the gate. *I shall go to Ramah. I shall seek Samuel. Yes! Samuel is a great prophet. The God of Israel is with him. He will tell me the truth!*

Kerem closed the door behind her and turned to her kitchen. A snake, a cobra taller than Kerem, swayed before her. Kerem's eyes locked on the eyes of the snake and the eyes of its hood. Slowly the face of her mother appeared on the head of the snake. "Sssss. You will not go to Ramah. You will never seek Samuel."

"You are not my mother! You are evil. You will no longer guide me. I will not call upon you again!"

The forked tongue of the snake tasted the air. "I could take you now. You are mine, my sweet. But I am not finished with you."

Kerem turned for the door but stumbled over a chair she did not see. Kerem fell to the dirt floor. She could not see her way to the door. She could not see anything. Kerem was blind. Slowly light, a dim light returned. Kerem began to see her mother, naked but for the golden belt and earrings, wearing the image of Asherah. Kerem saw others afar off, still coupling like animals in the wild. She heard their chanting, "Mother Asherah, you who eternally conceive but never bear, mother Asherah watch what we do! Let us entice you as you entice us—conceive! For to conceive is everything!"

Their chant was interrupted. "Kerem. My sweet. You are blind to everyone but me. You will do as I command. When I am finished with you, you will join those who you now watch. Those who forever conceive and forever chant."

Dav returned several days later and called upon Kerem. Kerem heard him knock, but she would not answer. "Kerem, It is me, Dav. You called at my house. I have come. Did you need something? No one has seen you in days. Answer me, Kerem!"

"Go away. I need nothing. I need no one! Why shame yourself calling upon an idolater?"

"Shame? You are my friend. You bring no shame."

"Your son tells a different story. And so does the elder. You are my kinsman but ashamed to say so."

"Kinsman? You say I am your kinsman? This I have never heard."

"My close kinsman. The son of my father's uncle."

Dav was quiet. He thought and then said, "In truth, I did not know. But I do remember my father saying we were to have no dealings with Micah and his whore wife. Kerem, I am sorry. I did not know. Kerem, you are kind and gentle, my truest friend. Kerem, you are hurting. Let me come in."

"Do not come in. I am cursed by an evil spirit. I have

wronged you, Dav. You came to me, and I commanded an evil of you, an offering to the gods. They deserve no offering—they bring only evil. Stay away from me, the cursed daughter of a whore."

Kerem no longer offered hospitality to the strangers. She did not welcome Dav into her house. Kerem went to the well after dark. She recognized night by the cool air and silence. Now blind, day and night made no difference to her. Her grain, oil, figs, and foodstuff were left at her door, where a pouch for payment hung.

Kerem sought out no one, but her gift was well known, and men and sometimes women, widows, sought her services as a seer. Once Kerem was satisfied it was only a seer they sought, she would crack open her door and receive them. She would need to be reminded to light a lamp after dark, and she offered no refreshment. "Who do you seek?" was all that she would ask before gazing her blind eyes into her pit.

Kerem repeated what her guide said and added, "The guide has spoken. Ten shekels." It was her business. She worked for her spirit guide, not the frightened people who crossed her threshold. She decided it was easier not to care, even when it meant crying for them when she lay awake at night.

Dav had long ago stopped calling at Kerem's door. So, it was some surprise to her when his familiar voice called out as he knocked. "Kerem. Are you there? Of course, you are. I know you only sneak out at night to go to the well. I know, I watch—for your safety. Kerem, if you won't open your door, listen to me. You must listen. King Saul has issued a decree. No one may practice divination. No one may play the seer in Israel. Did you hear me, Kerem? You are known. There are some in Endor who would gladly betray you. You can no longer conjure the dead. Hear me,

Kerem, it is on pain of death! Let no one come to you seeking your gift. Tell me you have heard my words."

Dav waited. Finally, he heard a soft reply. "You have accomplished what you have come for. Leave me in peace."

"Kerem, how will you live? Let me help you."

"Go away. I will live as I have always lived. Now leave me. I will say no more."

Not many months later, Kerem was awakened late at night by the loud knocking of a staff on her door. Surprised, she got up and stood behind the door. "Who disturbs me from my sleep?"

King Saul, disguised in the robes of a merchant, replied, "Call for me one from the dead. Bring before me the one I shall name."

Kerem replied, "You know what Saul has done, how he has cut off the mediums, the seers and the conjurers from the land. Why do you lay a trap for me to bring about my death?"

Saul replied, his voice strong through the closed door. "As the Lord lives, no punishment shall come upon you for this thing."

Kerem opened the door. Saul stepped inside the house, followed by two servants armed with swords and spears. Kerem listened to their footsteps and discerned the breathing of the two silent men. She walked to the pit and asked, "Whom shall I bring up for you?"

"Bring up Samuel."

"Samuel is dead?" Her eyes widened, and she screamed, "You are Saul! Why have you deceived me?"

"Do not be afraid. What do you see?"

Kerem's eyes focused on the pit. She heard a strong wind and did not feel the scales falling from her eye, only the wind blowing her hair back off her face. She saw a bright light moving like a cloud and then a shadow coming from the light. "I see a god coming out to the earth."

Saul said, "What is his appearance?"

The shadow came closer, the bright light behind it made it difficult to see, but yes, she saw a man, an old man. "An old man is coming up. He is wrapped in a robe."

Saul cried out, "Samuel!" And he bowed his face to the ground and paid homage.

The man from the cloud, Samuel, said to Saul, "Why have you disturbed me by bringing me up?"

Saul answered, "I am in great distress. The Philistines have come to war against me, and God has turned away from me and no longer answers me, either by prophets or by dreams. So, I have summoned you to tell me what to do."

Samuel replied, "Why do you ask me since the Lord has turned away from you and become your enemy? The Lord has done to you as he spoke by me. The Lord has torn the kingdom out of your hand and given it to your neighbor, David. Because you did not obey the voice of the Lord and carry out his fierce wrath against Amalek. Moreover, the Lord will give the army of Israel into the hands of the Philistines."

Saul fell to the ground upon hearing Samuel. Kerem felt the wind reverse as Samuel was drawn back through the cloud into the light beyond. She turned to Saul, still laying on the ground beside the pit. As he lifted his head, she saw the terror in his eyes. She said softly, "I am your servant, O King. I have obeyed you. I have put my life into your hand and have listened to what you have said to me. Now, obey your servant. Let me set bread before you. Eat that you may gain strength when you go your way."

Saul sobbed, "I will not eat."

His two servants finally spoke. "You have had nothing to

eat all day. The woman is right, O King. Eat and be strong."

Kerem said, "I have a fatted calf in my pen." Not waiting for a reply, she went out, killed the calf and roasted meat. She took flour and oil, kneaded it and baked unleavened bread. Kerem served the meal to Saul and his servants. When Saul arose from the table, he stood tall. He stood strong. His eyes burned with the determination of a man who knew his duty and knew it meant death. Then Saul and his servants departed into the darkness.

Kerem stepped out into the night and looked at the stars in the sky. Her sight now restored, she said to herself, "The Lord is God." When she returned to her house, she heard only silence. She walked to the pit. Still silence, not a hiss. Staring, she saw only dirt at the bottom of a hole in the ground. When Kerem opened her robe to bathe, she saw that her birth mark which had grown into a serpent, was gone. Her skin was clean and smooth as a young child's, without a blemish of any kind.

A week went by before the first report came to Endor. "Israel is defeated! The army has fled. The Philistines have taken Shunem, Jezreel, Harod, and many villages in the Jezreel valley. It is best to flee, north to Naphtali or better across the Jordan to Gilead of Gad or Ashtaroth of Manasseh."

Kerem asked, "What of our neighbor Dav and his son?"

The man replied, "Many have fallen. I do not know the fate of Dav or his son. If you are wise, you will leave now!"

Kerem waited for Dav. Two days later, he returned with his son. Kerem ran to meet them. "The Lord has preserved you. I prayed, and he heard my prayers. I am going to the Tabernacle to make offerings for my sin and offerings of thanksgiving."

Dav was surprised. "You follow the Lord? We thank you for your prayers, but—but the Philistines stand between Endor and Gilgal."

Kerem shook her head. "The Lord will be with us. He will shield us on our way. I go. Do you come with me or flee across the Jordan?"

Dav froze and stared at Kerem. "Marry me, Kerem. Marry me, and I will gather my household and go. We shall follow the mountain road south on the other side of the Jordan."

"You ask me to marry you?"

"I am your near kinsman—it is my duty to redeem you. I have always loved you, Kerem, but before I learned that we are kin, I had no money to support you. And when I learned I was your kinsman-redeemer, you would have no man. But the Lord has shown me that it is right that we marry."

Kerem stood stunned. Neighbors were running past. Donkeys brayed under their heavy loads. The air was filled with dust and the sounds of panic. Tears fell from Kerem's eyes. She pointed at the people rushing to the gate of the city.

"We must hurry. I will help you gather your household."

Dav waited. He just stared at Kerem.

Kerem turned to Dav. "Yes, I will marry you. It is a wondrous thing to be loved."

Three days later, Kerem approached Zadok, the High Priest, and made her burnt offerings, a sin offering, and a sacrifice of thanksgiving on the Tabernacle altar. When Zadok completed the sacrifice and brought Kerem her portion, he looked into her eyes. "You have been forgiven much, daughter. Know that the Lord has searched your heart, a heart filled with love for the Lord and love for your neighbor. He smiles upon you and makes you His. Tell me, daughter of Israel, your city and your father's name."

"I am Kerem from Endor. The man Micah of the tribe Issachar raised me, though he said I was not his. My mother, a Canaanite, played the harlot when she worshipped Asherah. I, too, served Asherah for many years. I conjured Samuel for Saul. It was Samuel who showed me the truth."

"Kerem, the Lord always accepts the sacrifice of a clean heart. Know that you are a true daughter of Issachar of Israel."

"Truly, the Lord has blessed me. He has saved me from becoming Baal's prostitute, from being sacrificed in Moloch's fire and enticed as Asherah's seer. The Lord sent my kinsman-redeemer to be my husband who loves me. I will love and worship only the Lord. He has saved me. For the Lord is the God who loves. It is a wonderful thing to love and to be loved."

Zadok paused. "It is as you say, beloved of the Lord. Tell me, Saul went to you? You were a conjurer, a medium? Samuel came up when you called? Tell me, Saul, what did he hear?"

"It is true. I was a seer. I was also blind, but now I see in truth. Saul listened to Samuel. He heard the kingdom was to be torn from him and given to David. The Philistines would defeat the army of Israel. He was told that he and his sons would soon join Samuel. But Saul regained his strength. I saw him stand tall. I saw strength in his eyes. He left like a king to do battle. Tell me, Chief Priest of the Most High God, King Saul, Jonathan, and his brothers, if they are with Samuel, are they not in the bosom of Father Abraham? Has the Lord redeemed Saul?"

Zadok smiled at Kerem. "No one is beyond the redemption of the Lord. He is merciful and gracious towards sinners who repent. The Lord has given the Kingdom of Israel to David, but he has not forgotten his servants Saul and Jonathan, whom David loved. No sin is too great to be forgiven, just as no one is free from sin or the attacks by the evil one. The Lord gives, and the Lord takes away. Blessed be the name of the Lord."

August

When Fall Comes Again
Maxwell DiMarco

a dim ray of light crept through the curtains, illuminating the darkness ever so slightly; it was morning. A new day. Winston's eyelids slowly opened to reveal his amber irises, his gaze drifting around the dim bedroom as he rose upright in his modest, twin-size bed. Yawning, he stretched his lightly muscled arms, reaching over to his bedside table and flicking on the lamp. As the shadows faded and the light illuminated an image in his mind's eye, he was pleased to find that everything was just as it should be.

Winston's light blue sheets were barely wrinkled from when he'd pulled them up over himself last night; he'd clearly slept like a rock. At the foot of his bed, the curtains were still drawn tight over the room's solitary window. Set beside the door, the small, metal clothes hamper was empty once again. And in the corner of the room, always remaining out of his way, the six figures stood. They were all too familiar to Winston, even with their faces obscured by dark helmets and tinted visors. Still as statues, their breathing muffled and dry, they stared at him with hidden eyes.

With no reason to go back to sleep, Winston got out of bed, pulled the covers neatly back over his pillow, and moved down the hall to the restroom. He could see the figures in the mirror as he brushed his pearly whites, now murmuring quietly to one another. Or maybe just to themselves. Winston could never really tell.

After taking a cold shower, Winston dressed himself, before heading downstairs to the kitchen. Today, Winston had picked out his favorite outfit: A camo-printed muscle tee, coupled with loose-fitting black shorts. The figures were watching Winston while he pulled on his clothes, and in turn followed him downstairs, making more noises Winston couldn't comprehend. Still, Winston paid them no mind, placing his phone to his ear as he began to prepare his breakfast.

"Morning, Frankie! Good to know you're still kicking," Winston placed a pan of eggs over the stovetop as he spoke. "So, ready to face another day, you ol' tree-hugging geezer?"

"Excuse me, just who are *you* to call me a tree-hugger?" Frank quipped. "And if thirty's the new sixty, then you're right there with me, buster!"

Winston laughed, shifting the pan over the burner as the eggs began to steam. "Nah, you know I'm just kidding, my man. For real, though, what have you got planned for the day?"

"Eh, same stuff as usual, really," Frank stated casually, Winston retrieving a plate and spatula as he listened. "Got the new fertilizer spread out last week, so now it's just a matter of watering a big fat square of dirt and hoping that this batch of seeds has life in 'em. Just another day for a 'tree hugger,' as you'd put it."

Winston chuckled at his friend's words, transferring the eggs onto his plate. "Frank, I'm telling you man, at this point it seems like a lost cause!" Winston replied plainly. He exited the kitchen and sat down at his round, two seater dining table with his food; the figures remained standing in the kitchen behind him. "How are you even supposed to know if they're growing right? We've had no point of reference for... well damn, definitely since before our ugly mugs were brought into the world!"

But of course, Frank was insistent. "Listen, Winston," He began, as he always did, "If I can pull this off, then we might actually get a chance to revitalize this stinkhole planet we're stuck on. Nature gave us plants in the beginning, but humanity beat out nature in the end; so with our modern technology, I see no reason why we can't try our hand at undoing the damage. Heck, man: In just a few years, you could be making your first non-abstract piece! I dare you to tell me that wouldn't mean anything to you!"

Winston let him prattle on, polishing off his eggs in the meantime. "Fine, fine, do your thing. But I won't believe it until I see it," Winston reaffirmed, sitting up and returning to the kitchen to deposit his empty plate in the sink. "And I'm talking, the moment they're fully grown you'd better be sending me pictures in both Spring *and* Fall! And don't you go thinking I won't notice if you make a set of cheap plastic models to screw with me, either! You *know* I have an eye for detail." Winston's words were stern, but his tone remained lighthearted and jovial. "Alright, always good talking with you, Frankie boy. I'll check up on you tomorrow; give the saplings my regards."

Winston hung up, discarding his phone before heading back through the dining area to the living room. This time, the figures resumed following him, coming to stand behind the couch as Winston sat down heavily with a resigned sigh.

"On that note... let's check what 'good news' we're

showing today," Winston muttered, lifting the remote and flicking on his widescreen television.

A resounding, flat tone filled the room, the screen displaying nothing but vertical bars of color. Winston's body froze up, as behind him the figures' murmuring became more chaotic, frenzied... and then, with a burst of static and a surge of electricity, the screen flickered to life.

"—tinues to advise all citizens to remain indoors until further notice." The screen showed video of a woman standing beside a square overlay of footage, dressed in a short-sleeved shirt and unbuttoned black vest. Her strawberry blonde hair was peppered with hints of white, but her pale skin was devoid of any blemishes.

As the murmuring behind him began to calm, Winston let out a spiteful chuckle. "And just who are they trying to fool here?" he asked, to no one in particular. "Poor Roxanne must be burning up under all that makeup... nobody's skin has been that porcelain-perfect since the early 2000s."

There was a noise from behind him at that, but Winston was now entirely focused on the broadcast.

"As temperatures are expected to reach lethal new highs in the foreseeable future, the ozone layer officially on its last legs, we can certainly agree that this is the safest course of action," the news anchor assented, her face solemn even as she attempted to maintain a removed, professional tone. "Rationing your essential resources, especially water and any other hydrating fluids, will be crucial going forward. Food and purified water will continue to be delivered to all recognized households as frequently as possible through the Hunters For Humanity service, but the heads of the project have asked us to reiterate that civilians should not assume that weekly deliveries will continue as conditions worsen."

"God bless those brave souls." Winston shook his head somberly. "Brave men and women, even at the end of days."

"These are all the morning updates we have for Monday, August Second," Roxanne stated plainly. "Thank you for tuning in. We will keep you updated as further information is provided."

The television switched off, Winston already standing back up from the couch. "Okay..." Winston grunted, cracking his knuckles. "...now that I'm in the know for the day: It's time to get to work."

Back into the kitchen he went, the figures tailing him like a fractured shadow as he climbed the stairs back to the upstairs hall. This time, however, Winston progressed to the end opposite his bedroom, coming to a second door with an abstract, green sculpture sitting beside it.

The figures' chatter began to rise again as Winston turned the doorknob, stepping into the dark room beyond. As he crossed the threshold, a smile flickered across Winston's lips. This was his favorite time of day. The one time that he truly felt like he had no limits, no inhibitions.

With a clap of his hands, the lights sparked to life, illuminating Winston's studio. The room was lined to the walls with blank canvas boards of all sizes, still untouched and wrapped in plastic. An easel stood directly before him, currently occupied by his most recent painting; its vibrant reds and yellows still left even Winston a little speechless. But of course, there was nothing to be gained if you never tried to improve yourself.

Taking his latest art piece delicately into his hands, Winston walked to the back of the room and set it down atop an ornate wooden dresser drawer. Then, opening the top drawer, he gradually retrieved his brushes, paint, and palette; each neatly sorted into ziplock bags.

Winston had intended to pick out a new canvas himself from his stockpile, but by the time he had gathered his supplies, he found that the figures had already taken the liberty of unwrapping and setting up a new canvas in his stead. This was indeed a rarity for them, but not unheard of, and Winston had never really objected to them stepping in. If anything, it just allocated more of his time to creating the finished product.

Returning to the easel and setting the plastic bags on an adjacent folding table, Winston looked over today's canvas. Normally, he would personally have chosen a classic, 16x20 rectangular canvas, with plenty of space to capture his vision. This time, however, the figures had picked out a smaller, 6x6 square canvas, barely taking up any of the large easel's wooden frame. Winston's eyes narrowed as he considered his options, the chattering of the figures evident, even with their hushed tones. This canvas wouldn't suffice for one of his full visions. But perhaps, it could still yield something new.

Picking out his first brush and dipping it lightly into the red on his palette, Winston told himself what he always did, every day: "Even when the world dies... my art will live on."

And then, his mind was lost to the colors. As he worked, Winston's thoughts and brush became one. His hand never faltered, his arm never shook. Each stroke was just as he intended for it to be, and each color of paint was the exact hue that was required. In the first moments that he stared at the day's canvas, Winston was crafting a vision for every inch, every millimeter of that pure, unbroken white. And it was his job to bring that vision to life, for the future to behold. This was what he lived for. His true passion, his own purpose in life. And through his art, he was set free.

The figures cautiously gathered around Winston as he gave one last sweep of his brush. In the only instance of the day, their gaze was directed not at him, but at the painting. And naturally, Winston was the same; this was his last moment of true freedom every day, and a moment to be savored. Together, they took in the shiny gloss of the still wet paint, absorbing the esoteric scene it depicted.

A layer of turf-hue browns, against a deep blue horizon. In the distance, red streaks rose from the ground, curving and twisting upwards like a geyser; segments of these streaks were shattered, tiny pieces of them crumbling away and tumbling down, revealing a barely visible pillar of green beyond.

As the canvas used is smaller than average, so too is the depicted subject observed from afar. Winston justified in his head. Around him, the figures' heads bobbed. He wondered if they understood his intentions.

And then, the thought was gone. Winston's arms stretched, a long, drawn-out yawn escaping his mouth.

"Whew, good stuff today!" he managed, his words nevertheless strained as he exhaled. "Still, even small paintings take their toll on the body. Guess it's time I turned in for the day."

With a second clap of his hands, the lights dimmed on his new creation. Leaving his studio, Winston crossed the hall to his bedroom, pulling off his clothes and discarding them in his hamper. Then, climbing into bed and pulling up the covers, his eyes slowly closed, and his mind went blank.

A bright ray of light forced its way between the curtains as Winston's eyes opened; it was a new day. Amber eyes drifted around the dark room, taking in his surroundings as he slowly sat upright. Stretching and yawning, Winston reached over to his bedside table and flicked on the light. As his eyes fully filled in the room's contents, he found nothing much had changed since he had last turned in.

The sheets were barely wrinkled from when he'd pulled them up over himself; the hamper was still upright; the curtains were still drawn as tightly as possible over the window; across the room, the six figures were already waiting for him. As before, Winston didn't leave them hanging.

Climbing out of bed, then adroitly making it, Winston stepped out into the hall and entered the restroom. The figures were quiet as he went about his morning routine, looking down at objects held in their hands. They had always held those objects, but Winston could only assume they weren't important to him. He couldn't identify them. And chances were, he never would.

After a cold shower, Winston put on a sky blue muscle tee, coupled with green cargo shorts. Today, before heading downstairs, Winston picked up his hamper, carrying it down with him through the kitchen and to the laundry room just before the front door. Whistling to himself, he emptied the hamper, putting it in the sanitizer for a six hour load. As Winston exited the room, the figures' heads were bobbing again, some of them chattering hoarsely. Giving them no thought as he returned to the kitchen counter, Winston retrieved his phone, putting it to his ear as he placed the eggs on the burner.

"How ya doing today, man?" Winston asked once Frank picked up. "Are the seeds showing any promise? Wouldn't mind some inspiration for today's piece!"

Winston listened intently while Frank explained, as Winston expected, that nothing had come of his project yet. He was about to remind Winston that it takes time, but he was cut off.

"Yeah, yeah, I get it," Winston relented, shifting the frying pan over the heat. "But we've both been doing our thing for a while, Frankie; not too crazy to check if anything cropped up." Winston's eyes widened as he realized what he said. "Ah, no, that was *not* intentional! Don't you go there, that's not even what you're trying to—" Despite his best efforts, a laugh escape Winston's throat, unable to help cracking up at his unintentional joke. "Eh, whatever. Nobody ever died from a bad pun. Anyways, did you catch the news yesterday? They've got poor Roxanne caked in makeup again."

Frank laughed scornfully at that, bemoaning the apparent need of the higher ups to maintain "standards of beauty."

"Yeah, I mean, am I right, man? Like honestly: Who are they trying to pander to at this point?" Winston chided, setting down the eggs temporarily as he reached up to the cupboard for a plate. "Any Caucasian I know has been permanently pale-red for at least as long as I've been alive; they're perpetuating an image that literally can't exist anymore." Shifting his phone to between his head and shoulder, Winston grabbed the spatula from the kitchen rack. "Plus, anyone with an eye for women can agree that Roxanne is still beautiful for her age. It's not like she needs the hel—"

At that moment, a rapid series of what sounded like knocking rang out from the front door. Winston cut himself off, turning towards the sound with a curious expression.

"I'll be... seems that I've got a guest," he mused to himself.

The figures began chattering between one another as Winston passed them by, their movements suddenly becoming quick and urgent. Particularly, one of them ran ahead to peer through the small glass window of the door, before Winston's arrival forced them to step aside.

Moving outside onto the porch, Winston gave a friendly wave. "Greetings, friend! I thought I heard someone out here!" His eyes scanning over the charred terrain surrounding the house, Winston saw no signs of life. "Er... well, I still can't *see* you, but— you're free to come inside if you want."

Winston's head slowly turned back and forth as he spoke, with the hope that he'd find the cause of the noise eventually.

"You can probably guess, but not a lot of people come by here anymore. Pretty much just me and my paintings now," Winston stated, one of the figures briefly peering outside behind him. "If you're looking for food or resources, I can't help you there. But, if you're curious how an everyday Joe made his way in this world? Well... I'm your man."

Winston laughed slightly, before staring down at the boards of the porch with a sigh. "Heh, look at me prattling on when I don't even know if you can understand me." He muttered to himself, "I guess at this point we just have to hope you can break the language barrier." Looking upright once more, he gave a smile to the empty air around him. "Well, anyway, I won't be very chatty from here on out, but feel free to come in. I'm not going to object to someone finally seeing my art."

Turning around, Winston walked back inside. He caught a glimpse of a small, winged corpse smoldering in the sun as he shut the door, but by then it was far too late for him to react.

"Alright, food's out of the way. Guess it's just about news time again." The figures were noticeably absent as Winston walked to the living room. Nevertheless, Winston sat down on the couch as before, retrieving the remote and leaning back as he turned on the television. This time, the screen turned on without any issue, its broadcast featuring the same newscaster as the day prior.

"This is Roxanne Chastain, with your news for Monday evening, August Second," Roxanne stated; her tone was far more somber than the previous broadcast, and her eyeliner was smeared ever so slightly. "It is with deep sadness we inform you that, an hour prior, we received harrowing news from NASA officials. As of today, all contact has been lost with Gen Ark: Prayer. With contact being severed prior to the Ark exiting the radius of NASA radar, we can only assume the worst."

"God…" Winston's eyes closed, his heart heavy. "…then that's it. It's official: Frank and I are all that's left."

"Launched a week prior, Prayer was already leaving Earth with the odds against it, but this only heightens the impact of its loss. Our hearts go out to any surviving relatives of the brave men and women who volunteered for this mission. May they be remembered as heroes, who ventured into the unknown in the name of all human kind."

Roxanne paused for a few seconds, her breathing uneven. When she continued, her voice was strained as she held back tears. "This concludes our evening news for Monday, August Second. However, in light of the Terrarium Project… we would like to take a moment and list the names of Prayer's crew, so that they may be immortalized for future generations, and hopefully, all those that come after."

Out of all the Gen Arks, Prayer had possessed the smallest occupancy, by far. More specifically, Winston had counted approximately three hundred names over the years. It was a truly pitiful amount, but it was all that could be brought together in the world's current state. He stared, unmoving, at the television screen, Roxanne reading out each and every life that had been lost. Not that Winston was allowed to react; only the final name was given any significance to him.

However, this week, he found there was one reprieve from that monotonous countdown. He couldn't acknowledge them prior, but Winston could now process that the figures had been in the room with him the whole time, barely visible out of the corner of his eye. Five of them were huddled on the floor, beside the television, exchanging hushed conversation; while the sixth was lying in the center of them, its breathing slow, and helmet discarded.

Winston couldn't express it, but this sight was rather interesting to him. Until now, he had never witnessed one of the figures lying down during the course of a day. Winston's eyes twitched ever so slightly for the remainder of the tribute to Prayer, as he tried to get a better look at the blurry scene. But, of course, he was unable to tear his eyes from the screen, even slightly, for any more than a millisecond.

"…Layla Chastain." Roxanne concluded. She let out a small sniff, barely noticeable to anyone save Winston, before addressing the camera one final time. "May the crew of Prayer Rest In Peace. Your memories are preserved in the hearts of your loved ones."

In a heartbeat, Winston snapped back to the present. "God willing, they're in a better place now," he stated solemnly, rising slowly from the couch. The figures muttered amongst themselves, glancing over at Winston as he turned back towards the stairs. "Well. Painting after *that* is easier said than done, but… let's see what I can do."

As Winston headed upstairs to his studio, only one of the figures stood up to follow him. The remaining four stayed behind, their sixth companion now silent.

By the time Winston had completed the day's painting, the rest of the figures had returned. Today, inspired by the smaller canvas picked for him the day prior, Winston had chosen a more unique canvas of his own accord: A 6x24 canvas, something of a happy medium between his preferred canvas size, and the previous day's 6x6 canvas. Though still limited in space for horizontal detail, the additional height made painting feel more natural to Winston than his preceding piece, allowing him to depict the full extent of his vision.

Today's painting was, in a way, an extension of his 6x6 piece: Now, several twisting and twining streaks of green branched off from the original, linear pillar, twirling upwards through wild tendrils of red, orange and brown. Small bits of color broke free from those tendrils like fire, drifting through that same deep blue sky, tumbling towards the earthy tones of the ground below.

But for the observant viewer, the most eye-catching detail was not the vibrant centerpiece of the painting. Rather, a small, messy dab of black near the bottom right corner, barely visible against the brown of the "earth." Compared to the rest of the painting—to say nothing of Winston's expected perfection—it was a detail that seemed very out of place; sloppy, even, as though Winston had accidentally pressed the tip of his brush against the canvas. But it was very much intentional, and while the figures observed the painting as a whole, he remained fixated on that seemingly insignificant splotch.

And then, just as he was about to transition back into his routine, Winston noticed one of the figures was also staring at the minuscule dot of black. Whether it was the same individual that had originally followed him upstairs alone, Winston couldn't say.

Nevertheless, when it realized he was looking at them, they lifted their head, as though to meet his gaze through their tinted helmet. A short, hushed string of noise came from beyond their visor, but it quickly trailed off. For his last moments of clarity, Winston and the figure stared at each other in solemn silence... until Winston heard the chime of his laundry from downstairs.

"Oh! That'd be the laundry, I'd say." Winston exclaimed, gathering his brushes. "After a painting like that, I'll leave the folding for the morning—I can already hear that bed calling my name!"

His thoughts pushed down as he left his studio, Winston didn't notice that the figure was watching him leave.

A wavering stream of deep orange light shone beyond the curtains as Winston's eyes snapped open; it was a new day. He took in the room around him, observing the walls bathed in the faint glow of the setting sun as he reached over to his bedside table and turned on the light. As his mind filled in the ambiguous variables the darkness provided, he found, to his mild surprise, that something wasn't right.

His hamper was waiting by the door, the curtains were still closed, and five figures were backed into a corner of the room, unknown objects held tightly. But today, Winston realized that his sheets were rather wrinkled, spread hap-hazard across the bed.

"Well, clearly something was bugging me last night!" Winston quipped to himself as he climbed out of bed. In some part of his mind, he knew perfectly well what had caused this. But he also understood that he wouldn't be allowed to process that for some time today. "Understood" being a relative term.

After re-making his bed, Winston walked to the restroom, the figures apparently keeping their distance today. Winston was left alone as he tended to his teeth, his toothbrush shuddering in his hand as it moved in synch with his arm. Leaning down and spitting into the sink, the residue disappearing moments later, Winston turned to the metal door of his shower stall.

After a cold shower, the figures met him outside. Returning to his room under their intent gaze, Winston put on a magenta tank top, coupled with purple cargo shorts. The figures remained close behind him as he descended the stairs, not uttering a sound between them. But as Winston tended to the pan of eggs on the stove, that silence was broken by an outburst of sound from outside the house.

The five figures whipped towards the door as one, the unidentified racket ringing out yet again. Their body language was tense as they looked back and forth between each other; in contrast, Winston turned to the door with the same calm as the day before.

"I'll be... seems that I've got a guest."

When the noise sounded again as Winston approached the door, it was more complicated. It was a voice, of some sort, overlapping with a resounding blast. As he stepped out onto the porch, the figures didn't hang back. Moving to stand around him with practiced fluidity Winston had never seen from them while they were a group of six, they stared out at their guest.

It was a humanoid individual, their body dripping with perspiration from the heat. While they appeared to be clad in attire similar to those of the figures, Winston could spy no further articles of clothing below that. As such, patches of their reddened, burnt features were left exposed to the light, save for the scarce remnants of shaved body hair, and a long, black object held at shoulder level; like those the figures held, but less compact.

Raising his hand, Winston waved to his guest, pleased that this time he was able to see them. "Greetings, friend! I thought I heard someone out here! Man, I'd bet you're probably sweltering in this heat—you're free to come inside if you want."

The individual replied by letting out a brief scream, motioning with the object in their hands. Winston couldn't respond, but the figures standing on the porch with Winston *immediately* stepped forward; a new voice came from his right, as one of them addressed the newcomer.

"You can probably guess, but not a lot of people come by here anymore. Pretty much just me and my paintings now," Winston continued, but his would-be guest's attention was now on the figure. Further torrents of noise erupted from its mouth in response to the figure, accentuated with the wild flailing of the object grasped tightly in its hands. "If you're looking for food or resources, I can't help you there. But, if you're curious how an everyday Joe made his way in this world? Well... I'm your man."

As Winston progressed through his speech, the figure to his right and his guest began engaging in a fervent back and forth. The intensity of their exchange was rising quickly, and the remaining figures had now raised each of their own objects to shoulder height, as well. "Heh, look at me prattling on when I don't even know if you can understand me. I guess at this point we just have to hope you can break the language barrier." Winston sighed, staring down at the porch. Looking upright, he smiled at his guest as it aimed its object in his direction. "Well, anyway, I won't be very chatty from—"

A voice screamed out, moments before a blast sounded and a barrage of hot metal pellets struck Winston in his left shoulder, severing his arm and tearing off the side of his torso. His voice cut out upon impact, but even if it hadn't, the ensuing assailment of rapid-fire bursts that erupted from the figures around him would have drowned out anything he could have said. Reeling back, Winston watched as his guest—his assailant, rolled out of the way as a stream of projectiles struck the earth, sending up a cloud of scorched, red dust. The individual broke into a fit of ragged coughing, trying and failing to aim the weapon in their hands, firing off a shot at nothing. For the first time in his life, Winston recognized these actions, as a solitary command rang out in his mind's eye, from a voice that wasn't his own:

"Get inside."

Painful, sparking sensations were shooting through Winston from his gruesome wound. He could barely think through the currents overtaking his brain, but his body somehow managed to turn without the use of his legs. The sound of gunfire continued all around him, as he was dragged back inside by the steel rod that served as his spine. As he neared the still-open door, the figures defending him were beginning to slump to the ground, moister seeping from their attire as something unseen sapped them of all strength. Winston heard his aggressor screaming in his direction as he neared the house, followed by the sound of a gun cocking. But the bloody sound of a bullet penetrating flesh replaced those screams of fury with animalistic howls of agony. The door automatically slamming shut behind Winston as he crossed the threshold, he began falling forward. Electronic feedback piercing his ears, Winston crashed to the floor with the resounding clang of metal, and his world instantly went black.

When he next awoke, Winston had been turned upright, so that he was lying on his back. Two figures were kneeling near him, looking away. Winston tried his best to look up at them, but his head was slouched to the side, and wouldn't turn forward. As such, he was left staring at a third figure laying to his left. Their weapon discarded on the floor, the figure's face was turned away from him, their helmet removed to expose neatly trimmed black hair. Unable to follow through with his tasks in his current state, Winston was free to process that their breathing was labored, and raspy. He felt a strange sensation come over him, as he realized: This was what he had seen the day before. Although, Winston didn't recall trickling red dripping down from the previous figure's midsection....

But at that moment, sparks erupted from Winston's wound, nearly causing his vision to cut out once more. He tried to fight it as long as he could, his eyes attempting to refocus on the figure before him... he quickly found this to be a hopeless effort. As his field of view began to break apart, the figure turned its head slowly upright, so as to stare up at the figures kneeling at their side.

"...It's okay... I'm not going anywhere," Winston's voice spoke reassuringly beside him; the falling drops of red the last image he could decipher, before Winston was pulled back into the darkness.

Winston's eyelids opened with a quiet whirring, the lenses concealed behind his amber eyes sparking to life. The bedroom was now pitch black. It was night; time had passed.

It was a new day.

Winston instinctively attempted to fully extend his arms, playing his morning yawn, but only one of his limbs still responded to his commands. Something was very wrong. Holding out his remaining responsive arm to the spherical device placed on the plastic bedside table, Winston triggered the lights' motion sensor, before beginning to analyze his current state.

He was once again in bed, although he was lying on top of the flickering "linens" at the moment. The hamper was where he'd left it, though now filled with yesterday's outfit, its incorporeality leaving it unscathed. The tantalum curtains were still shut, in order to keep out as much heat as possible. There were now only two figures in the room, standing at the foot of his bed, talking to one another. The only difference seemed to be—

And then, with a jolt, his left arm suddenly shot to life. Now able to fully see his body, Winston found that his wound had been patched with additional patches of high-melanin artificial skin, and any broken tubing had been restored. For all intents and purposes, he was good as new.

Climbing out of bed, the blankets snapping back into place with an electric pop, Winston moved down the hall and entered the restroom, the two figures remaining behind in the bedroom. A low hum sounding, Winston's toothbrush materialized in his hand, before he began miming running the projected image over his plastic teeth. This continued for a minute or so, before Winston "spit" a vague burst of light into the sink, where it instantly vanished.

As no water remained to use in a plumbing system, this was the only feasible alternative to capture the process.

With his dental routine out of the way, Winston's mental functions became fully automated, pulling him into the large, metallic box that sat where a human household would have had a shower. Moments after sealing the door behind him, a number of flush syringes shot out from the walls on mechanical limbs, sliding smoothly into the series of clear, vein-like tubes running in and out of Winston's skin. Freon gas poured through the syringes and into these tubes, directly cooling Winston's inner workings so he could make it through the day. Then, with a hiss of decompression, the chamber unsealed, and Winston was ejected, his mind acknowledging his protocol of a cold shower as fulfilled.

Upon dressing himself in the attire for Day Four of his routine, Winston retrieved his hamper and brought it to the sanitization room. He passed a figure lying on the floor along the way, its helmet discarded, burnt skin peeling off its face in dry shavings. After inserting his "laundry" into the room's solitary machine for the day, Winston returned to the kitchen. The blood-soaked body of another figure was knocked aside by the metal pole that connected Winston to his track as he stopped before the model stove. Tilting his head to complete the illusion, Winston's phone materialized from the projector across from him. His frying pan, already containing images of sizzling eggs, soon followed, as Frank's familiar voice was played through the holographic footage.

"Fr.Terraform. Greeting: 4."

"Hey, Frank," Winston began, staring down at what was supposed to represent his food, shifting over the non-functioning boiler. "You happen to catch yesterday's news report?"

Winston was silent as Frank's familiar white noise droned on. Eventually, the next sound cue activated, spoken by a monotone, robotic voice.

"Fr.Terraform. Response: 4-1."

Winston played a quiet "hmm" in response. "I'll admit: Didn't think Roxanne was up to it either. Losing her daughter and all. But I guess the station doesn't care about that… some things really haven't changed with time, huh?" The pan shifting off the boiler in synch with his arm's movement, Winston reached up to the cabinet, where the projection of a plate sparked into existence.

"Fr.Terraform. Response: 4-2."

"That aside, though." Winston's left arm let out a crackle of electricity before dropping limp to his side, and causing the spatula to seemingly rise from the kitchen rack of its own accord. "I guess the Terrarium Project crew's got their work cut out for them now, am I right? Not much more motivation to get off your lazy butts than losing our last Gen Ark and New York City erupting into a crater of lava within the span of a week."

"Fr.Terraform. Response: 4-3."

"God willing, anyway." Winston let out a resigned sigh as he sat down at the table, his left arm still immobilized as his utensil split off pieces of meaningless light from the meal. "Frank, old man... do you ever think, that we really can't fix this? That someday, you and I could be the last humans— heck, the last *beings*, left alive on Earth?"

There was a long silence, filled only by the Foley of Winston "eating," and the long, hissing frequency that was Frank's voice, which had continued playing over the phone the entire time.

"Fr.Terraform. Response: 4-finality."

"I suppose so." Winston nodded solemnly to himself, the intended contents of Frank's response being written out in his mind. "Well, I guess there's no point in dwelling on this. Have a good one, man."

His dish and silverware continuing to float without anything to support them, Winston deposited the imagery into a rough facsimile to a metal sink, in which they dematerialized moments after. Turning silently, animated as though deep in thought, Winston moved to the couch; the two remaining figures were waiting for him as he slid into place, one of them holding a new object—not like the others—steady in their hand.

Winston took in the colors of the screen in silence, the figure tampering with his inactive arm in the meantime. His mind was primed to recognize specific sentence fragments, but Winston had never been allowed to fully contemplate these archived broadcasts. There wasn't enough time to give him that ability… one of his creators' biggest regrets, in the end.

With a final jolt from the metallic object, Winston's arm returned to full functionality. The figure shifted back as the limb began motioning rapidly, attempting to catch up to the current timestamp of Winston's routine. It finally settled back into a resting position, just as the broadcast reached its conclusion.

"…first half of our late night updates for Monday, August Second," Roxanne stated to the camera. Across from her, a man clad in a short-sleeved button-up shirt and suit vest gave her a nod, before turning to the camera.

"Thank you for having me, Roxanne… and thank all of you at home for listening. May God give my team and I the strength to complete our work, and may he watch over all of you that remain virtuous in these times." He stated, with resigned solemnity.

Beside Winston, one of the figures stared down at their lap, letting out quiet sounds as the screen powered off. As Winston began shifting into his standing position, the other crossed the couch, holding them in their arms.

"And may the Lord continue to watch over all of you, as well."

The figures turned to look up at Winston, his eyes staring blankly ahead. "I have you five to thank for this. If we had never met, I would have given up years ago; I can pinpoint it down to the *second* it would have ended." Winston's voice was sincere, humbled, even though he was seemingly speaking to nothing. "I couldn't say it that day, but if you're hearing me now… my legacy is in your debt. My being, my creative voice, lives on because of you. And script be damned, I want everyone who finds us to know that fact. Godspeed; I hope that we can find each other again after this is all over."

Winston didn't see the figures as he left the room. He couldn't process the ragged sobs his speech had provoked, or the ramifications that entailed. But something felt different as he climbed the stairs to the upstairs hall. As he walked past that melty sculpture in its pot, and entered his studio, Winston was struck with a feeling of... finality. There had always been a disconnect between his recorded lines and his uninhibited feelings, but this particular sensation persisted, even prior to the restraining haze lifting from his mind.

As he lifted a new 16x20 canvas into place and pulled the plastic from its frame, something in his processor told him that he was nearing not just the end of his first official cycle, but the end of a significant phase of his lifespan. On this day, the vision in his mind's eye was not one that could be completed over the span of one work shift. It was imprecise, distorted. Even after creating so many abstract works, Winston found that he struggled to grasp even the core concept behind this new image. And so, as he was lifting his brush and preparing to take that first stroke, he stopped.

Instead, he returned the brush to the appropriate ziplock bag, and produced a mechanical pencil in its place. Holding up the tip to the canvas, Winston made a silent decision in that moment. In an electronic language incomprehensible to the human mind, he told himself: This was a piece he had to create. Because they were something that deserved to be remembered.

"Even when the world dies... my art will live on."

He remained focused on his painting as the figure entered the room—as they fully expected him to. They weren't even sure he knew they were there at all as they moved to stand beside him. They took a breath in... they could tell they couldn't wait any longer.

"I'm sorry. I don't want to bother you, Winston." The figure began, their voice muffled by their visor. "I... still don't know if you can understand me. Or, really, if my presence will have any impact on you at all."

The figure paused, shaking their head with a mirthless laugh. "Yet, despite that, I still decided to come and talk to you," they muttered. "Trying to fool myself into thinking I'm not the last of us to go. Complete, shameless hypocrisy, resting on the shallow end of a pool of red. Even when it's all over."

Winston continued painting, unperturbed, as the figure let out a slow, hollow sigh. "But I'm getting off-track. I didn't lug myself up here to talk about me."

Reaching up, the figure lifted their helmet off their head, before discarding it on the floor. Even that simple action caused sweat to fly through the air; they could feel the heat creeping through the insulation.

"I need to ask something of you, Winston. Just in case Liang really did manage to give you thoughts of your own, even with all our setbacks." The figure paused, running a hand through their short, sweat-soaked hair. "Hell, who am I kidding. Even if you can't acknowledge me... I don't want us to have left you without one final talk."

Crossing their arms, the figure's eyes drifted around the room, tracing the seams of the synthetic boards that made up Winston's studio. "You're the last of us, Winston. And maybe, you can tell this wasn't what we envisioned. But that's how it is." The figure didn't look at Winston as they continued, now simply staring into the middle distance. "Once I'm gone, you'll be all that's left... so please. If you did see us, when we were here. The best thing you can do for our memory... in the image of my best friend... is to keep creating. Just by existing, you're keeping humanity alive. But by *creating*... you'll be taking us further."

"Whew... I think that's all I can do today!"

The figure hesitated, turning to look at Winston as he began to put away his supplies. "You were making a multiple-day painting?" They asked rhetorically, looking at the canvas clearly for the first time... their breath caught in their throat at the image.

Elaborate sketch lines covered approximately one third of the canvas, their details yet to be fully realized. But the shadowy form that was beginning to take shape was clear. Broken, red flakes fell down around its dark, intricately shaded body, gathering on a tan floor and pooling together into a liquid. Deep shades of brown disrupted the darkness in order to depict a featureless face, looking out of the painting's world at someone unseen. And to the left of that face, still primarily in sketch form, was a hand. Its fingers extended, reaching out to the faceless entity. Even knowing that it would never reach it.

The figure stared at the painting in disbelief, the gravity of the piece washing over them. "You..." They began, the words barely escaping their lips. "...you did see him."

As Winston left the room, they couldn't bring themselves to follow him.

The house was shaking as Winston's eyes snapped open. His body felt hot. A red light shone through the curtains, but his processor was fighting against his lenses. It wasn't a new day yet. It wasn't time to wake up.

But he felt it. Something was calling him.

As Winston rose from his bed, a garbled drone began to emanate from his mouth. Voice clips overlapped, and his mind became overwhelmed with commands. Yet, when before he would find himself immobilized, Winston found that his clarity no longer faltered at the sound of his own voice.

Through the rush of electrical pulses, a question appeared in his mind. "Am I... free?"

And at that, he received an answer: "Come outside, Winston."

Winston didn't bother making his bed, instead immediately slipping on his first outfit of the week; the one he had once been told was his favorite. He followed his rail out into the hall, ignoring the commands urgently reminding him to take his daily shower—reminding him that without his Freon injections, he would melt into slag within mere hours. The voice in his head took precedence above all else.

The house trembled around him as he passed the corpses of the figures. He could see them all clearly now, lying with helmets discarded, their faces possessing only a mutilated facsimile of a human's features after days of lying prone in the heat. The holograms had triggered on their own, Frank's voice joining the din of sound in Winston's head. But he ignored it. He was approaching the front door now; the red light shining through the reinforced glass seemed to beckon him, as he reached for the doorknob.

The door opened on its own with a hiss of steam, and Winston came to a stop on the porch. The last remaining figure was standing there, the world bathed in red around them, facing away from Winston as they stared out at something in the distance.

As they turned to face Winston, speaking in brief instances of noise he couldn't comprehend, he saw a small, metallic object was held in their hand. Their hand trembled for a moment, and then threw the object to the ground. A crunch of metal and plastic was heard as their foot came down hard on the device.

The pulses faded. The voices ceased. For the first time, Winston's mind was clear, as he stared at the figure in confusion. Panting heavily, their face dripping with sweat, the figure looked up and met Winston's gaze. They began trembling, their mouth opening to speak, but no words would come out. Instead, they simply closed their eyes, and stepped aside.

There, rising out of the ground, splitting the dry earth, a pillar of fire rose into the air. Its flames danced in the wind, as it climbed upwards towards the heavens above. The sound of distant eruptions could be heard, as more and more of these flaming geysers appeared on the horizon. Magma poured from their bases, bubbling out of the dying planet into streams of orange and yellow. And through it all, from the sky, Winston watched as embers split off from the spectacle, and drifted downwards on the breeze. They filled the air, tumbling and turning; igniting the ground into further masses of bursting flames. Beside him, the figure cowered, shielding their eyes from the now blinding light. But even as he felt his lenses begin to smolder, and his skin begin to drip down into his endoskeleton, Winston couldn't look away.

A flat tone sounded from his throat, as his processor began rapidly creating amalgamations of thoughts and sentences. Until, finally, his feelings began to stabilize, even as his body warped ever further from its intended purpose and function. His thoughts slowed to a crawl, and the tone faded out. And as the remaining fragments of his voice played... for the first time, Winston's thoughts were set free from his mind.

"It's—"

Splice.

Search. Locate.

Splice.

"—beautiful."

End splice.

September

Haustblot

Hiromi Cota

You have to understand—I'm a good person.

I'm a good person, I swear to God. Gods.

I was just trying to help everyone—make the world better, you know? But now, it's all messed up. They're all dead, and it's my fault. It's—

I'm sorry. Let me start at the beginning.

It was a week before Haustblot. Haustblot? It's just this Pagan thing—holiday. Norse Pagan. I drove down for it then. I'd been friends with Alan and Samantha for a while. We met at a festival back in 2010, I think. We'd been talking about getting together for Haustblot for ages, and we finally thought, "This is the year. This is the year we do a big thing for the Blot this year." I know. I know. I keep using the Old Words. "Haust" just means autumn, and "blot" means sacrifice.

It's not like that. It's not like we were hurting anyone. Sacrifice is just a way of giving thanks. Sometimes, I'll just drop some of my food in the woods. Just sort of giving back to the Allfather. Sometimes, times aren't so tough, and the year was generous. Then, maybe, I'll bring a chicken or something and sacrifice it.

It's not evil or some kind of devil worship. It's just—you believe in one God, and I believe in a couple more. It's not that strange; our ancestors believed in Thor and Odin and—I'm just being traditional to my family.

Yeah. Alan and Samantha were also Norse Pagans. There's a lot of us, but I didn't know any ones in my town. Alan and Samantha were the closest. And, they knew some more that weren't on Facebook. Earlier this year, they said they found a big group of nearby Pagans, so we wanted to finally have that big celebration we'd been talking about. It—Haustblot—starts on the Autumn Equinox, so I wanted to drive down early to help Alan and Samantha with the preparation.

They said that there was gonna be at least thirty people, most showing up by motorcycle, so I figured it might get a little rowdy. I'm not saying that all bikers are roughhousers, but I've known some that were, so I figured it might be good to have a little extra space to keep things from getting too wild. So, we went out and borrowed some chainsaws from neighbors.

One of them, Caroline, wanted in on the fun. I guess she'd had the chainsaw since before her husband died, and he never let her use it, so she wanted to learn how. It didn't seem like a hot day and the forecast on my phone's app said it wouldn't get over 75°, but it was still plenty hot. I guess it was just because we were doing so much work, but we sweated up a storm out there.

My daddy taught me how to use a chainsaw when I was thirteen. Holdin' it back then felt amazing and terrifying at the same time. I was spittin' out wood dust for a while afterwards, and my arms ached for days. I'm bigger now, though. So, it wasn't that much trouble for me to get the saw started and give Caroline a quick class on it.

It must've been about noon by the time we got started, so the sun beaming down on us was mostly caught up by the trees and their leaves. I was out there starting to tell her about cutting out a notch cut when you're sawing down a tree, but she said, "Oh, that's just like doing it with an axe."

"You know how to handle an axe, ma'am?" I asked.

"Of course I do. It's hard growing up out here without knowing your way around tools, especially when you're as old as I am," she replied with an impish grin. It was about then when I realized that she knew how to work with trees just fine; it was just the chainsaws that were new to her. A few minutes of explaining how the chain works and how bad angles make the chain stop working, and she was already better than I was.

Along the way, we talked about our favorite Norse legends. She didn't know much about Norse Paganism, but she knew plenty of legends. We both really liked the wolf Fenrir. He kills Odin during Ragnarök, but that's kind of Odin's fault. It—

It's complicated. So, before the end of the world, there was a prophecy that Fenrir would eat Odin during Ragnarök. So, the Aesir—the gods—wanted to put Fenrir on an unbreakable leash to keep Odin safe. But, by trapping Fenrir with the fetters, they made him so mad that he wanted to kill Odin. It's one of those stories where you can read it over 'n' over and still not know who the good guys are.

I'm sorry. I can tell you need me to get back to my testimony. I just thought talking about Fenrisulfr—uh, Fenrir wolf—was important because of what happened later. I—OK.

By the time the sun was starting to set, we—Caroline, Samantha, Alan, and I—were all covered with wood chips. We even had some under our clothes and in our boots. But, we'd also knocked down a whole mess of trees and made us a nice series of stumps for sitting on. The wood wouldn't be dry in time to use for bonfires, though. So, we still had to go to the farm supply store and pick up pallets.

I know. Pallets aren't exactly the most traditional of ways to get wood for bonfires, but we wanted at least three fires since there'd be so many people. The idea was that if we had a few fires, the people wouldn't be clustered all around one. Keep groups smaller, keep them from getting too riled up. It also meant that if two of them bikers got heated up, they could just go to different fires and calm down.

We were originally only gonna buy enough wooden pallets for two of the fires, but we realized that it'd look weird if one was made of logs and the other two were made of pallets. So, Samantha paid a little extra and got even more pallets. I was kind of surprised that the store was charging for the pallets since they're usually free back where I'm from. I guess folks out here really like their pallets, makin' them worth selling.

So, anyway, we drove out there with a couple of trucks—mine and Alan's. We loaded them up with pallets so high, we needed to use rachet straps to keep them from spilling out. By the time we had them all set, it was almost night. Not exactly the best time to be hauling wood all over the woods, and we'd already done plenty of work that day. We still took the pallets. Don't get me wrong. We'd already paid for and loaded the things. No reason to not drive 'em back to Alan's place. Caroline was still with us. She said, "It's been lovely working with y'all. Been too long since I've put in an honest day's work. But it's almost 9, and I need to get back to my husband."

Her eyes flared and looked the ground when she realized what she'd said. "I—need to get back."

"You can have dinner with us, if you'd like," Samantha

said. "It's the least we could do since you helped us out so much."
It felt sincere, but I knew that Samantha was probably trying to
get Caroline to spend more time with us so that Caroline wouldn't
feel so lonely.

"Oh, I don't want to impose," Caroline muttered, like she
was excusing herself out of habit.

"We insist. After all, we wouldn't be as far along as we are
today without you. You helped us out a heck of a lot," I said,
working on breaking down Caroline's willpower. She gave in, and
came inside with us.

We had a mess of spaghetti with red sauce and meatballs.
Samantha had put a big ole pot of tomatoes and sauce on her
stove before we set out to get the chainsaws. It'd been going all
day long, and it was the best—

I'm sorry. I just need a minute.

It's going? OK. Yes, I can move closer to the microphone. Is that
better?

So, we had Samantha's spaghetti. It was good. It was
really good. Of course, we had leftovers. She made so much so
that we wouldn't have to worry about lunches for the rest of the
week. She's so thoughtful. I can't believe I almost went my life
without meeting her. And it—it was our last meal together, really.
We had another few days together, but we were all on different
schedules for the rest of the preparation.

Samantha was working on a feast for the first night of
Haustblot, taking her car around to get ingredients, rare meats
and vegetables. I don't know what she was cooking, but it all
smelled so good. But it also meant that she wasn't home for
mealtimes. Alan and I were hauling logs for a few days after that.
We both had trucks, but with that kind of terrain, we probably

would have been doing just as well to have done everything with chains, rebar, and rachet straps. We thought it was just going to take another day to get the logs cleared up, but—

Well, I did my best to get Alan to spill whether Sam thought of me the same way I thought of her. He never said anything outright; he just smiled and said it wasn't any of his business. I think he promised her he'd keep quiet. But we had plenty of other things to talk about. We had to; we were working together for hours and hours. We'd been chatting for years online, so we had plenty of in-jokes and topics to yammer on about. I don't know. I guess we probably talked about different kinds of Heathenism. Well, you see, Heathenism's just a big umbrella term. Not everyone likes it. But it's what we got. Sometimes folks just call themselves Pagans, but there's not as specific as Norse or Germanic Paganism. It's kind of like how you have Southern Baptists and Northern Baptists and United Baptists, and—you get it.

But I know we were talking about the folks that Alan had invited. There was a bunch of them, which was exciting, but Alan said that they sounded like Odinists, which—there's nothing wrong with worshipping Odin; he's pretty great. But a bunch of people who say that they worship Odin really worship power. White power. You get me? Again, I'm not saying that all of them do it or even most of them. It's just—it's just really worrying sometimes. I got Black friends. I don't want them getting the wrong idea about what I do. That's why I don't call myself an Odinist, or even a German Pagan; it's too close to those kinds of people.

Odin himself knew that other kinds of people could be great. He adopted Loki, who was a Jotun—a giant. And half of the Aesir were actually another group of god: the Vanir. He had a mixed family and—even if you don't think that Frigg and Freyja are the same god—anyone who knows the stories knows that Odin wasn't prejudiced.

What's wrong? I—I don't know what I did. I'm sorry. I'm sorry.

I'll talk about the night. That's what you want to hear about, right?

Other people started showing up a little after lunch. Mostly just friends, like Magne, and Erik. I didn't even know they were going to be there. I thought it was going to be too far for them to make. I knew Magne and Erik from the same online group I met Samantha and Alan. I think Magne said he flew out to a small airport near Erik's, and they drove out together. Must have been a long drive, but it was good to see them.

Magne was one of my oldest friends in the group. He's kind of weird, but I like him. He's pretty into Fenrir, wearing furs even when it's warm out. I never understood that, but more power to him if the furs make him feel closer to Fenrisulfr.

The furs? No, I'm pretty sure they're real wolf furs. I don't know how he got them. I never asked. Probably hunted the wolves for them, but you'd have to ask him. He—he got out right? I didn't see him—I didn't see him after it happened.

The bikers—the extremists—they showed up a little later. Had to be at least a dozen of them. Seemed like there were more of them, though. Even spread out around the clearing that Alan and I made, the area felt full of them. You know, I always thought of bikers as wearing a lot of leather, but aside from their vests, not many of them were wearing leather. A lot more jeans than anything.

Uh, they called their leader Bjorn. Bjorn Odinsson. He didn't look very Scandinavian, so that stood out to me. Most

Pagans I know wouldn't change their names. We're supposed to honor our family and ancestors; changing our names to sound cooler is kind of the opposite of that. Yeah, that's him. Those eyes are—were intense. Can you take the photo away, please? Thank you.

Bjorn was one of those people who just kind of fill up whatever space they're in. Sometimes that's a good thing, but not tonight. It wasn't like he was rude or anything, he just seemed a little too excited, you know? Like he was looking forward to the sacrifice part a little too much. And, even with as many people as we had in Samantha's backyard, I could always hear him. They had a goat with them. I don't understand how they got such an ornery creature to the Haustblot. I guess one of them had a trailer for his motorcycle.

It was still alive when I went into Samantha's to fetch her. It was almost sunset, and I hadn't seen her. I don't think there's any rule about when things are supposed to happen for the Haustblot, but I usually treat the sunset as the start. So, I wanted to make sure that she saw it. Also, I wanted to see her. I went in and the first thing I saw was the burners on the stove going, but there wasn't anything on the burners. That seemed plenty careless, but she *did* leave the spaghetti sauce going for hours without watching it, so maybe she was just a thing she did?

Once I got into the kitchen, I realize that wasn't it. There was red. There was—No, I can do it. There was red sauce and blood all over the kitchen. I think one of them tried something with Samantha. Had to be a fool to touch her. He had a knife in his belly and was just lying there, looking at me. Just staring and reaching for me. Like he was still thinking of coming after me. Just bloodlust behind those eyes. A true berserker.

Bjorn shouted, "Brothers and sisters! Our ancestors have

honored us with a glorious summer. So, we shall honor them!" And I snapped out of it and stopped staring at the dying biker. I heard water running in the bathroom. I didn't remember it being on before, so Samantha must have turned it on. Even thinking that she was washing blood off her hands gave me a little relief, because Bjorn shouting about honoring ancestors made me think for a moment that he was going to sacrifice her.

I don't know why I thought that. But I did. It almost would have been better than what really happened. The extremists start howling and shouting. It shook Samantha's double-wide, so when I got to her in the bathroom, she couldn't hear me coming and almost stabbed me. Her face was covered in blood. Just drenched. She said something, but I couldn't hear her over the hollering outside.

I grabbed a towel off the rack and wrapped it over her brow. She wiped her face off. The blood still stuck to her skin. I felt like it wasn't going to come off. But she started to sag, and I realized that whatever happened to her scalp wasn't her only injury. Her jeans were darker on one side. I helped her to the floor, and I almost sat down beside her. If I had, I don't think I'd be here.

As we checked her side for her other wound, I realized something that froze me for a second. Once the bikers realized that their friend was dead, they'd come for us. And all three of us were inside the house. All it would take would be for someone to miss any one of us and come looking. We found Samantha's stab wound and covered that with a towel, too. Her last one. I hoped that her towels weren't too dirty. Even then, I was still thinking about infection and first aid, not what was really happening.

I needed to get Samantha out of there, but my truck was still across the clearing, parked next to the last of the logs we needed to move. There's no way I could drive it to Samantha's house and load her into it without one of them spotting me. I prayed to Odin to make smart enough to get me and Samantha out of there. And to Fenrir to be strong enough to get her out. I realized that the closest car must be Samantha's, which meant all I needed to do was get her keys, help her inside, and then get to the hospital.

All without being seen. If any of them saw her covered in blood, they'd be after us. And there'd be no outrunning her. Not in Samantha's hatchback. I heard a shout roar through the backyard. I asked Sam for her keys, but she couldn't hear. I yelled over the ruckus, "Where are your keys?"

My ears started to ring a bit and she groaned out, "Over there," pointing towards the front door. As I scampered over to the door, I realized why my ears were ringing. Because it was silent outside. Had they heard me? Oh, Odin. I had shouted like a fool. They had to have heard. I could hear one at the back door. He pounded the wall next to it, rattling the whole house. The door must've locked behind me. I had to get Samantha out of there.

I snatched the keys off the wall and ran back to the bathroom. She was sitting on the floor, leaning against the door. Almost unconscious, but not quite. I reached under her armpits and reached behind her. I had to squat down low to get a good grip, but that made it real hard to lift her up. I fell against both sides of the door frame on the way to standing.

It's a lot harder to lift someone up from the front. I should have switched to holding her from behind, but I didn't think about it. I might have—No, I don't think there's anything I could have done. I waddled us over to the front door in time to seem the back door shake and flex. Whoever was outside was really pounding on it. I couldn't understand how they hadn't gotten in yet. Bjorn was shouting something. I couldn't understand most of it, but every few words, he'd pause for a moment, then his buddies would scream like people possessed.

It was awkward getting the door open, but I did it. When I pushed the screen open, the spring screamed. I thought for sure they heard me, but Bjorn growled out something. They started chanting it—Ofrinene. I knew it was part of some rituals, but I didn't know what it meant. I got Samantha out the front door while they were chanting it. We shambled against her car, leaning against it and gasping for breath, as I tried to hold her and get her keys out of my pocket. Thank goodness they only had Samantha's car blocked in from behind. The monsters—murderers kept chanting "ofrinene." I managed to get the keys out without doing something stupid like dropping them or falling over. But I accidentally hit her head against the car at least twice while getting her inside. I felt so bad.

I looked ofrinene up on my phone while I was waiting for you to arrive. It's Norwegian for "sacrifices." Plural. As in not just the goat. I looked back at the clearing and saw Alan standing on top of one of the big stumps we'd left for people to sit on. Bjorn was pointing a gun at him. I wanted to save him, to run out there and get him. But there were so many of them. I listened to their shouts get louder and turned the key in the ignition. The engine gave a staccatto cough as it started. But the noise lasted longer than the shouting. Heads turned our way.

I threw it into reverse and mashed down on the gas. We lurched backwards and slammed to a stop.

Their bikes. I saw them and then forgot about them.

Some of the extremists screamed their rage. Bjorn shot Alan in the head. The rest ran at us. I shifted into drive and pushed the pedal. For a second, the tire just spun against the dirt. Were we stuck on one of their bikes? Had I just given it too much gas? I don't know. But I pulled my foot back and eased back onto it, and we finally started moving. But they were, too. And we were heading right for 'em.

I turned the wheel hard and felt the back end slide in the dirt driveway, then snap back. We were suddenly going twice as fast. One of their bikes had been caught on our bumper, but it fell off and threw off our momentum. I thought I was going to crash into the bikes again, but only hit Samantha's mailbox.

I gave it as much gas as I thought I could handle. I'd nearly spun out twice driving this car. I know it wasn't my fault now, but then—I was worried. If I drove too fast, we'd crash. Even if we could still drive after the crash, it'd give them time to catch up. If I didn't drive fast enough, they'd catch up to us. We killed one of them and smashed a bunch of their bikes. We'd join Alan in a hurry. Oh, no. I just realized something. They didn't know any of that before they grabbed Alan. They were always planning on sacrificing us. Somehow, I knew that back then, too.

Dots of piercing white light stared at us in the rearview mirror. They were after us. I shoved the gas pedal to the floor. It didn't make as big of a difference as I thought it would've. Dirt whirled in a giant plume behind us, the red of dusk and the taillights bleeding into the dust trail. The ground whipped past us as Samantha's hatchback took us faster and faster away from the carnage.

Unfortunately, it wasn't taking us away from them fast enough. Three of them were close enough that I could make out their shapes, and one of them pointed a pistol at us. The windshield went white. I thought I'd blacked out for a second or was dying. But I wasn't seeing white; the window was shattered. And I missed a turn. I know because I felt us suddenly pointed downwards. Except down wasn't right in front of us. I wanted to turn back to the road, but something told me to steer towards the bottom. It probably saved me. I'd have rolled the car for sure if I'd turned the other way.

One of them rolled anyways. I saw their headlight crash to the ground and spin away. The other two plunged towards us. The car hit the bottom of the ravine, slamming us forwards, down, and back in the blink of an eye. I bit my lip, but the windshield had mostly knocked itself free. I could see again.

There was a boulder right in front of us. I yanked the wheel hard, but we still clipped it. My head slammed into the car's frame between my window and the windshield. This time I *had* blacked out. I woke up to water being poured on my face. I could barely see; even though it was night, it seemed too bright. Every point of light was like a needle in my brain. I held my breath and hoped they'd spare me.

"Nancy?" a familiar voice asked.

"Caroline?" Oh, thank Odin, I thought. But, when I sat up, I didn't see the scrappy, country grandma I had talked with the other day. I saw a she-wolf's bloody muzzle. I screamed. My skull felt like it split open, and I fell through the world.

"That's basically everything, Sheriff," Nancy said. "After I woke up again. I called 911, and they put me in touch with you after dispatching an ambulance." She stared off to the side of Sheriff Shaw's eyes, not meeting the law woman's gaze. A faint beeping from outside Nancy's room reminded them they were in the hospital. The sheriff pushed stop on her recorder. "I guess no one actually needed an ambulance."

"You did," said Sheriff Shaw, gesturing to Nancy's bandaged head.

"I guess I did." Nancy reached for her cup. Shaw picked it

up off the table, refilled it with water from the room's pitcher, and handed it to the weary witness. "Did you ever find Caroline?"

"Sure did. Got her all cleaned up and respectable, too," she made a show of putting her recorder into her bag. "But that's not something for the record. Neither are the last few seconds of your testimony, if I'm being honest."

"You don't think I saw a wolf with Caroline's voice?" Nancy fumbled with her bed's control, wrestling to sit up and finally look the law woman in the eyes. Shaw's fists gripped Nancy's tray-stand, as she leaned over it to return the favor.

"I think if you actually follow Fenrisúlfr, the Hróðvitnir, you'll keep your fucking mouth shut about Miss Ulfsdottir," Sheriff Shaw growled. Her eye's irises grew and glowed a hungry yellow. She smiled a predatory grin with too-sharp teeth.

OCtObeR

Hallow-umbus

Michelle Lee

Prologue

he shades were drawn in a dilapidated living room, darkness lurked in all corners, and a TV blared. In front of the TV sat an old man, his hair white and shaggy, his shoulders frail-looking. He sat on an ottoman that had seen better centuries than the one it currently occupied. The man was hunched forward, his head in his hands, his shoulders shaking uncontrollably while the reporter talked.

Breaking news on a local college campus, a block from the well-known frat row. It appears as if history is repeating itself, leaving a community devastated. In a scene straight from a horror story, our investigative reporter brings us news from this gruesome scene. Grace, have you found out what happened there?

Chapter 1

A week earlier

nside a stuffy lecture hall amidst the ramblings of a professor that only a few were listening to, a piece of paper passed through several hands before landing in the meaty fist of a glazy-eyed football player, where it stopped.

"Hallow-umbus?" the barely awake athlete mumbled. "What the f—?"

The professor's throat cleared unhappily, interrupting the curse that was about to spew from the popular male's mouth. "Mr. Mann, did you have a question?"

Discretely, Adam Mann slid the paper under his empty notepad in front of him. "No, sir. I thought I saw a bug."

"Your eyes would have to be open for that." The professor frowned, then continued his lecture with the occasional glance at the football player.

Adam waited until the professor of social anthropology was fully engaged in his lecture on morals and finding happiness. Adam was more interested in the social aspect of the party the paper that had landed in his hands alerted him to for the weekend.

The Gamma Psi Chi frat was hosting the party. They were an odd group, but their parties were usually memorable. Hallow-umbus, they were calling it. An Oktoberfest Halloween party where the costumes had to mimic the style of Christopher Columbus and his era. Adam shook his head in amusement and stored the information in his phone before passing the paper along.

Hours later, when the corridors we no longer filled with the voices of students and professors, the janitor cleaned. The wheeled cart dragging behind sounded loud in the empty space. It was ridiculous to think Crane, the janitor the students jokingly called Ichabod, was alone. Crane knew truths about the spirits roaming the grounds that were popular urban legends among the populace. Once upon a time, he was a student who thought the same way.

Crane bent over and picked up an identical flyer to the one that Adam Mann had seen earlier. Crane shook his head slowly, a low groan building to a crescendo in his throat. "Not again." Crane dropped to his knees, a keening sound spilling from his lips as he rocked back in forth. He was trapped in his memories, reliving the hell of his college days when he worked at a quarry to support himself.

The echo of a wicked laugh reverberating through the corridor snapped him back to the present, and he pushed his aching joints to a standing position. "Put a cork in it," Crane grumbled. "They are kids. Go feed at the prison; the souls of the guilty are already damned."

The evil that resided on the campus thrived when students stumbled into a historical fact and wanted to recreate the events for thrills. The effort was pointless. Minor differences happened over the years, but the result was the same—useless carnage and death. Crane would know; he witnessed it the first time.

Chapter 2

ude, I know Oktoberfest ends on the 3rd. That's why we are having the party on the 9th. Monday the 11th is Columbus Day, and everyone knows October is when you celebrate Halloween. We are just going to combine everything," Duke, a senior, patiently explained to his fellow frat brothers. "It's a party, and it will be epic."

"How do you expect that many people to find costumes

to simulate the clothing of Columbus's era?" Ezra, a new member, argued. "I mean, I get it. Another frat had a party doing the same thing fifty years ago that spawned a whole lot of stories is kinda cool, but we don't need to make it a costume party."

"That's what will set us apart!" Duke pounded his fist into his hand to drive the point home. "We're a relatively new frat, and we need to put our name on the map and school history. Gamma Psi Chi will be famous, and not for being comic book nerds."

Ezra shrugged, knowing Duke aimed that at him. "Whatever. What do we need to do?"

Duke gave each of the members tasks to complete to get ready for the party. They had a week to prepare, find costumes and get set up for the hordes of people that would show up. Ezra wasn't planning on being a large part of the festivities. Something about the whole idea gave him chills.

Ezra's research on the old fraternity party revealed nothing other than that frat name had been retired, and seventeen people had died on the location the current house resided. The causes listed were hallucinogenic hysteria and alcohol poisoning. *Witch trials, anyone?*

The '70s were known for LSD and magic mushrooms, granted, and frat parties were the cause of several cases of alcoholic poisoning, but killing seventeen people seemed a bit far-reaching. No matter how hard Ezra dug, he wasn't able to find more specific information; he only encountered roadblocks. The old house got razed to the ground, and a new one was built fifteen years after the event.

Once Duke learned about the old party, nothing Ezra said would deter him from recreating the event. Not the seventeen death's part, only combining Halloween and Columbus Day. Duke threw in Oktoberfest to ensure people knew that there would be plenty of beer.

In Ezra's mind, it was as creepy as people recreating the Titanic. There wasn't anyone alive who didn't know that the unsinkable ship sank and killed most people on board. Sure, seeing a replica of the Titanic would be cool and all, but sailing on it on the exact route that the original had sailed and sunk? No thanks. This party felt a bit like that.

"My girlfriend is going to come dressed as Pocahontas," Duke bragged.

"Maybe some hot female ghosts will show up, and we can poke-a-haunt-us," Blake, a junior majoring in smoking weed, joked while jerking his hips in case the rest didn't get the bad pun.

"Pocahontas was alive about a hundred years *after* Columbus," Ezra pointed out with an eye roll. "That costume isn't even accurate for the era."

"Man," Duke bent forward and patted Ezra's arm. "It's okay to let go for one night and have fun. I promise. I even found a guy who makes homemade brats from scratch that he'll sell me for super cheap. It's perfect and way under budget for our normal parties. He brings all the ingredients with him and makes them right in front of us."

"How'd you find him?" Blake asked.

"Professor Kline," Duke smirked.

"The humanities professor?" Ezra piped up, looking confused. "She's strange."

Duke shrugged. "She hooked me up with a killer deal. Plus, she's kinda hot. I told her to stop by if she was so inclined."

"You invited a professor?" Blake looked astounded. "She could bust us."

"If that were her goal, I don't think Professor Kline would have given Duke the lead on the brat guy," Ezra pointed out with a frown. "Slow down on the smoking trees."

Blake flipped Ezra off and lit a joint, dragging deep. "Maybe you should start."

Chapter 3

twenty-year-old Ezra was a soul of diverse beliefs. His parents raised him to believe in God, though they never pushed any denomination over another. Ezra also believed in worlds unseen, parallel realities, ghosts, and species that others said were nothing more than imagination.

Theoretically speaking, legends, stories, myths all stemmed from somewhere. The universe was far too vast for humans to be the only living species that existed, considering earth was one of the younger planets suspended in that sky above him. Humans are probably the most immature species.

The reason he joined this particular fraternity was the name. The Hulk was one of his favorite Marvel comics when he was a kid, and gamma rays changed him. Psi chi, well, it sounded like psyche. Ezra knew he was a geek and different from his frat brothers, but he didn't let it bother him. He was one of the younger guys in the group, and he often found that they looked to him to be a voice of reason, except in cases of epic parties.

Ezra's job to help prepare was to make sure there were plenty of cups, plates, toilet paper, napkins, and ice. Duke was taking care of all the alcohol, and Blake was in charge of making sure the brat guy had everything he needed, and the rest of the house was to make sure that things were secured and cleaned—for a frat guy, Duke was a neat freak in a house full of slobs.

Ezra sighed and closed his laptop, sliding it into his backpack. He planned to head to the store and pick up the items on his list for the party. He strode out of the lecture room, and his step faltered as the janitor moved right into his path.

"Are you a part of that fraternity that's having the party?"

Ezra looked up at the looming man, a frown on his face. "Excuse me?"

The janitor held up one of the flyers that students passed around. "This. Are you a part of this?" His voice was a low, growling rumble as he held the paper right in front of Ezra's face.

People didn't easily cow Ezra, and he swatted the flyer out of his face. "Obviously, you know I am a member of that house if you are asking me. I didn't see you asking anyone else. And so what if I am? What's it to you?"

The janitor moved a step closer, invading Ezra's space. "You don't know the forces you are dealing with; you'd be wise to cancel these festivities."

Ezra snorted. "I tried, man. They don't listen to me. I'm no one. Take it up with the frat president. I'm the peon, not even legal to drink yet. Also, festivities? It's called a party."

"Listen to your elder, child," the janitor fumed. "I'm trying to save your life."

A chill ran through Ezra as he glared back at the man. "Really? Save it from what?" Ezra snapped, unnerved despite his best efforts.

"The likes of which you have never laid eyes on; things not of this world," the janitor warned and moved faster than Ezra imagined possible, walking away from him down the corridor.

Ezra shrugged the weird encounter off and left the hall, heading to his parked heap of crap to run to the store. The drive passed in a blur as Ezra puzzled over the janitor's warning. The conversation was playing out over and over in his unwilling mind.

It stuck with him even as he wandered up and down the aisles of the party supply store with his cart, grabbing the items he needed. By the time he made it to the checkout line, it had overflowed with everything that could be required.

The cashier gave him a flirty smile as she began to ring up the supplies that Ezra unloaded from the cart. He recognized her from one of his classes and smiled back at her while frantically trying to figure out which class it was they shared.

"Maybe I'll see you there," the cashier, her nametag declaring her name Nelly, told him.

"The chances are good." Ezra winked. "You know since I live there and all."

Nelly hadn't needed to specify the party since it was the talk of many students, and it was evident that Ezra was buying for a party. Theirs was the only one going on that weekend. It was another point that Ezra had brought up to Duke, trying to get him to change it to a weekend when other parties were happening to lessen the chances of them getting busted.

Nelly giggled. "That does give me pretty good odds. Watch for me, and we can have a drink. I'll be wearing a bright pink corset dress."

Ezra moaned. "Are people really going to dress in costume?"

"Well, yeah," Nelly answered. "That's what makes them so fun. Themes are a tradition in frat parties."

"Not themes that celebrate a man who massacred the indigenous people who lived in the territories he landed in," Ezra argued fruitlessly.

Nelly shrugged and pursed her lips. "Maybe, but get in the spirit of it anyway without focusing on that part of it. It's original, combining all these holidays into one party."

Drunken idiots that were celebrating a murderer for a holiday that had spooky undertones. Right? Get into the spirit of that. "Anyway, I'm sure I'll see you and keep a lookout for a bright pink corset dress," Ezra promised as he dug into his pocket for the wad of cash Duke had given him.

"Oh," Nelly exclaimed, taking the cash. "I'll also be wearing a wig the same color as the dress. That should help me stand out. Not exactly in line with the era, but it *is* a costume party."

Ezra loaded the supplies back into his cart with a grin. "I'll definitely be watching for that."

Chapter 4

Crane moved silently through the woods behind the Gamma Psi Chi house. He was searching for signs of the otherlings, as he called them. Those that weren't a part of this world. This ground had become saturated with the history of them being here, doing nefarious things to the unknowing.

Crane himself was an otherling now after surviving the massacre that never made the news because there wasn't television back in those days—it happened right here on this land. Natives had warned him and his friends that the ritual they were doing was dangerous, and much like the groups that came after him, they didn't listen.

Crane had gone along with the plan due to the woman he was courting. Molly Kline was beautiful, well respected, and a teacher. Crane had been nothing more than a quarry worker, yet the lady saw something in him worthwhile and accepted a date with him.

It wasn't until they courted each other for a couple of months that she revealed she was part of a coven, a witch she called herself. They wanted to do a harmless ritual that would allow them to speak to the spirits of the area to see if the industrial growth was harming them.

Crane saw no issues with that, and he didn't believe in ghosts or anything similar to that nature. As he thought back on it now, hindsight allowed him to see how foolish and naïve he used to be in the name of love. Now, look at him, old, withered, and decrepit looking, while Miss Molly Kline looked as if she hadn't aged a day since October 9th, 1871.

The ritual that Molly and her coven, along with some others she never put names to, performed a spell that soaked deep down into the very earth. Sealing the magic with the blood of the fools believing they were attending an elite and illicit secret party dabbling in things they found intriguing and fun in an exciting way. Crane had been one of them; only his blood never shed. Instead, he survived, and the magic bound him to Molly Kline for eternity.

Every fifty years, the scene was recreated, the magic brought back to life, and more sacrifices to keep it alive. Crane tried to stop it each time and failed. This generation, it was only the party in 1971 that anyone remembered.

No one knew of the one in 1921, or the first, where it all began, locking Crane into servitude of the witch he once loved wholeheartedly. They didn't know of the otherlings, creatures that were nothing more than a myth. They only believed in ghosts, and those were bad enough.

The cast of her crew was still alive one hundred and fifty

years later, ready to perform their renewing ceremony once more. What worried Crane was the number of people that were going to show up at the party. Only this time, the innocents weren't so innocent, except maybe the kid he accosted as he came out of the lecture room.

Ezra woke with a start, a nightmare teasing the fringes of his memory. It felt important for him to remember the content, only every time he tried to focus, it slipped away. Ezra reached out and touched the face of his watch to illuminate the screen: 3:23 AM. It was the third time he had woken at this exact time from a nightmare he couldn't remember.

Coincidences happened, though Ezra didn't think this was coincidental. It felt like a warning, only far more sinister than what the old janitor had tried to impress upon him. He was under no illusion he had precognitive abilities; he was just a man-child. At least that's what his father called him.

Ezra slumped back in his bed and did his best to fall asleep. It hadn't worked the previous times, but he managed to nod off for a bit this time.

Ezra took a few cautious steps and looked around the area. Woods that looked familiar were in front of him, and he was standing on a type of clearing, possibly a place where someone was planning to build something. It had been cleared of vegetation mostly, the dirt churned up, and some type of berry vine with thorns, probably blackberries, was poking up through the earth.

He could see the sun setting in the west, and he paused, giving his brain a moment to catch up to his gut. It looked like the frat house's property, only way back in time since no other buildings were around. Weird.

Ezra moved fifteen feet to his left and looked closely at the ground. That was the area that one of his frat brothers had made a garden. He reached down and ran his fingers through the soil before rising again. He turned in a full circle and then decided to head to where the street was or should be.

Instead of a driveway and front yard, it was wheat stalks, but a gravel road existed on the other side of them. What year was it? The entire street, as far as he could see, was undeveloped. Yet back where he was standing had been cleared as if an excavator had ground up the earth.

Lost in thought, Ezra didn't notice the group of horses headed towards him until the hooves hitting the gravel road penetrated his ears. To his utter shock, there were riders, and the person leading the pack was Professor Kline.

The period of dress confused him, and he considered that the rider wasn't Professor Kline but perhaps one of her ancestors that was identical to her. It happened that way sometimes. However, something niggled at the back of his mind, just out of sight.

When Ezra's eyes focused on the person directly behind her, he saw a younger version of the janitor that had come at him after class with the warning. That was no coincidence. What were the odds the two of them had ancestors that looked exactly like them and that the ancestors were together? Ezra was betting those were slim chances.

None of the riders appeared to notice him standing there staring at them, so he made no move to acknowledge them and watched silently as the horses turned and walked through the wheat stalks, stopping near a cluster of trees. The riders dismounted and tied their horses.

Only after the janitor guy flicked his eyes at Ezra with a stern look did Ezra think that somehow the old janitor was behind him having this vision. Too many pieces were missing for him to figure out. So he followed behind the mystery group to see what was going on.

The young version of the old guy hung back out of the way and leaned against a tree with his arms crossed, and watched the Professor Kline look-alike order around the others in the group. Time seemed to jump then, and soon the sky was dark, and numerous people were milling around talking and casting excited looks at what had to be some sort of witchcraft circle.

Black candles were sitting in particular positions, and Ezra could see bags of what looked like herbs and some bells. It wasn't a séance; he didn't think. He wasn't sure what was happening.

Ezra didn't want to walk closer because that look from the janitor dude made him think he could see him. On the chance that others would, Ezra stayed right where he was and tried to make sense of what he was seeing and putting together things he couldn't see or identify with what he knew.

Time moved fast again, and Ezra saw a pale man ruthlessly kissing a woman who wasn't objecting, his arms holding the woman up while she let his mouth travel over her face and neck. Another pale female was doing the same to a man, which seemed highly odd for this time period, which had to be the 1800s or somewhere in there.

The two people receiving the kisses dropped, and Professor Kline began to chant, and all the people outside of that circle moved in closer to get a good look at what was happening. Ezra couldn't see through them, but he did catch sight of two giant wolves on the other side of the circle facing out towards the woods.

What was he witnessing? In the following minutes, bedlam broke out amongst the viewers. He could see mouths moving in horror and screams, but he heard nothing. Something muted the sound. It was just as well since the facial expressions bore panic and terror.

Soon blood was spraying, and no one was able to flee to save themselves. What had to be a group of forty people was quickly reduced to five people, covered in blood with manic smiles spread across their faces, and the two wolves.

Ezra was shocked at the carnage of the bodies scattered everywhere—torn to shreds, insides ripped out, limbs severed, and the earth stained red with the blood soaking into the ground. The lady who Ezra now believed was Professor Kline was tearing flesh from a corpse and making the janitor eat it.

Ezra heaved, his feet finally unfrozen from where they had been, and he ran back towards the gravel road, screaming in his mind to wake up.

Chapter 5

Whoa, why are you here?" Duke barked out in surprise as Ezra walked into the kitchen.

"Yeah, I know." Ezra shrugged sheepishly. "I slept past my alarm. Hey, have you seen that old janitor that cleans the rooms by Professor Kline's class?"

Duke wrinkled his face. "Yeah, some of the assholes call him Ichabod. I think it's kinda mean, but hey, to each their own. Why?"

"He stopped me coming out of class yesterday and was warning me about the party. Told me that lives were in danger. It was eerie. Then I had a dream where I swear, I saw him and Professor Kline together in the 1800s doing some sort of ritual,"

Ezra tried to explain, knowing he sounded crazy.

Duke laughed, throwing his head back. "Oh man, I've had dreams about Professor Kline; she's made for pleasure. Damn, though, she's not old enough to be that old!" Duke chuckled again then waggled his eyebrows. "Maybe she's one of the undead and never ages."

Ezra knew Duke was joking, but there might be some sort of kernel of truth in there. He was more confident than ever that the person in the dream was Professor Kline. Yet, the janitor showed age from that dream to now, so whatever they were, they weren't the same.

Duke moved past the weird dream. "You've never overslept before, have you?"

"No, it feels weird. I already sent my professor an email asking for today's lessons and assignments," Ezra defended himself.

"No judgment, man. I've done it more than once, though I try not to make a habit of it," Duke assured him. "Ready for this weekend?"

Ezra shrugged again, not wanting to voice his apprehension. "It's a party. The cashier at the party store said she was coming and told me to look for her."

Duke raised his eyebrows. "Maybe you'll finally decide it's the time."

Ezra frowned, wishing he'd never mentioned that he was still a virgin in a weak moment of needing to feel like he had a close friend. "Maybe. Regardless, there are other ways of getting pleasure without going balls deep."

"I fully plan on being that deep with my Pocahontas." Duke grinned. "I hear you, though. Do what you got to do, Ezra. Did you find a costume?"

Ezra shook his head. "I didn't even look. Figured I could wear a pair of joggers and find myself an oversized shirt I can cut up and belt it."

"Blake is buying himself a pair of women's leggings," Duke laughed again. "He's gonna find there's no room for his junk in those. He should have planned to do what you are doing. I found a wig that looks like the pictures of Columbus you see in the books. That curly look, you know? And I found a sword."

Ezra rolled his eyes. "Yeah, I'm not taking it that far. Anyway, I'm gonna try to catch someone from the biology class and see if I can copy whatever notes they took. I'll catch up with you later."

"Later, Ezra." Duke moved and bumped shoulders with him before he took off up the stairs towards his room.

Ezra felt unsettled, but he headed for campus and did his best to brush it off and go about business as usual. Though, he found himself looking for the janitor that people called Ichabod. He actively sought the man out and failed at every turn.

Since that endeavor hadn't panned out, Ezra went to the library to start researching the types of rituals he witnessed in the nightmare. He couldn't call it a dream anymore because that was pure crazy bullshit. Maybe Dahmer was a part of Professor Kline's bloodline. Ezra's stomach rolled at the thought of cannibalism.

He found a quiet corner, tossed his backpack on the table, and whipped out his laptop to begin the disturbing search. Ezra lost time, and he dove deep into reading accounts of similar things. When the daylight streaming through the building windows began to fade, he looked up and realized that it was already evening.

Closing his laptop, Ezra cringed and made a note on his scribbled-on notepad to email the rest of his professors and ask for the day's lessons. The research he completed revealed several concerning things that sounded more like a movie plot and left him with more questions than answers.

More research could get done when he returned to the frat house. Mentioning any of this to the guys would land him in a psych evaluation lockdown. So Ezra planned to do the digging in the privacy of his room.

He picked up some tacos from a fast-food restaurant on the way back, nodded hello to the guys in the common room, and went to his, closing the door and locking it behind him. Ezra pulled out his notepad before the laptop and read over the various notes written down. There were multiple options to consider, and not being all that well versed in the occult, he wasn't sure where to start.

The urban legends surrounding this area, the school, and the region were where Ezra started when Duke began talking about the party. He wasn't able to find concrete evidence of anything, in particular, only several stories that read like something one would tell around a campfire to spook people.

Today's search in the library unveiled several things he would need to look further into, but he had no way of knowing if he was on the right track or not. At least not without talking to the janitor guy, which might prove to be pointless if he wasn't in a sharing mood.

Vampires, werewolves, witchcraft, possession, demonology, voodoo, necromancy, ghouls, cannibalism, fairy-folk, and plain old hauntings; those were the things that came up with the keywords he'd searched with earlier. Well, cannibalism was one of the keywords as well. He'd also used wolves, magic, rituals, black candles, bells, and various combinations of those.

It was a lot to digest, and Ezra's mind was spinning

furiously. He tapped his pen against the notepad as he mentally went over the more well-known legends about vampirism and the werewolf curse. Those tales were many, and some vastly different than the mainstream thoughts about creatures of that sort.

Ezra sighed and dropped the pen. Was he seriously considering that vampires and werewolves existed? There was a slight chance that his nightmare was simply a product of an overactive imagination. Yet, if that was the case, why did the janitor deliver his ominous warning? Maybe that encounter spawned the nightmare? Did he genuinely want to travel down this path of thought?

Ezra flopped back onto his pillows and stared at the ceiling. Vampire tales went back centuries, and so did werewolves. Those stories also spanned several faiths and belief cultures. It would take Ezra weeks to sort through all of that, and he only had a few days.

Witchcraft was an authentic thing; Ezra knew that as well. Wicca was a faith, and there were centuries of beliefs and stories linked to spellcraft, magic, and witches. Starting there would take a long time to unravel those mysteries.

However, many stories spoke of witches that never aged because of some sort of spell or ritual performed. Ezra couldn't discount that. But if he were to follow that vein of thought, he would need to bring back in werewolves and vampires since they were well-known for not aging.

Perhaps starting with demonology might be better, or possession, since that kind of went together. Necromancy was in that category too, and it at least gave Ezra a place to start to narrow things down.

Ezra pulled his computer out of the backpack lying near his feet, plugged it in, and made a shortlist of topics to search on and blogs to try and find. Somewhere in the vast knowledge that the internet held was a grain of truth, and he was determined to find it.

Chapter 6

Friday night before the party, Blake unveiled a project he'd worked on all week. Cardboard imitations of Columbus's ships, the Nina, the Pinta, and the Santa Maria. Ezra was a little speechless since those displayed some serious work, and truth be told, they were rather impressive.

Duke was hyped and wouldn't shut up about how this party would be the party that ended all parties. Ezra was a little afraid that it might be the truth. He'd been unable to find the janitor again, and he even stalked the halls at night, watching for any sign of the man.

Thankfully no more nightmares plagued him, though he continued to wake for no reason at 3:23 AM. He wasn't used to sleeplessness. It made him irritable.

Stuffing his face with the pizza that one of the guys had brought home, Ezra patted Blake on the back. "Nice work, man. I'm heading to bed, guys; lack of sleep is dragging me down."

Without waiting for a response, Ezra headed back into the house and up to his room. He didn't bother pulling the blankets off the bed. He just crashed on top and said a silent prayer to the sandman for a solid night of sleep.

When Ezra woke up in the morning, he didn't remember any dreams, though he felt unsettled and assumed that was because the party was today, and he still hadn't figured out what all the warnings meant.

Wiping the sleep from his eyes, Ezra began his daily routine and soon joined the rest of the house downstairs, where everyone was in prep mode. Duke was delegating in a clipped tone, and his frat brothers were scurrying around to get things done.

Ezra saw Duke pointing him to the cups and other items he had picked up at the store, and Ezra nodded his acceptance and set those out along the counter where Duke typically set the hard alcohol. That was how the morning passed, an endless list of chores to prepare for the fun that was to take place later.

Once it was all satisfactory, Ezra went back to his room to enjoy the quiet before chaos settled upon the house. He tried one last search but came up with nothing new. He had learned there were guilds for some of these groups that blocked you from information on the web. That was curious and frightening.

For example, the necromancy site he'd found listed rituals, but only in a series of numbers and sequences that made no sense to Ezra. Demonology he'd been able to dig a little deeper, though he'd stumbled on some arcane references that Ezra dug deeper on and been scared about the things he'd learned with people summoning demons.

Ezra couldn't say that information wasn't out there; he only didn't understand it, which might not be all that bad of a thing, considering. Giving up on the searching, he leaned back on his bed and closed his eyes, wondering if all that research put him on the radar of the government.

The pounding on the door jolted Ezra awake three hours later. His heart racing, he snapped out, "What the fuck is wrong?"

"Get ready, man!" Duke yelled through the door. "People are starting to show up!"

Ezra glanced at his watch and was surprised to see it was

seven. "Okay," he grumbled to the sound of Duke thundering down the stairs. "Stupid costume parties."

Ezra pulled on the makeshift costume he'd thrown together and checked his appearance before heading down to join the others. It wasn't perfect, but almost everyone there would be drunk and probably not remember what he wore anyway.

Drinking wasn't in Ezra's plans, not after that dream and the janitor. The noise level grew louder when he stepped out of his room, and he made his way down the stairs. He shook his head, seeing the costumes that spanned at least three or four centuries, but there were a few that got it right.

Once he neared the kitchen, the smell of cooking meat assaulted his senses. Whatever was grilling smelled nothing like the bratwursts Ezra was used to eating. It prompted the memory of his dream again, and Ezra fought the urge to heave. It didn't look like he would be eating tonight either, not after that thought.

Ezra wandered into the backyard and was surprised to see how many people were already here and in the swing of things. Off to the side near the garden was the guy with the grill. Duke hadn't exaggerated; the guy came with everything. He even had a meat grinder set up next to him. Whatever herbs he was using had a pungent smell that didn't agree with Ezra, but others didn't appear to have the same feeling about it as he did. People were chowing down.

Duke had kegs set up on the corners of the patio, and people were milling around between the cardboard ships. A few had started their version of sword fights with wooden swords and the cardboard ones that Blake had crafted.

Ezra had to hand it to Duke. People were having fun. Not

only that, the number of people had doubled in the five minutes that he'd been down here. Music was playing, though not loud enough to piss off the houses next to them. Maybe they'd get lucky, and the cops wouldn't show up this time. Maybe.

Then Ezra spotted Professor Kline mingling. What struck him absolutely stupid was her costume. It was the exact thing she had worn in the dream he'd had. His feet wouldn't move from where they'd frozen to the ground, his mouth hung open, and his heart thudded painfully against his ribs. It was real.

Chapter 7

ey! Remember me?" Nelly stood in front of Ezra waving her hand in front of his face. "Are you okay?" Her neon pink wig wasn't complimenting her complexion. It gave her skin a waxy appearance. The dress, however, fit her nicely and gave Ezra a moment of pause as he appreciated the sight.

"Hey, Nelly. Of course, I remember you," Ezra tried to smile. He was watching her devour the brat she was holding. His stomach rolled again. "You look great."

"Can you believe Professor Kline is here? Mind-blowing that she would come to a frat party," Nelly giggled, halfway drunk already. "Her costume is killer, though."

A chill raced up Ezra's back. "Not period-accurate, but it looks cool," he agreed to make Nelly happy.

"Phew! It's hot in here," Nelly fanned her face dramatically. "Why aren't you drinking?"

Ezra held up the plastic cup that held only soda. "I am. You know you are outside, right?"

Nelly giggled again. "Oh, yeah. Those boats are wicked."

"Blake did a great job on those. I didn't even know he could do that," Ezra nodded, watching Nelly's face. Something didn't seem right.

Ezra didn't even excuse himself from the conversation with Nelly. He just left and casually walked to the edge of the woods and turned to face the party, like nothing was wrong. That was when he caught sight of someone creeping through the woods.

Ezra glanced at the grill master brat guy and visibly started. He recognized that face from the dream, too. The blood-covered apron was a bit much, but he seemed to be in his element and was chatting with each person he handed food to, smiling. What was happening?

"Don't move," a low voice behind Ezra said into his ear. "Don't acknowledge I'm here. No one can see me with you."

Ezra moved and leaned against the tree, still facing the party. Nelly had moved on from his absence and draped herself over some burly-looking guy who was guzzling beer and shoving brats in his face as quickly as he could, like it was a contest.

"Why?" Ezra asked softly.

"Don't eat or drink anything." The voice that Ezra identified as the janitor he had been seeking forwarned him again.

"Wasn't planning on it," Ezra confirmed.

"Only this, drink this." A cup appeared in front of him. "It will protect you from the effects."

Ezra frowned but took the drink and smelled it. "What is this?"

"The only thing that will keep you alive," the janitor growled. "I can't make you trust me, but I saw you searching. You know something is wrong. You saw the first party that was here."

"How can you be here?" Ezra almost turned to face the man.

"I'm not human anymore. Follow me," the janitor commanded him.

Ezra heard faint receding footsteps and glanced over his shoulder to see the old man walking deeper into the patch of forest. Wanting more answers, Ezra followed. Worry for his safety should have crossed his mind, but it didn't because he believed the old man didn't mean any harm even though he was certainly creepy enough.

Finally, the old janitor stopped and turned to face Ezra. "What do you see?" The janitor was pointing down to the ground.

"What's your name?" Ezra asked, pointedly not looking down yet. He could at least be civil and not barking at him.

"Call me Crane," the janitor answered. "Now tell me. What do you see?"

It was dark enough where they were that his vision wasn't as straightforward as it should be yet. It was still adjusting to the darkness. Yet Ezra was able to spot a pile of bones with flesh still hanging off of them. He involuntarily took a step backward and paused, not quite believing it.

"Are those human?" Ezra whispered, afraid of the answer.

"They are," Crane confirmed.

Immediately the vision of the two giant wolves popped into his head. "Did a wolf kill someone?"

"No. Those wolves are drinking with your friends," Crane sneered. "Think, boy!"

"Think about what?" Ezra lashed out. "All I get is warnings, fucked up dreams, and puzzle pieces but no real direction for me to follow. What's with the cryptic bullshit?"

"Drink that!" Crane snapped, ignoring Ezra's outburst.

"Please," he added as an afterthought.

Ezra hesitated and smelled the drink again. If it would get him answers, he was willing to drink the concoction. Ezra truly believed the man called Crane wasn't out to hurt him. He'd had plenty of opportunities so far. Ezra slammed back the drink.

"Happy now? How about those answers?" Ezra challenged Crane.

"I'm an otherling," Crane snarled out in a furious whisper. "All those people you saw in that vision of the past are too—nothing you can do to stop what's about to happen. The magic is already at work, you little fool. I tried to warn you."

Ezra blinked in surprise. "What the hell is an otherling?"

"Not human. Something other. I don't know what to call the beasts, so I use that term. Molly has me trapped, my soul bound to hers until she releases me. Some dark magic at work here, child. It wears thin every fifty years, and the ceremony has to get repeated. But she's twisted, that woman," Crane spit out with venom.

Ezra did some quick math that put his vision at 1871. "So this is the fourth time?"

Crane shrugged helplessly. "The fourth time I've been a part of at least."

The horror of that statement settled on Ezra's mind. "What is she?"

"Otherling. She has death magic," Crane whispered. "For fun, Molly plants ideas of a Columbus Day party in the minds of youth. She calls the spirits forth of Columbus and the crew he took with him on raids on lands and offered up the youth as sacrifices to appease the dark spirits she uses for her deeds."

"What the fuck?" Ezra muttered, trying to piece it together. "Death magic? Is she a demon?"

Crane shook his head. "Maybe she has the heart of a demon, but she is not a demon."

"Necromancer?" Ezra's eyes widened as the implications began to sink into his bones.

Crane cocked his head to the side and shrugged. "When I knew her, Molly was a school teacher with a sweet smile and lips that tasted like sin. I never knew that term until more recently, as the people of today are far more interested in these dark arts than they were in my time. Necromancer is as good of a term as otherling."

"Columbus," Ezra muttered insanely. "What did you mean the magic is already at work? Are those bones from someone here? Where's the rest of the body? I should call the cops." Ezra patted his pockets for his phone only to realize with dismay that it remained in his room. "How did she extend your life this long? She looks young, yet you have aged. Am I going to be the virgin sacrifice?" Ezra continued to fire off questions.

"Molly made me eat the cursed flesh," Crane declared sadly. "It did something to me."

Ezra's head swam. Whether it was from the information drop or whatever he drank, he wasn't sure. His knees wobbled, and he dropped to the ground.

Chapter 8

When Ezra opened his eyes, Crane was gone, and he lay with a pile of bones that might have once belonged to someone he knew. The thought made him sick. He pushed himself to his feet, needing to get away from the sight.

The smell of burning flesh hit him as he moved closer to the party, and he halted in his tracks. Ezra hadn't thought incorrectly in those initial thoughts he had about the brats being wrong. The blood on the apron, the meat grinder, the odd smell.

"Oh god," Ezra groaned and bent over at his waist. He didn't want to puke in case whatever was in that drink that Crane made him drink really would keep him alive. "People are eating a person or persons. Cursed meat." The whisper was barely loud enough for Ezra to hear it.

If Crane was correct, history was about to repeat itself. Ezra witnessed the horrific scene in the dream, add in the party that was a school legend, and whatever other times it had happened other than those two.

The sound of giggling made Ezra straighten up in time to see a bright pink dress get shredded as the gown was torn right off Nelly's body. She appeared in a trance, under the spell of the guy running his hands up and down her body.

Ezra turned his head, not wanting to see Nelly and the stranger going at it. The groans were enough to let him know what was happening. Fascinated horror had him peek and saw the guy sink his teeth into Nelly's neck while she rode him with no shame.

Fuck. There's a real vampire here. That means there is a female one wandering around too. Ezra kept his mouth closed, but he was powerless to stop the thoughts.

Ezra's thoughts quickly scrambled as he tried to remember what happened next in the dream. Wait, how long had he been in the woods? He could still hear music going, people laughing and talking, the fevered groans coming from Nelly. *Didn't the professor have to make a circle?*

He shook it off and boldly began to walk back to the

house. Maybe there was a possibility he could save a few people from whatever fate was about to take them from this plane of existence, despite what Crane said.

The closer he got to the backyard, the air felt thicker and had a current to it that buzzed along his skin like electricity. Something scratched at his arm as he moved, and he paused to look down and see a thin line of blood beading up.

"You look cute," a perky female voice said, making him raise his head.

Ezra fought the urge he had to wrap his arms around the female. "Not interested," he managed to get out.

"That says otherwise," she pointed to his hardening crotch. Her voice was like velvet. Sensuous and husky.

"My dick lies." Ezra forced the words from his lips, his mind feeling like it wasn't his. Everything in his body told him to go to the woman. The beautiful lady only needed him.

The only thing that broke that compulsion was a drunk guy stumbling up, his skin the same waxy tone Nelly's was. Ezra moved away from them both when the poor sucker started stripping off his clothes with superhuman speed.

When the backyard came into view, Ezra stopped and took in the scene. The man grilling was closing his station up. Professor Kline was in the center of a circle of drunk and dancing idiots. Their skin was all the same wax-like appearance, their eyes dilated, and utterly unaware of anything. Guess Professor Kline had her circle prepared.

The only people noticing Ezra were the ones that showed up in the dream vision Crane shared with him. The fact that his skin was normal and he wasn't a part of whatever Professor Kline had going on caught their attention.

Seven people started to move in Ezra's direction, and he

didn't have the slightest clue on how to ward them off or protect himself. The only thing that popped into his head was to try and wake these people up, and he dove for the hose that lay not too far from him.

Ezra landed hard on his elbows, rolled, and snatched up the hose, praying that the water was on. It typically was during these parties as a preventative measure against fire, because you know, drunk idiots. He squeezed the nozzle as hard as he could and sprayed the hose into the crowd with reckless abandon.

Not even a flinch from one person as they got doused with icy cold water—nothing. And the people were still after him. A hose certainly wasn't a good defense, and panic began to lace Ezra's thoughts.

It was then that under the sound of the music, Ezra heard chanting. His head swiveled between Professor Kline and the advancing otherling people. He wasn't sure which was more dangerous.

Chapter 9

The air began to look like a shimmering pool of water, undulating in time with the bodies surrounding Professor Kline. Something was happening beyond his pathetic understanding.

What felt like an invisible hand belonging to the Hulk slammed into his body. Ezra flew backward, his back crashing into the house's siding and his feet sliding out from under him as he sunk to the ground.

Ezra's head was ringing. No, wait, that was the sound of bells, not his ears. For some reason, many tinkling bells paused the otherling creatures from whatever nightmare they had planned for Ezra. As one, they turned toward Professor Kline.

The music in the house died, and with the last of the tinny sound fading, the air pulsed. Ezra's skin crawled, and his feet scrambled to find purchase to escape whatever the hell that was. Everybody in that circle, and there had to be at least sixty, stopped moving at once.

"The waxing crescent moon calls to you," Professor Kline drawled out. "Give yourselves freely to my friends." Her arms rose in the air.

It was as if the crowd were puppets on a string. Heads tipped back in supplication to the moon, arms rose, reaching for the waxing crescent moon. A man carrying Nelly crossed the yard, deposited her in front of Professor Kline, and likewise, the woman who had been trying to seduce Ezra did the same with the man who had stripped.

Dark wisps rose from the ground like stained fog and hovered in front of some crowd members. A quiet laugh filled the sky, the voice menacing and promising pain. Ezra couldn't move.

There was no line of sight to what was happening in the circle, but the gurgling sound gave him a good idea that Nelly was no longer alive, or possibly, human. A coppery scent filled the air that still bore the smell of burnt flesh, nauseating Ezra.

At least the virgin sacrifice wasn't me, Ezra thought guiltily. *Though I can't say my chances of surviving this are any better.* Dark humor, but it was the only thing keeping him sane—barely.

The black masses began to writhe and sank into the bodies they claimed. There was a flicker of something across the faces of those people like they knew what was happening was awful and couldn't stop it—a last conscious thought.

"Ah, Christopher, my dear friend. I have brought you to a

new place with a new tribe that needs conquering. Please, claim this land." Professor Kline spoke with a friendly, sweet tone as if she were delivering a gift to a child. Only Columbus wasn't a child or even alive. He was a mass murderer ghost.

To Ezra's horror, Duke stepped out of the crowd, his eyes blank and skin the color of parchment paper. He spoke no words, simply nodded at Professor Kline. Duke grabbed his girlfriend by the neck and dragged her five feet, crushing her windpipe before dropping her. The sword he had found to go with his costume appeared, and he violently stabbed down into the prone form, killing her instantly.

Ezra was going to be sick. That first death sparked a melee; only this time, no one screamed as opposed to the dream. Either someone magically silenced their voices, or Ezra's ears went on mute. That couldn't be right. He could hear the death gasps, blood dripping, flesh-ripping, and bones breaking.

There was nothing Ezra could do to avoid the spray of blood. He couldn't look away, move, speak, or try to help. It felt like the earth was holding him in place, making him bear witness to the massacre of his friends; *by* his friends.

Two giant wolves joined the fray, though they performed no killing. No, this was their dinner, and they feasted. Crane was nowhere in sight, though he had to be somewhere nearby if he was bound to Professor Kline.

Ezra's mind was shattering at the massacre taking place in front of his eyes. Piece by piece, it fractured apart with each limb torn from a body, broken apart with each life that stamped its loss on his soul.

Tears slid unchecked down Ezra's cheeks as he couldn't move to wipe them away. His tumble into insanity was slow, painful, and an unstoppable descent. He no longer cared for his safety because he would have rather died with everyone else than to sit there and helplessly watch their violent ends.

The last straw came with disgust after the final person succumbed to their fate. Professor Kline and her crew of otherlings ripped the hearts out of each person. They shared a bite before moving on to the next. She was eating their lives, using them to extend her own.

At last, Ezra was able to close his eyes. He welcomed the dark, quiet recesses of his mind that took him to a place where he wouldn't remember this. He couldn't; no one would believe him. No one would ever know the truth—no human, anyway. With his eyes shut, Ezra never noticed that his digital watch froze at exactly 3:23 AM.

Epilogue

The shades are drawn in a dilapidated living room, the darkness lurking in all corners, and a TV blared. In front of the TV sat an old man, his hair white and shaggy, his shoulders frail-looking. He sat on an ottoman that had seen better centuries than the one it currently occupied. The man was hunched forward, his head in his hands, his shoulders shaking uncontrollably while the reporters talked.

Breaking news on a local college campus, a block from the well-known frat row. It appears as if history is repeating itself, leaving a community devastated. In a scene straight from a horror story, our investigative reporter brings us news from this gruesome scene. Grace, have you found out what happened there?

Scott, I am standing in a scene that defies your worst

nightmare. *More than sixty people are dead in a mass murder more horrendous than you can imagine. Police are tight-lipped about what happened here, and in my opinion, they don't know. Words are hard for me to come by at the moment, so please forgive my rambling.*

I have learned that there is a lone survivor that the police are calling a person of interest. The young man was found alive, covered in blood with no apparent injuries and weapons all around him. As I speak, the crime scene units are still cataloging the scene and working on identifying the victims.

From the whisperings I have picked up, not all of the bodies are in one piece. I overheard one officer calling it carnage. If that doesn't paint a picture for you, I don't know what will. In all my years of experience, I have never seen the first responders so sickened and scared at the same time.

What I will say next is not fit for all viewers and has not been confirmed by anyone in an official capacity. A medical examiner rushed from the scene earlier, mumbling about victims having human remains in their stomachs.

Crane reached forward and shut the TV off. He knew what happened. Crane had seen every last bit of it, right up to the point Ezra was found unconscious and alive in a sea of blood and body parts. He watched from the recesses of the forest as the police escorted the young man to an aid car for care as it was evident he was in shock. Ezra was no longer present, though he drew breath.

Crane's shoulders shook again as insane laughter bubbled from his lips. He'd thought this time would be different, that Ezra would heed the warning no one else would. Crane had hoped for the first time in a long time, only to have Molly thwart him again. She would never willingly release him.

Crane's laughter wasn't in jest; he was no longer capable of tears.

november

Silver Harness

J.W. Capek

The abandoned fairgrounds traded its shadows for the daybreak mists. From his third story apartment window, Phillip could see the track just beyond the residence shrubbery. He could remember the sounds of the dirt raceway even on this late fall Morning: The hum of crowds of excited people, announcers calling races, artificial trumpets, and most of all the pounding of hooves as the sulkies raced. Pounding. Pounding. Pounding.

Being gobbled up by developers, acreage had already been turned into medical buildings, assorted businesses, and senior residences. Parking blacktop covered the former placement of colored tents and boisterous fairgoers. Only the dirt racetrack and bleachers awaited the highest real estate bidders. The dilapidated buildings lingered beside a remaining forest wood with autumn leaves. Soon, it too would fall to the bulldozers and construction. Not silently.

The sport of Harness racing, like the fairgrounds, was in the throes of dying: The drop in betting income, the rising costs of maintaining horses, and a social change in attitude towards horse racing all contributed. The white haired man at the window had witnessed it all.

Phillip was a tenant of Billy Dale Senior Residence and Rehabilitation Services. After a life of loving horses, he was relegated to gazing out his window with a re-built hip, physical therapy, rehab, a walker, and a pacemaker. The tinnitus in his hearing was dampened by the racing hooves. He could feel the anticipation of a Race Day in his memory, contrasting with the empty dirt track now shouldered to the Residence outside wall.

By late afternoon, in the Residence Recreation Room, Phillip sat at his computer station fingering little plastic horses. He had brought his own gaming accessories when admitted to the Rehab care facility. His computer station dominated the other computers on a nearby table, and the other residents avoided interactions with it. It was part respect and part awe of the desktop tower with its colored lights, console, and large monitor.

"Hey there," a voice said gently, "that's quite a stable of horses you have there." An older man stood next to the table with a prominent "Volunteer Jack" badge on a lanyard.

"That's a stupid remark." Phillip said gruffly. He didn't like being interrupted when he was thinking. The lines in his face deepened with his annoyance as he began working with the deluxe gaming console. He reached for the head phones that would eliminate the man's talking.

"Then what are they?" the man pursued in a condescending tone, returning attention to the tiny horses.

Phillip looked at the volunteer and saw a man near his own age who was probably another of those do-gooders who came to the Residence to take care of the ol' folk who had dementia. Sarcastically, Phillip said, "They're plastic markers for my international MMO digital game played on the Internet which I designed and sold to a gaming company for three million dollars!"

Not offended by the brusque tone, the volunteer laughed. "I have some plastic gnome markers at home for my international MMORPG digital game on the internet which I designed and sold to a company for five million dollars!" He sat down in the vacant chair next to the table and looked Phillip in the eye. He held that look with a twinkle until Phillip's face softened and he almost grinned back.

Holding out his hand, the man said, "I'm Jonathon, but you can call me Jack. Glad to meet you, Phillip of the international digital gaming set."

Phillip hesitated. The man called him by name. Jack had called his bluff, had a friendly face, and held his hand out to shake like a man, not one of those sissy fist bumps or elbow rubs. Still not grinning, Phillip set the headphones down and shook the offered hand. "And I'm Phillip, but you can call me Phillip. I have royalties every month," he stated matter-of-factly as he casually rubbed the old scar under his chin. He returned his eyes to the curved monitor of his personal station. His fingers played the buttons on the mouse and his attention never wavered. He was dismissing the man with the volunteer badge.

"I have my game coming out next month as a graphic novel," Jack said proudly. Not to be ignored, he bent in towards Phillip. The boast broke into Phillip's focus.

"My hardcover game novel will be released in the spring," Phillip said even more proudly. He leaned forward in his chair and stared directly at the man named Jack.

"My game will be serialized in a television series next month." This was becoming serious fun for both men who could have been arm wrestling with their bragging. Their eyes never wavered.

"My game is being produced as an epic Spielberg motion

picture." Phillip was reaching for the finish line.

"My game... my... Oh, never mind. You win!" Jack held up his hands in submission as he laughed.

Phillip could hear the crowd in the stands cheering. Even trumpets sounded as he eased back in his chair, relaxed, and finally let a slight grin escape. He decided to let this man interrupt his thoughts and he gathered his horses into their little plastic bag. He could use them another day.

Twice a week, Jack would spend the afternoon with Phillip. They had both worked as Information Technicians. Both were widowers. As Phillip's hip needed exercise, the two men would walk the deserted track and Phillip would tell stories about his passion for Harness racing. He was surprised at his ease in talking with Jack. Maybe it was just because Jack listened.

"I loved horses for as long as I can remember. Kind of a... what do they call such kids now... a nerd? Horses and computers," Phillip offered, shaking his head. "At least the tech work paid for the horses."

"Did you actually race the horses?" Jack asked.

"Naw. I'm too big for a driver in races. I did my share of training though. For a while I owned one. My mid-life crisis. Other guys bought expensive sport cars or played around. I bought a horse." He added, "They say the best two days to own a horse is the day you buy it and the day you sell it." He chuckled.

"I thought that was said about boats," Jack corrected.

Phillip nodded. "Unfortunately, it could be said for both!"

"What about your wife?"

"Ella loved 'em too. That's how we met. Her father had a trotter and she helped with the training. Sometimes she was a driver as well. Hanging out with her meant being around the horses. The horses brought me to the track, but Ella kept me there. When you clean stables with a woman, you get to know the real person." For a moment, he could remember her smudged face with straw in her hair. "She's gone now." Phillip's smile dimmed as he moved the walker forward. Jack had put oversize tennis balls on the walker feet so they wouldn't sink in the soft track dirt.

"Any kids?" Jack asked noticing the distant look in Phillip's eye.

"What?" Phillip questioned.

"Kids, did you and Ella have any kids?"

"Who?"

"You and Ella." As a trained volunteer, Jack knew there was sometimes confusion for the residents, but he didn't expect it from Phillip. They were only a few years apart in age. The two teased each other about who was "an old man." Phillip was quick with remarks and jokes and was only at the Residence to rehabilitate his hip. Jack paused to watch his new friend's hesitation.

Standing there in the old track, Phillip heard the pounding hooves. They were louder now than in his apartment. Nervously he turned his walker back towards the resident building. "I gotta get better," he murmured to himself, shaking his head and determinedly shoving the walker ahead. Today's walk was over.

Jack's schedule of only two days a week left Phillip restless. He pushed himself to the limits allowed by Milton during the physical therapy sessions. Milton had retired after his Afghanistan deployment as a medic and was working to get his kids through college. Phillip was a favorite client for the Therapist because he worked so hard to improve.

On Jack's next visit, he observed Phillip was now striding behind the walker hardly putting any pressure on it. "For a computer jockey who can only play games with toy horses, you are looking pretty fit, Gramps," Jack joked.

"I'm not a Gramps!" Phillip snapped back. "My horses are AI and can run the fairground track faster than you can say 'Update!'" Phillip retorted as he led the way beyond the Residence, through a short path to the end of the abandoned track. The fence had been removed for resident's access.

The track was moist from the weather changes. "Winter is definitely on the way. We may not take walks here much longer," Jack said. He looked over at the woods where trees were now bare of leaves.

"I suppose you'll be going south like some snowbird, too wimpy for a brisk mid-west day," Phillip ridiculed but never stopped striding while Jack matched his pace.

"Oh, don't give me that crap about driving trotters through the snow so high you could only see their ears above the drifts. I know the harness racing circuit moves south for the winter," Jack responded and laughed but then, abruptly, he saw Phillip stop.

Holding the walker, Phillip stood tensely. He didn't move but tilted his head as if listening to something. Jack turned his head, then his whole body but could hear nothing other than some distant sounds of traffic. "What is it? What...?" Jack questioned.

"Shut up! Listen. Old Man! One of the trotters has broken the pace." Phillip gripped the walker, and stood for long seconds, listening attentively. "Hear the difference? The horse started to gallop and the driver has to slow it down. He had to move to the inside, to run on the pegs until it resumes its pace."

"Pegs?" Jack asked.

"The inside rail," Phillip explained still listening intently.

Finally, the rhythm changed to the desired trotting. The hobble straps on the horse's legs encouraged the timing, he thought. Phillip relaxed slightly and rubbed his hand over his forehead "It's okay now, he's back, but the others have passed him. He's out of the race," he murmured mostly to himself. The energy disappeared from his step as he began shuffling back to home. He didn't raise his eyes, he was too absorbed on missing any pot holes as he walked. The track hadn't been groomed since the season closed.

As they walked, Phillip kept thinking about the break in pace. *Maybe it was a young horse, or an inexperienced driver.* At the porch entrance to the Building, Phillip looked sadly at his companion. "Some horses just can't stay the pace in the turns. They just can't finish the race with the others." With a sigh, he dragged his feet over the threshold to go into dinner.

The next volunteer day, Jack paused to talk with Milton in the entrance archway dividing the Residence into two distinct sections. Jack had caught Milton as he was exiting the REHAB side and going towards the MEMORY doors.

One set of doors with a sign MEMORY CARE listed staff names, service locations, and an admonition to check in at the admittance desk. The opposite doors said REHAB and listed other staff, service locations and a direction to sign in at the desk before visiting the activity rooms. Elevators were centrally located to give access to the residential quarters upstairs.

"Milton, a quick question. How do you divide people into these sections?" He gestured to the signs.

"It's all doctor directed. The medical diagnosis comes with them, we just follow orders."

"I've seen you moving back and forth, do you work both wings?"

"Yeah, I'm certified for both, Memory Care or just Rehab."

"Like Phillip?"

"I can't talk about individual clients," he winked at Jack, "but we have number of older people without family or anyone to take care of them while they recuperate. Some get well faster and go home, or assisted living, others stay for a while to get rehabilitated. We once had an older lady coming in who was terrified because she thought she was being condemned to an old folks' home. She thought she wasn't wanted anymore. Her fall injuries were severe, she needed rehabilitation but was frightened. Her son told her, 'Look Mom, there are two sides here and you are going to Re-hab. When you're recovered enough, we'll take you home again.' That was enough, she worked very hard to get on her feet again." Milton smiled at the success story. So did Jack.

"Thanks, most of my time has been spent on the rehabilitation wing. I'll let you go." Jack watched Milton as he swung whistling through the doors to the other wing while he entered Rehab where Phillip was in the REC room.

"Did you really create this game?" Jack asked suspiciously as he came upon the gaming station. Phillip was so intent on the monitor he was surprised when Jack touched his shoulder.

"What? Oh, Jack" he said, relieved. "What did you say?"

"I asked if you really invented this game that put you into another universe."

" Oh—I was IT for the County Fair for years. Office work, scheduling, maintaining the electronics. My early love of horses always brought me to the stables during off times. That's where I met my wife…."

"Ella." Jack interrupted but Phillip just went on talking.

"…and learned about harness racing. It fascinated me. So

one day, I turned my hobby into a game, sold it, and retired!"

"Information Tech? Me too, but my hobby never inspired me to create a game."

"What was it?" Phillip asked, now interested. "The hobby, I mean."

"Nothing."

"Look, if you don't want me to know…?"

"Nothing! Doing nothing was what I liked best and never could think of a game for it." The twinkle in Jack's eye was a tell. "Come on, it's too rainy outside to walk, show me your game. Were you a big gambler at the track?"

"No, never had much use for gambling," Phillip boasted. "Gambling put the pressure on the money and the risks. I loved the horses, working with them, training. The kids who race with me on the internet game always bet to win but I've got more points than any of them!"

"You developed the game! Don't you think you're taking advantage of them? They're just kids," Jack chided.

"Nope! I'm teaching them! Never bet more than you can afford to lose. And the players are more than kids! The company that bought me out added my game as a sub platform to their major racing collection. A lot of the players use the game to fill in days when their favorite track is closed." Phillip's eyes moved to the window and he called out, "Rain shower's over, let's walk so I can show off to Milton."

"The track's a mudhole, why don't you play your game instead, I'd like to judge if it's as good as you boast." He moved a chair closer to the station.

In the sulky race on the computer, the drivers were all young, mostly men but women too. It was a mixed-sex sport and both men and women could qualify if they were over sixteen. One young driver seemed to stand out with his bright smile, black silks and Number Seven. A pretty young woman in turquoise silks accompanied him and posed for pictures while petting the horses. The game included fans in the stands and Phillip chose Seven for his driver. There was a lot of pre-race activity and the audio announced races and numerous types of bets. The horses with their light-weight racing sulkies lined up behind the starting gate of the mobile barrier. The vehicle with the hinged gates started a slow steady drive around the dirt track as the drivers guided their horses into the starting position. Stop motion graphics gave a realistic feeling of the track and characters in the video. The pace established, the gates swung open, and the race began! Horses surged around the starter car as drivers juggled for places. Jack was surprised at the sound effects and quick camera angles. He forgot he was watching a computer game except for Phillip's quick maneuvering on his console. Rounding the last curve, the competition was between Number Seven and Number Three. The horses were racing each other but controlled by their drivers. Animated muscles reflected the equestrian energy being expended. Long equine noses reached out and pulled back in rhythm. The crowd in the stadium was screaming, the hooves were pounding! Number Seven won by a nose! The crowd went wild and Jack and Phillip joined in the cheering. Until.…

They were met with complete silence by the rest of the occupants of the game room. Jack looked around and realized they had been the only ones excited by the little sulky race on the computer monitor. Everyone else was quietly playing chess or pinocle. Milton was standing in the corner watching them while trying to contain his laughter. The rest of the crowd just stared at the two grown men who had raced horses in a residence game room.

A bit embarrassed, Jack coaxed Phillip to shut down the computer and follow him. "You're right, the rain has ended. Let's walk around the parking lot to stay out of the mud."

The two friends walked silently. The exercise was therapy but the blacktop was not as friendly as the track. Phillip kept pausing to listen but heard nothing. As they rounded one parking bay, Phillip turned to go to the woods.

"Where are you going?" Jack asked.

"Home!" Phillip said firmly. "It's almost time for dinner. My wife hates it when I'm late." He continued walking until Jack caught up and touched his arm.

"This way," Jack coaxed with a nod back to The Residence. He repressed his question about 'the wife.'

Phillip turned with a surprised expression. He looked at the Residence with confusion. "I live there?" Then, nervously he shook his head and looked away. "Oh well... um... I was just thinking of the woods... back home" he mumbled to cover his mistake.

Thanksgiving Day, the Residence parking lot was filled with volunteers and family members pulling food stuffs out of their trunks and cars. Everyone was in a good mood bringing contributions to the food fest being prepared for the Residents: Turkey and dressing, ethnic selections, specialty foods for special diets, colorful decorations, forbidden desserts.

Jack had a box of bakery fresh breads and was carrying them to the entrance when he saw a young woman hesitating at the main door. She watched the people going into the foyer but held back. She appeared to be searching faces. Dressed rather strangely for the upcoming holiday, she looked like a groom or someone in Phillip's game. There was something vaguely familiar in her clothing.

"Hello, can I help you? Are you looking for someone?" Jack asked.

"Oh, no... I was just wondering." She rubbed her hand nervously on the sleeve of her turquoise shirt and seemed ready to run away.

"The staff inside can help you," Jack offered, as he juggled his box of breads.

"No, don't bother anybody." Her face changed to puzzlement as she looked over the facade of the front entrance. She questioned, "Has this building been here long? I thought this was all part of the fairgrounds."

"All this area is being developed. The racetrack and bleachers are the last to go." Jack saw the disappointment in her face.

"And the stables, are they all gone?" A sadness in her voice reflected her forlorn expression.

"Gone, just like the horses and people," Jack admitted quietly. "Please, come in, you can talk to people inside." He held one hand out to her while shifting the box to his hip.

"No, no, my boots are dirty, and I'm not sure what I could ask them." Again, her eyes rapidly viewed the façade. Her expression changed to consternation when she saw the complete signage, 'The Billy Dale Residence and Rehabilitation Services.' She asked, "Is that true? Is that the name of this building?"

"Well, yes. I've been told Billy was the all time winner at this track. He was kind of a local hero, I guess. People got it named after him once the County sold the land parcels and developing started."

"Is he here now?" Her tight lips barely allowed the question.

"Oh no!" Jack answered while wondering at her interest. "I heard he survived a terrible wreck, then Billy went into a slow decline and suffered serious memory loss in his later years. He died in poverty. I think that's why this Residence was named for him."

The young woman became visibly distraught. She was on the verge of tears and quickly turned away to move off the portico and to the car loading zone. Jack looked down to adjust the box in his hands. When he looked up, she was gone.

In the evening, the guests and volunteers had all left, the residents were back in their apartments, and the halls were quiet. Phillip stood at his window staring at the race track. The pounding of the horses never seemed to stop now. Memories faded in and out as he tried to focus. Yes, the horses were trotting at top speed, at the final quarter mile. In a fraction of a second, the course was broken when one horse in the pack seemed to trip. It went down with a flurry of legs, the sulky flipping over the horse. Following sulkies slammed into the collision, drivers were trampled over, and shattered carts heaped upon each other. One horse without a sulky or driver followed the leader and raced to the end. Officials ran onto the field, the crowd groaned. Cameras snapped and replayed the calamity. One driver was up and holding the railing, the rest were retrieved or walked around dazed. An emergency vehicle pulled onto the track and its siren was louder than the pounding hooves had been. From his vantage point, Phillip could see into the middle of the melee. One driver in turquoise silks covered in mud was not moving.. Abruptly, the siren, the pounding, and horses screaming all stopped! Phillip was breathing rapidly, his fists trembled but his body was rigid. His heart beat against the inside of his chest and he grabbed the window sill. He remembered! He remembered it all!

Ella had been excited to be driving in a race with Billy Dale. It was a dream of her career, a two-minute flash of competing with the best. It was the final turn when the forward horse went down. Ella was caught in the middle of flailing horses and carts. The chaos was a bedlam of horses, and humans, and spinning wheels. While drivers were moving through the debris or gathering the reins of horse, Ella lay motionless: emergency technicians hurried to place her on a stretcher. She did not move when lifted into the ambulance. She did not respond as the vehicle sped away from the mayhem. Ella did not survive the ride to the hospital. Phillip became a shadow of himself, retreating more and more to the solitude of his computer game.

This night, the aching old man turned away from the sight in his mind. Phillip's legs gave way and he slid down the wall. Crouched down, he wrapped his arms about his knees, and began to rock gently. He was wailing as he had never sobbed before. He had been there. He had watched. He had forgotten. He remembered now.

Answering the tense morning call after the holiday, Jack rushed to the Residence to meet Milton waiting for him at the entrance. "What is it? What's happened?" he asked anxiously at the look on Milton's face.

"It's Phillip, we can't find him anywhere!"

"Since when?"

"Our early morning bed check. He was there last night after dinner but when the Breakfast call was made, he never appeared."

"His room?" Jack's own tension was rising. Milton was always so calm around the residents but now his anxiety was catching.

"Of course, we checked his room!" Milton said nervously. "His walker was there next to the bed. We inspected the rest room. The library. The game room where his Harness racing game was on the monitor. The rehab room. . ."

"Did you check outside?" Jack started to grasp at straws.

"All the doors were checked for safety, like every night." Before Jack could ask, Milton said, "And yes, we've already called the sheriff and a team is on the way."

Jack looked over his shoulder at the track in the distance. The end of November had brought an overnight dusting of snow to the abandoned Fair grounds. There were footprints, probably Milton's, going around the building perimeter as he had scrutinized doors and windows. A light snow flurry promised a winter snow as the day grew later and Jack needed to do something! He pulled his jacket and scarf tighter and started walking around the residence calling Phillip's name.

The snow was beginning to fall in larger flakes and Jack's anxiety was growing. At the corner he saw another set of footprints leading towards the track. They had been partly obscured by early flakes and were now filling in more quickly. Jack had never thought of himself as a great tracker but now he started towards the raceway in the gentle flakes. He kept calling "Hey, Phillip, it's me. Where are you, guy? Answer me, ol'man!"

The tracks under the flakes led to the downed fence and onto the track. There was a stumble marked by mixed snow and dirt. The marks showed where knees had landed and hands, then feet shuffled up and continued down the center. At the midpoint, Jack was confused by the number of hoof prints rounding the curve and churning the turf. Soon, they would be obscured by the snow but now they were defined by it. They had better find Phillip soon, it was getting colder, the snow thicker. He continued on the track where the trampled ground caught up to the footprints. At that junction, the footprints disappeared. Meshed into the hoof tracks, gradually being covered by snow, a few strides further and all traces of the man's footsteps disappeared. The prints of the hooves continued a few more yards, then also disappeared. The track beyond was smooth. Undisturbed.

Jack turned to look in all directions, he could see no further evidence. Nothing. He called even louder and looked to the fringe of woods. There were no hoofmarks, no footprints. The traces ended in the middle of the racetrack. Puffing into his hands, Jack knew he couldn't search the woods himself and he was fearful of what he might find if he did. He sighed and trudged back to the residence where once again, Milton was waiting. Now, there were search teams as well.

Milton's face expressed more than the concerns of the volunteers and team members with the canine unit. It was cold, snowing, and getting worse. The dogs were becoming anxious to start searching. "Come inside, Jack, they'll locate him." He guided them both into the warmth of the main hall. Reluctantly, Jack looked over his shoulder but followed Milton.

"I couldn't find him!" Jack tried to explain through his cold lips. "The footprints, they must have been his, they just disappeared into the middle of the racetrack. There were no exit traces. I couldn't see anything leading to the woods. They just disappeared in a mixture of hoofprints." He shook his head slowly, biting his lip as he spoke. "What could have happened?"

"It's okay, Jack. The search teams will find him." For all their sakes, Milton hoped he sounded more confident than he felt. "Let's go get some coffee." The two men tried to shake their dread as they passed through the game room on the way to the kitchen. On the computer table, Phillip's monitor was flashing, its screen a myriad of colors.

Stepping quickly, Jack glanced at the monitor, still playing a copy of The Silver Harness! Trotters were rounding the curve and animated drivers followed in their bright colored silks holding the harnesses, racing in the lightweight sulkies. Tiny, delicate persuader whips flicked the horses or carts to give directions. There was no snow, just bright sunshine and maddening cheers from the crowd in the stands. The intense faces of the drivers transmitted the exhilaration of the race.

In the moment when the animation closed in on one driver, Jack gasped. This was not possible. No, no, no. The driver exalting in the thrill of the race was an old man, Number Seven, a caricature of Phillip, the lifelong scar on his chin. There was a glimpse of a woman driver in turquoise silks holding second place. Jack tried to take his eyes away, he grabbed and gestured toward Milton, but he could not look away from the video. He was unable to even form the questions galloping in his brain! *Did Phillip just disappear in the woods? Was he spirited away by the race track? Did he evolve into the game?* Jack looked at the semaphore board on the screen and it was clear—Phillip was going to win this last race. All bets were on him. After the last turn, the sulky in second place made its break and moved to the outside just behind the leader. It was a dangerous move because the horse had to race farther and faster than the inside leader. The challenge was to cover more ground and swing ahead to match the first position and then take over the lead. It was not a strategy for weak judgment or with a lax horse. For Ella, it was neither. She was still the young girl who loved horses, loved Phillip, and talked with Jack the holiday morning. Her sulky edged forward until she was abreast of the front set. For the fans in the stands, the scene was in fast motion. It was just seconds of great harness racing neck and neck. For drivers, Phillip and Ella, it was a long stretch to a photo finish.

deCeMbeR

Consummation

Bree Indigo

I first met you in the Spring
        a spark of something unknown
as I gathered lilac sprigs
crocuses and hyacinth
I could feel your eyes
            your gaze
                your need
watching, waiting
and I wondered if you were
        a greenman
        or a forest guardian
but when the sun broke
through the clouds
        you were gone
and the flowers I had gathered
        were wilted

summer came with
unbearable heat
a heavy, thick presence
inescapable, impenetrable
and it was then that I began to dream
my body asleep but
my mind suddenly
        awake
            alert
                alarmed
        aware——of you
like a thick sheen of sweat
covering every inch
        of my skin
and I couldn't move
screams gathered
        silent, caught in my throat
my chest tight
with barely enough room
to draw in breath around a heart
that couldn't beat any harder
without escaping
        through a broken sternum
and I began to pray
every conscious part of me
focused on the ancient words
        at Tara in this fateful hour…

ochre and burgundy leaves
through my window
damp earth and petrichor
filled my lungs
finally Autumn arrived
and I felt like
        I could breathe again
and though you hadn't left
on the westerly winds that
blew away the oppressive heat
you weren't unexpected
in this season of death
        the hanged man reminded me
                to find perspective
        the wheel of fortune promised
                the consistency of change
        and the high priestess asked
                I acknowledge the darkness
so when you came in the night
I was ready, waiting
anticipating you
finding the stillness
        the priestess required
while her mother, the empress
showed me how to find the moon
and you filled me
        with your shadows

the frost came early this year
December settled in
like the weight of
a comfortable blanket
        worn thin
            by the memories
                of all it has seen
the forest grew quiet
and the days grew shorter
but I had already prepared
            for Winter
and I could feel you
watching me from the shadows
the weight of your gaze
following me in the garden
as I trimmed away
dead leaves and old growth
making space for the
            promise of new blooms
the wheel of fortune
always moving, reminding me
of the impermanence of death
            and the cycle of rebirth
so when the sun set
on the Winter solstice
giving way to the longest
deepest night of shadows

I surrendered myself
        to the darkness
like grief, demonic activity
comes in stages
        infestation
                oppression
                        obsession
and the final stage
        is possession
you thought you would
devour me—you expected
resistance, a fight
but I rode out your attack
like a wave
        my feet pulled away
                from the earth
        trying to keep my head
                above water
        struggling to
                find air
        my chest burned with
                a deep fire
and I opened my mouth wide
a voiceless scream
        I will not be consumed
you seized the moment
taking root as I choked
the thorned tendrils of you

beginning to grip tight
my mouth closed
and you thought you had me
but I am no longer
              p a r a l y z e d
                    s i l e n t
                          or h u n t e d
you struggled to escape
not yet knowing
you had already been
         devoured

I am the shadow keeper
              she who hunts the darkness
          daughter of Hecate
                protector of the night
bring me your demons
for Winter is coming
          and we will no longer
                              be
                          consumed

thirteen

Conventionality

David Mecklenburg

he air conditioning on the coach is not failing, but it cannot really do the job. Perhaps it's just too hot here. Perhaps under "ordinary" conditions, the air conditioning would be fine. The Oxford collar chafes the back of my neck in that uncomfortable way fabric does when it is damp. You know, take a damp linen napkin, and rub it across your lips. I am not drenched in my own sweat: not yet, but this maroon wool-blend sport coat I wear does not help.

We all wear them. The children, a mixture of 9-to-10-year-olds, also have the same sort of coats. Except theirs are dark blue. This is the only difference. Even among us adults—there are about 10 of us, one for every two children—there is no difference in the cut of our coats. Regardless of age, I think we are all wearing the same black gabardine pants. I like the feeling of this fabric, I always have. There is a strange mechanical squishiness it has against my skin. I can't say that by looking at it, I must feel the warps against the skin of my thighs and hips, but especially on my hamstrings when I am seated.

"And interestingly, it is always black."

"Always?" Tarum asks me this question.

"Was I speaking out loud?" I ask. Tarum sits next to me. Don't ask me how I know the child's name, I just simply do. Coming out of the daydream of gabardine, I just know 'Tarum' is associated with this particular child, just as I know the one sitting there by the window is called 'Celia.' I try and remember when I learned their names. In this way I can perhaps better attach myself to this journey, or whatever we are doing. The sweat begins to run on the back of my head, down channels of my hair and further moistens the crisp pleat of my collar. I look over at Celia's neck, which is bare because she has short hair, and I see the same small sheen of perspiration. At this I think of salt and wish I had some.

"Yes, but you do that a lot when you nod off," Tarum says.

"Oh, I was thinking about the fabric of our pants," I say.

"Is that gabardine?" Tarum asks.

"No," Celia says. "Well, yes in a way. Gabardine used to be a special kind of coat. Now it just means a kind of twill."

"What is twill?" Tarum asks. The two children discuss the fabric and I look past them at the desert we all move through. It is not a picturesque desert where dramatic dunes that look like the ocean slowly move beneath the wind and sun. There are no rocky outcroppings in the sand sea, standing like lone island sentinels. The way is flat. It is a mixture of grey, grease-green, some color that is also the memory of tan or healthy yellow, like the blush of a sunflower gone senile. Faint life crackles through the dry bushes and yet water is a miserly object, cherished within the plants that sprawl amongst the deposits of saleratus, soda ash, and calcite. This place is no garden for a human, such as me, and presumably these others. We are thinly separated from this dry garden—this symbol of death—by a thin sheet of bitumen laid across it, heading in the direction of the Convention Center.

I close my eyes, listen to the droning of the tires, the fans, and something like a faint radio that fades in and out of a jazz station. They are playing something familiar, something I have heard before but not through this modality or tempo.

"What will we do there?" I try to ask Mindy before I fall asleep. Mindy sits across the aisle from me. She is a petite woman, neither young, nor old. I would say she's 'just right.' Strong and funny with enough room left to grow, but wise through her years. She has a storehouse of inside jokes and knows the histories of tangential subjects.

How do I know that? This question has been vexing me for the entire trip.

"The darkness is too palpable. There are too many ways in," she says.

I don't know if she is answering me or not.

My first view of the Convention Center is a single flare of white light flashing on the horizon. As we draw closer, the coach's movements allow the light to differentiate, like the facets on a diamond, yet in this case the refracting object is much larger. It must be miles across and I can discern no structure to it. Yes, it is there, but it is not a tower, or a dome or anything like that. Closer still, I can see some of those architectural expressions make up different parts of it. Once we are close enough, the ends of the Convention Center disappear from our view and I can make out individual floors, balconies. Some have specks of people on them.

"So, there it is," Tarum says.

"What is it exactly?" I ask.

"Didn't they tell you?" Celia asks.

"No, I just know it was some place we were going to. I'm

new, remember? I don't even know what I am supposed to do except follow you around and makes sure you get where you need to be."

"How will you know that?" Tarum asks.

"I don't really know. Perhaps I will ask someone. Danael, or Mindy. Are they your teachers?"

"No, I've never met them before, but they seem to know what they are doing."

We glide under the first overhanging cantilevered slabs of the Convention Center and the coach finally begins to feel more comfortable. We pass innumerable bays until the driver slows down and pulls into one.

Danael stands up at the front of the coach. "This is it." He looks straight at me. His dark brown eyes are expressionless. They are richly holding back a secret. "Just follow us," he continues "and gather up your things, everyone. We are here."

"Wherever that is. | I can't wait. | I can | You've been waiting for this all your life. | Give me that back, my mom gave it to me. | The math must be interesting. | I wonder if there will be a comet | Who knows. | Everything is here. | I've heard we're not staying long. | That's because we're going somewhere else. | I could learn to like you. | I'm afraid. | Don't be. It's what you have to do. You can't avoid it anymore by flunking out. | I'm hungry. | Me too." The voices are all cut off as the coach's doors hiss open.

I get up and Celia and Tarum follow me. We follow the rest out into the heat which feels like someone shoved our faces into an open oven. We all quickly walk into the relative darkness of the building. It is cool inside, and the low entryway soon opens out into a huge atrium contrived of stone, glass, and massive textiles that seem to have no purpose but to wave in the artificial wind that belies the work of enormous machinery.

Danael and Mindy are not leading us. There is a woman in a mid-calf skirt, white shirt, and a strange cap that is more of an artifice, a crowning bauble to her uniform, and she leads us to a massive desk. The concierge there is a tall, impeccably beautiful man, in his mid-forties dressed in a crimson single-breasted suit that is so dark it seems almost black. A small silver feather is pinned on his lapel. His tie is a deep bronze color, which, like this building is made of a remarkably complex weave so that it appears to be many geometries of pattern at once. I look around and yet cannot find the exact source of light illuminating us through the enormity of the interior, and which shines on the man's shaved head.

"Welcome. I am your managing concierge. You must all be hungry. If you will follow me, you will soon be refreshed."

How many moving staircases do we go through? I am not sure. There are long stretches of straight corridors we walk down. Entire rooms serve as elevators to silently send us aloft into the shining upper floors of the Convention Center. Some of the floors are made of opaque glass, others seem to be cut from pure obsidian and I have a strange urge to take off my comfortable shoes and feel the cool smooth surface on the balls of my feet and heels. We pass masses of artwork: carefully installed in abstract jumbles of metal, frescoes of people cavorting naked underneath the baleful gaze of bloody lipped one-eyed giants whose hands each have five ruddy thumbs. There are still-lifes of pomegranates, persimmons, and plums. There is a splayed colossal cephalopod made out of exquisitely blown quartz. We walk across a massive bridge towards a small opening in a gigantic wall that must be at least six stories tall. As we arrive at the small door and file in, I noticed that the herringbone pattern of the walls' masonry is made of thousands upon millions of tiny sperm whales. Each appears to be slightly different and unique. I cannot imagine how it was made.

Beyond the door is a massive cafeteria made of twenty different overlapping mezzanines. I remain close to Tarum and Celia. We find ourselves in a line. Camson then tells us goodbye. "You will find your lunches there upon the table."

A small cityscape of scarlet boxes tied with black ribbons awaits us. Our names are on them.

"We're all staying together. You can eat at your own tables but we're all eating together on the fourteenth mezzanine. Then, we'll wander around for a while." A tall woman with short blonde hair going gray announces this. I remember her name: Carmina. I think. I look down in reflex at my chest and see there is no name tag. No one else possesses one, either.

"So, what is going to happen exactly?" I ask Mindy, whom I have sat next to. She has opened her lunch box and is poking at the different subsections of food. She drinks water from a blue bottle that was carefully tucked inside.

"What do you mean? Here? They're all going to grow up is what I figure."

"That's inevitable," I say with a little laugh. "But I mean right now…"

"It's good you know that's inevitable," Danael says.

"Do I know you?" I ask him.

"We've met before, I think. You look very familiar to me. But maybe I'm just remembering someone else."

"Or dreamed about," Mindy adds. "I don't mean *that* way. You know what I mean. That's one of the weird things about this place, because I've never met either of you. But I know you've done this before," she says this pointing at Danael, then me: "and you haven't." She then held up some nori and rice. "This is actually quite good."

"The food here is always delicious," Danael says.

"What do you mean, 'or dreamed about?'" I ask Mindy.

"Look, I've been here before and the first time I was just as surprised as you are, but the easiest way to explain this place is…" And she looked off into the light streaming in from the upper floors. I noticed it had darkened in hue from the cyan color of a bright sky to something yellow, like the heart of a dandelion petal. "…it's where all the déjà vus come from."

"Déjà vus?"

"Yes, you know. Especially if you go to sleep here. It's not a big deal. After my two charges wandered off last time, I just found a nice couch in one of the atriums and fell asleep. Then you'll dream of everything you've seen and later you'll forget about it…"

"…if you're lucky," Danael adds.

"But then you'll be somewhere else, and it comes back like a mask without a face beneath it. You lift it up and its blank underneath. It's not scary. Well, not always. It's mostly the fear that comes when you've first lost them that comes back. But don't worry. You won't be able to name it."

"It takes some getting used to," Danael says. He is eating some kind of salad made of bean shoots, daikon radish, and peanuts. "Eventually, you'll get sick of it."

"Have you?" Mindy asked him.

"It never gets easy, but you get used to it like everything. No, it's all these beautiful things we'll see here. Things we might do. But if they're only supposed to come back as confusing memories when I tie my boots before hiking… that seems like a waste of time."

I don't know why, but I say "But time doesn't work here

the same way. We'll be either millions of years older, or we'll have just left."

"I thought you said you've never been here before," Danael says.

"I haven't. But now that you say it, I'm not so sure. How did we get here?"

"The coach, as always."

"We didn't swim?" I ask. I don't know why I ask this. I can remember the coach-ride, the feeling of my collar, which is now dry and comfortable here, but I remember some massive swimming cavern. I won't even call it a pool. I am sure there is one in this Convention Center somewhere.

"You swam? That's interesting," Mindy says.

"There is a pool," Danael says. "More like an underground lake, but there might be several of them. I've seen people getting out of it. Huh, but never wondered how they got in it."

As he says these words, I remember it clearly. A huge underground cavern. The water is cool, but not unpleasant. People are treading water, some are exercising. It is dark, but not terribly so. I am not wearing a bathing suit, or anything. Nor is anyone else. I remember swimming to the side and a concierge handed me a towel, and a change of clothes like the ones I'm wearing, but they were new. I remember that. *How?*

This memory of the lake becomes an idée fixe that overpowers my thoughts as we finish lunch, find our children and begin to explore. There are arcades full of rusting games and farming equipment. In one area, we experiment with ancient tubes of glass and electricity. Other groups of people move along with us. One is a large party, perhaps 400 people dressed in silver blouses and blue tights with ludicrous crescent moon hats. They seem to be having some annual convening. Their intake of alcohol and other drugs is off-putting, both to the adults and children, although Danael says I may join them once the job's over. He turns his head then and runs off after his two charges: a pale haired boy and a girl with beautiful purple and gold hair extensions, so I can't ask him for details.

I follow Celia and Tarum up to a massive platform. It was glassed in and cool. I still think about the delicious feeling of the water on my skin. I remember the dark tunnel I had to swim through with other people. Everyone swimming, or sitting by the lakes edge, was nude and chatting. We were all ages, some were not able to stand, and so others carried them gently in the water from conversation to conversation. Blue phallic shaped lanterns were everywhere giving off the pale imitation of moonlight along with yoni-basins full of clear effervescent water laced with hints of cucumber, raspberry, and mint. We simply drank it with our hands and laughed at the tickling it made on our palms.

Now, when I follow the children up to the glass, the vision dies away in the grand expanse of the desert. Finally, we are high enough in the Convention Center, and evidently near an edge of it so that we look out across the terrain we have crossed. Or perhaps I had swum under. *which is ludicrous, look how far it is, you're remembering something else.*

I walk up to Celia near the window. We are high over the desert, how many stories, I cannot tell. This is not, as you may expect, because of immeasurable height. No, it is because the architecture of the building, while composed of mostly right angles, a few curves but nothing you could call organic, piles itself upon itself in misleading geometry. I imagine a brief image of four enormous arms sprouting in the middle of a great wasteland. The wasteland was not merely what we call someplace that doesn't have anything 'worthwhile' in it... no, it was like a vast spill of broken concrete, sand, glass, steel, rubber-waste, and it was deftly pulled in by the arms and built up anew. I feel for a moment that I witnessed the birth of this place, which is now so vast, plumb, and cool—at least on the inside. This random piling, this placement of block upon curve upon galleria upon colonnade, renders perspective and depth perception useless.

This place was never planned, and if there had been some grain of order—even based on one plus one, then two plus one, and three plus two and so on—it had spun out of control. Celia and I look out over the desert, and see in the distance, a long line of hills, perhaps even mountains.

"Was it like this, where you were from?" At the point of her asking, my mind drifts off into the sky, skimming over the projections of lavender blue upon the hot air above the edge of sight, what we call in the simplicity of illusion a distance almost naked save for the sheer slip of mirage.

"*Where I was from*" and I move in memory, through memory. I am in a car or wagon or some vehicle without a roof and rows upon rows of dark towers form a trench whose bottom I travel along.

"The Towers. I see them too. What are they?" she asks me.

"They are not trees. Do you know them?"

"Trees? Yes, I will someday. I have read of them. Some are good and helpful, and some are rotten and very dangerous. Their real strength is in armies, for together they do not need to move, only have someone move through them toward madness."

"How do you know that?" I ask her.

"I said. I read about it. But you're new. You won't know me very well. I'm sorry."

"I wouldn't know you, you mean."

"No, you won't know me. Or should I say: 'will not?'"

"Tense is a tricky thing with them. You'll get used to it." Danael says this as he walks behind me. He is following his two children along the viewing platform.

"What do you mean?" I ask her, pretending to ignore him.

"Come on. I'm growing up. You know that. You've done it yourself. Don't you remember?"

"No. Evidently. What were we talking about?"

"Trees and towers."

"The towers I drove through on the way here are not trees. Understand that. They are not columns from an ancient civilization. They are enormous, yet they are not monsters frozen into that form. I don't know. No one built them, not on purpose, but they are there none the less, and they blot out most of the sky so that it is only a strip of blue, or grey that water comes from."

"The rain?"

"Yes. But that is not where I originally came from. The land I came from was full of rolling hills and oak trees. The grass was dead there, but a beautiful gold, like the blondest hair you will ever see."

"Does the rain make it green?"

"Yes, but it depends where you are. I remember the green in Spring, when the rain still fell on my homeland. The hills would erupt with poppies, millions of them. Orange, not red. They all would die away in the furnace of Summer."

"But the desert, it comes to life, briefly? It's what the kind voice always says in the shows I watch. Or something like that," she says, and her forehead wrinkles a bit at her brows. She looks down for a while, and then suddenly, she snaps up her gaze to meet mine and says: "I don't know, though. I am beginning to question everything you know. It's what happens when we get older. You learn things. You learn how grownups lie to you."

I looked at her and for some reason, I smile.

"I don't mind talking to you," she continues. "I don't think you're lying. You don't have any reason to. You're new. And generally, I don't mind grownups lying because they always seem to mean the best of it. It isn't like other kids lying to you. They are lying to get something from you. A piece of candy. A secret they can use."

"That doesn't change," I say.

"Are you lying?"

"I wish I was."

"The rain comes. See." Celia points toward a distant line of clouds forming above the mountains.

The sudden sight of them prompts an involuntary memory. Like a trigger. A match. A flood of urine. A spark. A gust. A gasp. A sudden hand upon your back from one who is not there.

My grandmother had a bottle of ink. I knocked it into the toilet. And there it spread out. No, my grandmother never used ink bottles. By the time I was around she and the rest of the world had switched to ballpoint pens.

That's because it wasn't your grandmother's ink bottle. It was our grandmother alright, but it was the bloody catarrh she spat into the toilet. Remember? When she was dying?

The clouds move in the sky like blood in a toilet, expanding and searching with a cohesion suggesting tentacles, or at the least the evolutionary promise of them. The water turns red, a dark rotten red saturated with black bile. We stand there, and watch it come across the wide expanse towards us, towards this collection of geometries. Towards our memories, ourselves and what we are, were, and going to be.

"It will be here soon. The blue, see. That means it is getting closer." Danael stands next to me and points. Long trailing arcs of blue light, like illuminated clouds reach down like the filaments of an undiscovered jellyfish.

"I've never seen a storm like that."

"It's not really a storm. We call it that, mostly because we don't have any other word for it. Where are your children?"

"I don't have any."

"I mean the ones here."

"Oh, they're here." I motion toward Celia. I do not know where Tarum is. "Oh god."

"Don't worry, he's probably here somewhere. They never really go far, until the end of course. I think that's your errant rabbit over there." Danael points to a crowd of children. They have all different manner of hair, of color, but the style is remarkably the same.

"Excuse me," I say and walk over toward the children, all the while keeping my eye on Celia. She stands in tiny relief against the cancerous storm spreading itself over the vanishing blue sky.

"I don't want to grow up," Celia says as Tarum and I approach her.

"You don't have to. Just scream and it will break the glass. Then you can throw yourself out the window," Tarum says.

"Ha, ha," Celia replies. "Have you looked outside? It's not exactly promising."

The light from the sky has nearly disappeared. The storm undulates softly and then suddenly changes its mind to reach out quickly with a great wing of clouds, illuminated in purples and greens from the discharge of electricity within it. I stare at it for how long? I don't know. I keep trying to imagine it in some smaller form, like it was in a tidal pool—note my continued use of aquatic, invertebrate imagery, especially non-bilateral symmetry—and then I will have an idea of what it is. How it thinks. There is no doubt in me at that moment that sea urchins think. It's just what they think might seem rather banal, or uncomplicated. As with urchins, this storm seemed to simply think with its entire form. What does it think of? How?

Is it attuned to the disruptive frequencies and confounded realities of dark matter? Can it contemplate them like a cuttlefish? I feel the children huddle closer to me, like small trees in a vast forest, as though we stand on a precipice looking out over an ocean that is mostly peaceful but often overcast in a grey blanket of life we call water. I thrill at the thoughts of all the unique particles of dust carried aloft in the dark rain clouds. Each one could be counted like a star, and thus represent a dream. I feel cellulose and lignin structures compile themselves from my feet up past my knees, my hips, my vagina, and my chest. My blood is clear, fast syrup. The children's hands sprout tender shoots, and we speak our anemotic language through the rustling of our leaves. But it is cold in this dream, and I feel my head forever cloaked in a hood of foggy water, and I am bereaved of the sight I had so long enjoyed without consideration.

"C'mon" Celia tugged at my hand, and I shake my head. "You're going to get us in trouble." The rest of the mezzanine is empty now, and a clapping sound raps against the air, sending shockwaves through my body. It is the storm; it has begun to embrace the Convention Center.

"We should go that way," Tarum says. "I think it's where everyone else went. We're going to all see something." I see the lines of children and adults descend the wide stone stairs that seem to float like concrete clouds in their curious way, for deep within the building, the cantilever weights lie hidden, only suspected, and only connected by an unworldly alloy of metal that takes on mysterious qualities of reflectivity. It is not so much invisible as it refracts light in so many confusing ways that I cannot tell where it is. The steps seemed buoyed in the air like so many regular, architectural clouds.

"They never said it was going to be like this. Never so big or weird. And I thought grownups knew what they were doing," Celia looks up at me as she says this. I try to remember why I care about these two specifically. I like them, but when had I been assigned them? What were my choices?

Celia studied me and her expression is momentarily telling, but she then swiftly relaxes her facial features into an emotional void capable of either the most awkward social ignorance or a vast taiga of spiteful variations on the larch of antipathy. "You'll do quite well as a grownup with a face like that you little bitch," I say it without thinking. Her eyes start wide. I want to slap her. But I don't because it feels like *something else* wants me to hit her—hit both of them. For a moment I am a stranger and I scorn them just for being what they are. This very thought arouses the nub of a memory, but like some iceberg in a stormy sea, it slips back below the waves. The music, I realize, is a variation on that same melody about some place, a paradise where I never lived but would just before I die. The jazz moves in its inimitable improvisation and then retreats having done its work on me.

"I am sorry, I didn't mean to sound so…"

"We know," Tarum says.

"Actually, we don't. But we heard that can happen sometimes. No worries."

We have to catch up to the class, I remember.

We reach the floor where the rest of our 'class,' if I can call it that, has gathered in a sort of lobby. The large lights, the kind that broadly illuminated the ceiling and the walls began to fail. Tarum points up. "See?"

There are faint twisting coils of... smoke? That is one way of looking at it. Another is as some exquisitely jewel-like creature of non-carbon formation, a silicon slime mold, which I had read about in... and I suddenly sense the door close. Celia grabs onto my hand.

"I'm sorry. Let's get through this," she says.

"Yes, together."

"You don't get it. We aren't going to be together. Just get through this. But not 'with' me, you know."

"Let's get through this near each other," I offer.

"That works. I have to pee."

The three of us all agree we should "go" before the next event, whatever it will be. We follow two other children and Mindy. The restrooms are not difficult to find and like everything else in the Convention Center, they aren't what you expect. They are attended, for one thing. A tall old man with thick white hair stands near the entrance in a white shirt with a craftsman collar. His shirtsleeves are rolled up to his elbows and he wears red silk arm-garters just below his biceps. Over this, he wears an apron striped in deep red and whites. His trousers are dark and look just like ours in cut and fabric. He wears black rubber clogs, which makes sense given his occupation and location. His hands are enormous, perfect for playing the piano. He opens his hands and waves us into the restroom with a gesture of welcome but says nothing. He smiles.

The restroom itself is large, its flooring made of dark grey slates polished to a high gloss. There are sinks with elaborate bronze handles and taps offering hot, tepid, and cold water. None of the taps take any regular form, but swoop and curve like the necks of water birds. The toilets are further on, each one an individual stall. Nothing is segregated by sex or gender. All manner of humanity can use these facilities. A group of gaudily dressed people in feathers and tight silk dresses stand near the parfumerie, a long counter to the right of the sinks where cosmetics and unguents can be used. The people all possess thick, rich lips colored with every hue of the rainbow: no color is natural or desaturated.

Stepping into one of the toilet stalls I see the partitions are made of the same stone as the floor. Strange curls of the smoke collect in the ceiling above me, and I detect no tobacco, or any other kind of burnt matter. The only smell is a heavy lingering pong of lemon verbena and musk that somehow covers up all the other odors. After I finish, I wash my hands and notice the water run widdershins as it empties into the drain. *Have we crossed an equator? How strange.*

As I wait for the children, Mindy comes up to me.

"How are you holding up?"

"Fine, it doesn't seem to be very difficult. This place is amazing."

"You should see the main toilets on the Alexandria Center Mezzanine." She describes them to me as an entire attraction unto themselves. Perhaps it would be good to ask her about the Storm.

"About that Storm outside. It comes often?"

"Outside? Whatever made you think it's outside. Look up."

I see the same strange thickening fog or smoke. It resembles the inside of a mussel shell, save that it moves with currents of blue and aquamarine gas blending into one another, then separating.

"Chad, where is Kyle?" Mindy asks. A young boy stands next to Tarum and Celia who have also finished washing their hands.

"I don't know. He's not here?"

"He was in the stall next to you." As Mindy says this, she points toward two doors, one closed, the other open. As though waiting for the last of us to look, Chad turns in the direction of Mindy's pointing finger and the door opens. Out steps an adult. From the white double-breasted chef's jacket, houndstooth pants, and humiliating headgear that resembles a paper pot, the person appears to be some sort of cook.

"Oh God, the first one," Mindy says.

"Is Chad gone now?" Kyle asks.

"Probably," Celia says. "I don't think he turned into that chef."

The chef walks up past us to use the sink.

"Sir, was there a boy in that stall?" Mindy asks. He looks surprised and worried.

"She didn't mean it that way," I say. "We thought someone in our party was there and when you stepped out it seemed strange."

"Oh, I see," the man replies, relieved to be free of suspicion of pederasty or worse. "No. But you know there was the ozone smell in there. I didn't think anything of it really. That's usually..."

"...I know what it means. Thank you," Mindy says and then turns to me. "Well, I'm down to one now. Maybe it won't take as long. Come on, we'll be late for the show." I look around and no one else is nonplussed by the event. *Had it even happened,* is my first thought. We walk out and catch up with our party. We enter some kind of large hall. Like everything in the Convention Center, it is enormous, a curved room full of red chairs facing the same way.

"Mindy, I'm sorry. I'm so new. What is going on?"

"We're here, and they won't be for much longer."

"They?"

"They, the children. Tell me, are yours talented? Chad was. A prodigy at piano. The only thing preventing him from playing the Konchiev Sonata was the fact his hands hadn't completed growing. Danael says the talented ones go first sometimes. Depends on the talent."

Many people, both children and wards file into the hall. As I grow accustomed to the dim light, I realize the room is something like an ellipse, as though we are on the bottom of a very large pan. On the inside of the curve is a raised platform. Whatever lies behind it is obscured by enormous, burgundy-colored curtains. The ceiling throbs with the searching tangled plasma of the Storm. It does not strike me as strange by this point, but it does not comfort me, either. Somehow, in the initial darkness of entering, we had separated from Mindy.

"Celia, Tarum, what is going on here?"

"I almost wanted to ask you if you knew that or not," Celia says to me.

"I don't know, either." Tarum says. "I just know my mother is coming here to pick me up."

"SSShhhhhh!!!" someone hisses at us. Instinctively, I forget about the vanishing child, Mindy, Celia's bold statement and Tarum's admission. Instead, I become the neurotic sort of person who worries about being in one's seat when the performance starts.

"Do you know what we're going to see?" Tarum asks. We find three seats together.

"No, of course she doesn't. She doesn't know anything. No one told her." Celia says.

"Then do you know what it's going to be?" Tarum asks her.

"No, I don't even know what theatre this is. No one gave us a map or a program."

The lights dim further, and I assume the performance will commence. Tarum stands up and looks around the darkened theatre. He is polite, for he still hunkers over a bit so as not to block the stage, even though the closed curtains, huge, and maroon colored velvet, continue to billow softly in some draught of air.

"Is your mother here?" I ask.

"No. You will know her. She has hair like yours," Tarum says.

"Your mother does?"

"Yes, although she isn't my real mother. I say that because it's easier when I talk to someone like you. Actually, I don't remember my mother. I just know that the woman who is in charge of me isn't who I was inside of." He looks at me for a moment with pleading eyes. Then a low rumble from the storm shakes the room. He looks up, and I followed his gaze.

"Inside of…" I say.

"Yes, my mother."

"How sure are we of any of that?" I ask.

"Some are sure."

"Perhaps they are refutable, but the fact they exist is not."

"Do you know how much longer it will be?"

"No. I thought you had been here before. I'm just a substitute."

"I have never been here before. Not that I remember. That would be like being a baby."

"Like what we were just talking about?"

"*Ssssshhhhh.* It's about to start." We wait and wait some more. The fog, or smoke, the storm-plasma as I like to call it, grows thicker and begins to swirl as though it were a complete meteorological system. I have the sense of seeing this from some other perspective. As though I can somehow see these things from the other side... like I am flying on top of the clouds, or someone told me about it? *Was it grandfather? or Cassandra? Who told me about how and where the storm-plasma would go?*

Slowly, gradually, music made of long, drawn-out pentatonic notes, begins to wail behind the curtains. It sounds like a daughter and her mother perhaps, mourning the death of someone, or wishing for it. A male voice then comes in to explain something in the same plaintive voice. This continues for quite some time. I have the impression we are never going to see what is happening behind the curtain, and yet we are left with the sense that something is happening. What makes it all the more maddening is I recognize the melody. It's *that melody*, the same as the modal-jazz. I can put together enough of the mood to know someone pines for a life that never was. The dream glorifies the most mundane things, like digging potatoes and boys playing together. The singer is dying and prays to not be released from this fragile world, or else let the afterlife be just like this world that did not really exist. The voice finally cracked in some kind of agony. The plasma shifts above us. Whatever is going on is not 'made up.' If it is a performance, it is one that is really happening.

"I think we should go," I say.

"Why?"

"I don't like this. It doesn't feel safe. Do you hear the horns?"

"I think it's kind of creepy," Tarum says.

"You would. But I think she's right. We should go somewhere else." Celia says in rare agreement with me. Side exit doors begin to open and light streams in from them, a blue, long light: the kind that stirs the plasma into further strange configurations and impossible tendrils.

"Where were you before this?" I ask Tarum.

"At school."

"What did you learn there."

"Nothing. Seems like. There's my mother."

At the end of the aisle, close to us, is a very beautiful woman. She does have hair like mine—black, thick, shoulder-length with bangs—only cut and styled by much more talented hands. Her bangs look like a single perfect wave. She has blue eyes, pale skin, and bright red lipstick. She wears a business suit. What color, I can't tell in the theatre although it does not appear black. Perhaps navy blue. She is very shapely, with a thin waist and voluptuous hips. She wears silk stockings beneath her skirt whose hem dips just below the knee, and beautifully shined black patent leather heels. Although fully, professionally dressed, I can somehow feel her nudity beneath the clothes. I feel like I know her.

"Are you ready to go?" She asks. The blue light from the outside flows around her.

"Yep." Tarum stands. "Thanks. Maybe I'll see you again." And he squeezes right by me before I can say anything. The woman holds out her hand.

"Do you know her?" Celia asks.

"No, yes. Kind of...?"

"Don't you think that's kind of weird? She doesn't look like his mom."

Tarum reaches the end of the aisle and with his mother's, or... the woman's hand in his, they walk towards the blue light. At that moment I realize Celia is right. I don't know what I am doing, but I should say something, make sure. ID her? I get up.

"C'mon. You're coming with me," I say to Celia and tug her along.

"Fine."

We follow them and it seems like the auditorium, or whatever it is begins to stretch. They make it to the door. The music swells again. Individual drums sound, followed by a string instrument, then some sort of horn.

"Hurry," I say. We make it to the door and the outside is thick with the Storm. It feels oddly dry and searching, like a desert wind and not the stickiness I expect. As they walk away from us deeper into the blue light that fills the mezzanine outside the auditorium, I see again just how shapely the woman's figure is.

"Jane!" I yell but they gain on us into the light that grows so bright I eventually cannot see them.

"That's not her name," Celia says.

"How do you know?"

"He told me her name is Bettie."

I become aware then that the light is failing. Other children and their wards move around us like they have somewhere else to go. Mindy is alone. She walks past and looks up a me.

"Oh, you've lost one already. First one's are the hardest. Mine are all gone now. I'm going to get drunk."

I turn back in the direction "Bettie" and Tarum had gone. The way is empty save for a thick nest of fumes doubling in on one another and then vanishing into the upper, darkened part of the great hall.

I cannot say we are fleeing the storm. It is everywhere. It knocks against the glass here on an observation deck just like any windy storm. We are deep inside the Storm and therefore close to the giant bolts of spider lightning that flow through it with deafening roars that shake the glass and steel around us. I have seen it come up steps like a billowing snake of plasma, enveloping everyone on risers until they disappear from view. Then it dissipates and a few people are missing. Always children. It does not take them all. Not yet, I suspect.

It passed over Celia at one point when we went looking for a Zoo someone had told us about. Celia wanted to see a hippo. The tangling arms of red and black smoke, the blue plasma, moved over us, but I never felt her hand give way. Never turned to see empty air.

"Are you going to die?" I finally ask her. We sit in another cafeteria drinking milkshakes. It seems like the thing to do. Mine is chocolate and hers is cherry. "Look, you know I don't know what's going on here. I should be following you. You seem to understand this better than I do."

"I don't think I'm going to die. It looks that way, but that's not what I heard happens back at school. If nothing else I'll probably look back on this, the time before, with some kind of... oh what's the word you use when you're homesick for something."

"Nostalgia?"

"Yes. Although it sounds like a pain."

"What?"

"Changing. But I want to. I'm sick of being small. No one really listens to you because they're always 'looking out' for you." She makes finger quotes in the air and rolls her eyes. I blink and she is still there although for a moment it felt like she was inside of a glass vase, with muted words talking to someone else. "...it's all natural. Blah blah. Like I should be scared of it or something. Were you?"

"What?"

"Were you scared?"

A flash of the spider lightning arcs outside and in reflex I glance to the side and feel goosebumps all over my body. I know these are each tiny hairs reacting to the electricity. But they say something. I look back and Celia is gone. Her straw is there. The cherry milkshake is half finished. I don't even look under the table. I don't understand, but I certainly know she's gone and that's it. Mindy's desire to go get drunk seems like a completely rational plan now.

It is. Danael and I have one of those meaningful conversations where he finally tells me all about this place. That we are somehow supposed to guide these children to the Storm, and it takes them, and we never know what it does with them. We comfort ourselves here on the summit of the trip, knowing that the children did not seem to be abducted in wrath or depravity. We never discover their hands and bloodied stumps in some Sadean grotto. And we aren't going to remember any of this. "Only I am because I'm not going back with you and I'm not drinking anymore of that watermelon flavored red water. It passes through these tanks you see. They're made of quartz and inside is an aquaphillic mycelium which is most likely sentient. The water enters from the north and exits from the south, colored red and tasting of watermelon, of summer. Of the time before. Green carpet. Swamp Cooler. The Light of August," I say all of this and then put the cup down on the bar. We have been drinking Irish Coffee which seems the best way to be drunk and awake at the same time.

"Let's go to the conservatory," Danael says. "It's so peaceful there, I looked in and it was a green carpet of plants, but not the gross prickly dry kind that leave those horrible burrs in your socks. There're no blackberry bushes, no gorse. No manzanita. Just lots of cool plants with gentle, lobed skin parts, succulents, water lilies, a nest of tender mint-green ears like the leaves of tulips, and everywhere the water is running through the cress and the grass like our mother's hair the way it waved in the wind, like wheat when she was young, and the world had not yet been broken. My life was tall. If only for a short time. Perhaps in the Storm, we can be wide. we can embrace the earth and travel across the West until the last notes. Do you hear them?"

I listened hard. It's that melody again. A melody that suggests what was, but never really was. There is a rich baritone.

"Yes, but are you hearing the same thing? Probably yes and no. I can expect that kind of answer now," I say.

"A song you can't name," he says. "Your grandmother loved it. Or maybe someone's grandmother. I think this act is considered remembrance. It just doesn't have to be ours. Remember," says Danael, putting his right index finger to his nose "is the whole point of this place. In one way or someone else's other."

The TV above the bar shows nothing but a view above the desert, an illusion of perspective.

"It is in memory, where we are human." Danael says this

to me. The statement sounds like an answer, yet I had posed no question. I learned quickly that a great deal of our discourse is like this—an answer given for now.

"But what if someone has lost their memories?" I ask.

"They are beyond hope," he says. "But whether that is good or bad remains a human judgement." He looked at me then intently. "I think I know you."

"We have always known each other," I say. "I will be there when you die. Can you please, for God's sake tell me why I just said that?"

"There's a TV show that sort of explains it."

"Did we watch that as children?"

"No, that was another show, but it lived in the same world. It had the same flagellums. Anyway. Did you remember where the lake was?"

"The lake?"

"The one you said you swam through to get here once."

"Yes. I remember. They served the same water there."

"Lethe-water no doubt."

Beyond us, the desert, as I have said before, did not undulate in seductive rhythms of dunes, nor did it stretch in the manner of an arm or a dream. It simply is, and that means flat, grey, green, greasy and without counterpoint until one's gaze eventually finds the horizon above the lilac mirages and that unreachable line of sun-blasted hills. The red and yellow of the sunset have disappeared in the mercy of night and the storm blows back from whence it came. What souls does it bear, if any, or are we all graduated, sublime codes of memories suspended in the absurd fluid of itself? The cloud, the droplet, the sand, and the pebble.

Author Biographies

Lauri Boren

Lauri, raised in Washington, navigated the ins and outs of suburban life, and earned a doctorate in terror, like every middle school survivor. Working as a school bus driver enriched that understanding, if understanding is possible. After forty years of teaching mostly preteens, she's fully accredited in the concept of horror. Living on the edge of a primordial woodland was disappointing.

Lauri has a Masters, a BA and far too many credits in professional development in-services. She now studies Mindful Doglish, while she tutors her dogs and cat as they pursue advanced degrees in quantum physics, evolutionary microbiology and genealogy, respectively.

J.W. Capek

From reading children's books to grade school students, to creating the Senior to Senior Intergenerational Communications project, J.W. has always appreciated the art of storytelling! Growing up in Arizona, teaching high school and raising a family in California, J.W. moved to the Northwest to be an author. The *Deerwhere Codex* trilogy creates a Science Fiction world with quantum computers, epigenetics, and three unique sexes: Female, Male, and Uniale. It is a twenty-fourth century tale of a community survival of a pandemic. J.W.'s short stories span the human experience from tragedy to ridiculous. Check out www.jwcapek.com for current information.

HIROMI COTA

Hiromi Cota has been a special operations heavy weapons expert, an adjunct professor, a rave journalist, and the flaming-sword-swinging lead in a heavy metal opera. They (singular) have lived in nations around the world, but have settled down in Seattle with their spouse Randi and their (plural) dog Nasus. Outside of crafting queer horror, Hiromi writes and develops roleplaying games, programs video games, and gets into sword fights as a member of the Seattle Knights actor-combatant troupe. Their numerous books can be found at HiromiCota.com

JENNIFER DIMARCO

A PNWC and Bumbershoot award-winning poet and Seattle Times bestselling novelist, Jennifer DiMarco first toured nationally as an author when she was nineteen years old, having written novels since the age of ten. The first sixteen years of her career included the publication of contemporary drama, high fantasy, science fiction, poetry, and mystery novels as well as the production of two short films and three stage plays. During a twenty-year hiatus from prose, DiMarco married, raised two children, and worked as a filmmaker writing and directing more than a dozen feature films, half a dozen mini series, and more than a hundred short films. She returned to prose with *Body of Work* in 2020 and will celebrate forty years as a storyteller with the re-release of her bestselling poetry collection, *Season of Fire*, and an all-new creative memoir, *Sabbath Rising,* in the winter of 2021. DiMarco lives in the Pacific Northwest with her wife, composer and actor Brianne, and their adult children, author and illustrator Maxwell, and actor and illustrator Faith.

MAXWELL DiMARCO

Author, illustrator, and award-winning actor and filmmaker, Maxwell DiMarco has been writing professionally since he was a pre-teen, with stories and novels published in *Tales of the Slug, Super,* and *Ghost Sniffers, Inc.* In addition to these family-friendly adventures, DiMarco has written stories for all three volumes of *Unnerving,* where he explores the darker aspects of society through both physical and psychological horror. He lives in the Pacific Northwest, where he works as a special effects editor and the host of the weekly children's series, *Seriously Cereal.* He is a huge believer in community, acceptance, and seeing the world from all perspectives, striving to always provide his readers with an intriguing, thought-provoking narrative, no matter the genre.

BREE INDIGO

Bree Indigo is a poet and songwriter. She enjoys astrology, exploring Washington State's Olympic Peninsula, and local mushroom foraging. Her favorite authors include Madeleine L'Engle, Holly Black, and Laurie Halse Anderson. Indigo lives with her wife and their children in the Pacific Northwest. Her first memoir, *Unreliable Narrator,* is forthcoming from Blue Forge Press. Find her on Instagram or Twitter @bree_indigo

C.M. KANE

Born and raised in the Pacific Northwest, CM Kane was fed a steady diet of sports, particularly baseball. Having this love of the game instilled in her at an early age, she found that nothing was better than getting lost in the game. Storytelling was another gift that was encouraged in her youth, and she's taking to the written word to explore a new aspect to the game she loves.

MICHELLE LEE

Michelle Lee is a Pacific Northwest native with an imagination open to possibilities. Growing up, people often saw her with her face buried in a book, and not much has changed in that regard. She's living her life dream of writing books that set her imagination free and explore the possibilities she sees in the mysteries of the land around her.

Michelle's eight book series *The Raven's Journey* and her novella-length series *I.S.P.I.* can be found online at Amazon. Keep up with Michelle on Facebook at www.tiny.cc/MichelleLeeWrites

DAVID MARTYN

David Martyn, retired from a career in the Maritime industry, lives in Gig Harbor Washington, with his wife Karen. David writes Christian fiction. His Biblical series of novels, *The Hall of Faith*, include *The Praise Singer*, *The Oak of Weeping*, and *The Epistle*. David's historical fiction series, *The Robert Curtis Mysteries*, include *Called into Service*, *Soldiers of the King*, and *Lords and Ladies*. David's short stories can be found in the anthologies *Unconditional* and *Unnerving: Volume 2*. A complete list of David's works can be found at blueforgepress.com

DAVID MECKLENBURG

David Mecklenburg was born in Sacramento, CA. but at the age of 22 he moved home to the Pacific Northwest, where he received his MFA in Creative Writing from the University of Washington. In short fiction, novellas, poetic essays and novels, he unveils worlds upon worlds in the fabulist tradition that reveal the multivalent condition we call being human. His short fiction has appeared in Silver Blade Magazine, Adelaide Literary Review, The Dark Fiction Spotlight among anthologies, such as Blue Forge Press's *Trinity* series. His longer work includes *The Nightingale's Stone*, a fictional memoir, along with Graphic Illustrated Essay collections such as *Hyperborea* and *Deukollectrum* also available from Blue Forge Press.

SUSAN NORDMAN

Susan Nordman is an award winning poet and author. She has written *Ascension: The Psions of Janus* as well as several short stories. Together with her father Vern Nordman, she co-authored *Project Voyager* and they are diligently working on the second book of the series titled *Sanctuary*. After living in the Pacific Northwest for many years, Susan recently relocated to Myrtle Beach, SC.

LAUREN PATZER

Hailing from Tacoma, WA, Lauren has been an information technology guru, actor, writer and film producer among other pursuits. His love of horror began with a non-stop reading of *The Amityville Horror*. With two novels and over fifty short stories published now, his most recent work is the top-rated horror anthology *From The Shadows*.

JAMES LOWELL SNYDER

James Lowell Snyder was raised in Arizona. He worked as a civilian logistics specialist with the US Air Force for over twenty-five years, which included writing and teaching instructional courses. After retiring, boredom set in so he decided to write fiction. He began that risky career by contributing several short stories to J.W. Capek's *Ever Aequum*, part of the *Deerwhere Codex* series. Emboldened by success, he decided to create his own fictional sphere.